The Last First Day

The Last First Day

•

Carrie Brown

PANTHEON BOOKS, New York

Copyright © 2013 by Carrie Brown

All rights reserved. Published in the United States by Pantheon Books, a division of Random House, Inc., New York, and in Canada by Random House of Canada Limited, Toronto.

Pantheon Books and colophon are registered trademarks of Random House, Inc.

Library of Congress Cataloging-in-Publication Data
Brown, Carrie, [date]
The last first day / Carrie Brown.
pages   cm
ISBN 978-0-307-90803-2
1. Middle-aged persons—Fiction. 2. Marriage—Fiction. 3. Private schools—Fiction. 4. Self-realization—Fiction. 5. School principals—Fiction. 6. Childfree choice—Fiction. I. Title.
PS3552.R6852937 2013 813'.54—dc23 2012050988

www.pantheonbooks.com

Jacket illustration and design by Joan Wong

Printed in the United States of America
First Edition

9 8 7 6 5 4 3 2 1

To John

PART I

The Last Day

1

That morning, in anticipation of the party to be held at their house in the evening, Ruth unearthed the vacuum cleaner from the front hall closet. She had to move aside a heap of belongings to reach it—umbrellas and boots and musty-smelling coats—as well as Peter's old film projector, heavy as lead in its mossy green case, and half a dozen cartons containing reels of footage from their early days at Derry. A brand-new teacher then, his enthusiasm like a light inside his face, Peter had recorded everything during those first years, endless hours of slow-moving football games, canoe races on windy spring afternoons with the boats shunting jerkily across the lake, the winter evening Robert Frost came to read his poems in the chapel.

Mr. Frost had been aloof that night at dinner, attending vaguely to the conversational gambits offered by the school trustees who had been assembled for the occasion. The meal had been splendid fare by the dining hall's usual standards, stuffed clams and lobster with melted butter, corn and boiled potatoes, blueberry pie. The evening had been a triumph for Peter, who had arranged it, and an honor for Derry, which then had no real standing among boys' schools of the day, its pupils drawn historically from poor families rather than the well-heeled aristocracy of New England.

The trustees, already worried about the school's financial future, however, had begun to entertain ambitions for wealthier students, and even those men who did not read poetry—which was probably all of them, Ruth had thought at the time—understood that Mr. Frost's appearance conferred distinction on the Derry School, a reputation for intellectual seriousness that the school could not otherwise acquire no matter how much money it raised, or how many prosperous families it attracted. Poetry, the reading and writing of it, was understood to be a hallmark of patrician gentility. It was evidence—however baffling to the practical men of industry and commerce who made up Derry's board of trustees at the time—of refinement. They were in search of pedigrees and the resources that came with them. If a poetry reading had to be part of the bargain, so be it.

Mr. Frost had eaten his dinner with apparent appetite but without saying much, his head bent over his plate. His face was so shut away and expressionless that Ruth imagined he had suffered recently a personal loss of great severity.

But when he began to read in the chapel later that night, coming up to the podium after Peter's introduction with the slow steps of a man accompanying a coffin to the grave, his voice was surprisingly strong. Ruth knew that even the philistines among the trustees could not have failed to be moved.

I have been one acquainted with the night, Mr. Frost began.

A light was trained on the page before him, and he put his palm against the open book on the podium as if to crack its spine. He paused. Then he looked up, and he did not look down again for the duration of the poem.

I have walked out in rain, he recited, *and back in rain.*

When he read the line *I have outwalked the furthest city light,* Ruth thought that every boy, every teacher sitting in the cold, hard pews of the chapel with its smudged smoke stains on the white walls, and its old glass windows full of air bubbles, and the tall hurricane globes on the altar containing the candle flames—every one of the listeners in the chapel that night— was made aware of the miles of forest surrounding the school, the tumbled, rocky coast of Maine at the edge of the forest and its terminus at the sea, the black restless body of the Atlantic Ocean. Surely they felt themselves at that moment as alone as a man could be, Ruth thought, as alone as the lonely speaker of the poem, unwilling to meet the eyes of the night watchman whom he passes in the dark. Surely they understood that this lonely feeling was inside of them, too, even if it had lain there mostly a thing concealed from them by the blessed ordinariness of their days.

Yet the occasion had been miraculous as well as solemn. The poem reminded them that the world around them lay beneath what Mr. Frost called the dome of heaven; Ruth pictured images from her art history classes at Smith: St. Peter's Basilica in Rome, the Hagia Sophia in Istanbul, the gilded onion domes of Moscow, their golden beauty. And that night, as if to illuminate heaven and its arch above them, the sky had been filled with a meteor shower, streaks of light descending through the darkness.

Outside the chapel after the reading, in the cold night air

that smelled of the pine trees, everyone had stopped to stare up at the sky, some of the boys straying off the path into the snow, where they stood alone, heads tilted back, mouths open, faces upturned toward the stars. They had looked so vulnerable there, Ruth had thought, so faithful and willing, like those sad believers who trudged to the tops of hillsides in their old garments and with their heads shaved, expecting to be delivered up to God.

She remembered Mr. Frost beside Peter, their hands deep in their coat pockets, their faces calm but watchful, everyone silent.

Peter had studied with a professor at Yale who knew Mr. Frost, and it was through this man, actually a childhood friend of Robert Frost's wife, that Peter had been able to secure the famous poet's presence at Derry that night. As the assembled school stood there, the sky above them electric with light, Ruth had wrapped her arms around herself inside her coat. She had been absurdly pleased for Peter, as if he had orchestrated the display of meteors as a flattering tribute.

How small she had felt that evening. Mr. Frost had read his poems to them in a voice of judgment, not benevolence; he had seemed in some way hardly to see them at all. Yet she had felt the importance and the beauty of it all, as well, a sense of imminence in the world, something about to happen.

Later, reading in the library, she discovered that the meteor shower, common in December, was named for an obsolete constellation no longer found on star maps. The meteors visible to them that night had been orphan lights, travelers from a vanished source.

. . .

From the hall closet she lifted aside the old round film cases, cool and smooth and heavy in her hands, in order to extricate the vacuum cleaner's cord. Long ago it had ceased to retract properly, and it lay now in an impossible tangle.

When had they last looked at those old movies? She got to her knees and began stacking the film cases on the hall floor beside her. The last time, it had been for some event, she thought. The school's centennial? She couldn't remember. Peter had taken down the painting of the ship in the living room to bare the wall, and they had turned out the lights. He had been afraid the old projector might not work anymore, but after a moment's delay, the reels had begun slowly to turn and a light had streamed toward the wall.

At first they saw just a splatter of cracks and creases, hash marks on the film itself. Then, abruptly, a scene emerged: a track meet on an afternoon at Derry, the big oak trees in full, late-summer leaf, their crowns an undifferentiated black, their shadows pooling across the grass.

There must have been enthusiastic shouting that day, bystanders urging on the runners. There must have been notes of birdsong, whistles blown.

But as Ruth had settled herself on the couch next to Peter to watch that evening, there had been no sound accompanying the images on the film, only the whirring of the projector's motor and its metallic-smelling heat.

At first Peter had focused the camera on the boys, following them as they ran around the track, boy after boy, the white numbers on their backs flashing past. After the last runner had gone by, Peter had panned over the crowd standing at the edge of the field behind a white rope. Suddenly there was Ruth among the cheering onlookers, clapping and smiling. A boy standing beside her had spoken to her—she'd leaned toward him, clearly trying to hear him over the shouting. Peter had lingered on Ruth's face, the runners forgotten. Then, as if feeling his eyes on her from across the field, Ruth had turned and looked straight into the camera.

Seeing it so many years later, she'd felt again the power of that moment, her bodily awareness of his gaze, Peter looking at her through the camera from a hundred yards away. She'd felt again the way the distance between them had collapsed, everything else fallen away, the chattering boys and the shade beneath the trees and the afternoon's high clouds. It was as if his hand had reached out to cup the back of her neck and pull her close for a kiss.

On the film she had given Peter a little wave from the other side of the track.

All right. Enough of that now, her wave said.

But he had kept the camera steady, even when she'd turned her face aside.

After a moment, she had looked back. She'd smiled, and then she'd made a dismissive shooing motion with her hands, her lips moving, though of course he couldn't have heard her from that distance.

What had she said? Stop it! You're embarrassing me.

Sitting in the dark living room watching the footage, Peter beside her, Ruth had stared as if at a stranger at this vision of her younger self. She was a tall woman, and she looked disconcertingly enormous in photographs with the boys, towering over all but a few of them. Her mouth—my big mouth, as she liked to say—had been open wide as she'd shouted to encourage the runners. The dark lipstick they'd all favored back then had been a mistake on her, she'd thought; her mouth was too large for it. Her hair had been held back in the wind with a paisley Liberty scarf given to her by her friend Dr. Wenning; it was the nicest item of clothing Ruth had ever owned, and she'd loved it. At the time, she'd thought it made her look sophisticated. But all those years later, an old woman looking back at her younger self, she could see only a fairy-tale giantess, an old peasant. Where was the chicken under her arm? The goat tied to her waist with a rope? The bucket drawn up from the well?

What on earth had Peter seen in her all this time?

It was a mystery, wasn't it, why people loved one another?

But she had closed her eyes, resting her head on Peter's shoulder, remembering the sensation of his gaze on her that day, the heat of it.

That old love between them.

The noise of the vacuum cleaner was deafening, but she pushed it grimly through the rooms downstairs. How long had it been since she'd used it? She'd never been much for housework, especially in summer when school was not in session and visitors to the house were rare.

There must be something wrong with the old thing, she thought, to make such a racket now. She'd have to take it in to get it fixed.

Once she had imagined that a point would come when such

duties would fall away from her. After decades of diligence—
the headmaster's house ought to be kept properly, and she had
tried never to leave undone that which ought to be done—she
had thought that perhaps a sort of exemption would be granted.

Now she knew she would cook and vacuum and dust until
she was no longer able to do so. And after all, she thought, she
supposed she was grateful for the wherewithal and ability to
keep even an untidy house.

She would not lug the vacuum cleaner upstairs, however.
No one would go up there during the party anyhow. She bundled it back into the hall closet and fetched one of Peter's old
undershirts from the ragbag hanging on a hook in the back hall.
In the living room, she ran the cloth over the bookshelves and
end tables, the frayed silk lampshades, the tufted chair backs.
Dust rose, accusing her. After the vacuum's noisy vibrato,
the silence rang. She sat down at the piano and played a few
emphatic bars of a Mendelssohn march, feet pumping the ped-
als, but her hands faltered, the melody lost.

There was work to be done anyway, she thought, rising. She
could not sit and play all day.

The mirror over the fireplace needed polishing. She dragged
in the shaky old stepstool from the kitchen and climbed the
steps. But as she reached for the eagle at the top of the mirror's frame, the stool swayed alarmingly beneath her. In the
glass, her reflection lurched to one side, like someone falling
off a cliff. She backed down carefully, clutching the mantelpiece. No need to break a hip, she thought, just to prove a false
assiduousness.

In the kitchen she turned on the radio, tied on an apron,

and set about making three baking sheets of the cheese puffs she always fixed for social occasions at the school. They had a French name—*gougettes? gougères?* She always just called them cheese puffs. In the refrigerator she moved aside the jars of mayonnaise and mustard and pickles, half-empty bottles of salad dressing and tubs of yogurt, balancing the warped trays on the crowded shelves.

Then she made herself a ham sandwich. She ate standing at the sink, dropping crumbs.

Outside the window, goldfinches mobbed the thistle feeder. On the radio, a piano opus by Schumann commenced. She recognized the piece: "Tangled Dreams, Confusing Dreams," it was called, something like that. The station played a lot of Schumann.

She and Peter had seen Rubinstein play this particular piece once years and years before, she realized, when Peter was at Yale. Ruth had a remarkable memory for music, though never the aptitude for which she had longed. Rubinstein had been the height of elegance that night, silver in his hair, and dressed in a forked tailcoat. They had sat where they could see his hands, big as a longshoreman's. At the time, he had seemed to them impossibly old, though he couldn't have been more than seventy. Younger than she was now, she thought.

It had been early spring then, the evening they'd heard him play. Water from the snowmelt had been running in the streets in New Haven. After the performance, she and Peter had gone home to their three-room apartment, theirs exactly like all those issued to married graduate students. Pocket doors separated a bedroom and a tiny sitting room with a hissing radiator and a leaded-glass window on a crank. A hallway led to a narrow kitchen with a two-burner stove. The toilet and a stall shower were concealed behind a curtain in a space no bigger than a broom closet.

In the sitting room, Peter had put the Schumann record on the turntable. Ruth had watched him from bed, the blankets pulled up to her chin.

She had loved that sound, dust blown from a phonograph needle.

Peter had joined her between the sheets, pulling her to him, naked and warm.

In Peter's arms, Ruth had listened to the quicksilver notes. She'd wanted, as she sometimes did, to say how the music made her feel, to describe it. She and Peter had watched on a friend's television set Leonard Bernstein's first live concerts for young people. She'd been held rapt by Bernstein's analysis of Beethoven's *Waldstein* Sonata and "The Blue Danube" and boogie-woogie. She loved how Bernstein would say, *I've missed you!* to the children at the start of each new broadcast. She felt exactly like one of those lucky children sitting in the audience. Bernstein asked them if they, too, saw colors when they listened to music. A brass sound made Bernstein see fiery orange, he said, and Ruth had known just what he meant.

Over the years she and Peter had listened to all kinds of music. Billie Holliday and Herb Alpert, the Rolling Stones and the Jackson Five, Gregorian chants and the Red Army Choir. Their taste for the classical repertoire, though—especially for the piano—had outlasted everything else.

But the piano made Ruth want to talk. She couldn't help it.

That night, Schumann's music filling the room, Peter lying on his back beside her, his eyes closed—had reached over and put his hand over her mouth just as she opened it. Then he had turned to face her on the pillow and smiled.

He kissed her.

I forgot what I was going to say, she said. Thanks a lot.

Let's play it again, he said.

He got up and crossed the floor to the sitting room. He was so tall and handsome, Ruth thought, with his long legs and lean belly and broad shoulders. She'd watched him, admiring.

There was that wonderful sound again, his breath on the needle. It was as if he had blown into her ear. The sensation sent chills over her skin. Then the music started.

Peter climbed back into bed beside her. He pulled up the sheet and blankets, tucking them in around her shoulders.

Fantastic, she thought, listening as the music began, closing her eyes.

Rubinstein's hands had moved like lightning that night in the concert hall. How *did* the music sound? What color was it? Black and silver, she thought. Like the ocean, its pennants of light, its adamantine swells, flooding into pools like mirrors along the sand.

She had turned her head and slept then, her cheek on Peter's arm.

Those had been such lovely years.

Now she brushed her hands free of crumbs, put her plate in the sink.

As she did so, the music on the radio ceased abruptly. A dead silence fell into the quiet kitchen.

Ruth turned away from the window.

The radio was on a shelf mounted over the radiator. Three warning blasts blared from a siren, and then, after a moment, a computerized voice announced the threat of tornadoes in a distant county.

A line of dangerous thunderstorms was moving eastward.

On the radar maps that Peter consulted, such storms were conveyed as comic-book explosions of red and yellow and green.

She glanced out the kitchen window again.

The sky was empty, a formal ceremonial blue.

She turned on the tap to rinse her plate.

Years of living with Peter, whose interest in the weather Ruth considered obsessive, had acquainted her with the habits of storms. These would dissipate long before reaching them so near the coast, she expected, their force dissolved by the wall of warm air gathering offshore and advancing inland.

She even knew, thanks to Peter, the name of this effect: the marine influence.

She had never seen a real tornado, only the ones captured on television. How sinister they were, she thought, their scale so . . . biblical.

But Peter would tell her not to worry now.

She ran hot water and washed the mixing bowls, glancing up at the sky from time to time.

She had always done the work herself for parties at the school. There had never been any extra money for help, and she wouldn't have asked for it if there had been. The school had many other, more urgent needs. There was no skill to making cheese puffs anyway, as she'd told Peter when he fretted that all the labor fell to her. She'd made them so often she could do it in her sleep. She'd rather bake a cake—and eat one, for that matter—but one didn't eat cake with gin, and gin was what they would all want at the end of this first long day of the school year.

It was a private satisfaction to Ruth that those who had worked at the Derry School all the years that Peter had been headmaster had come to expect cake on their birthday. She made several kinds—lemon, coconut, apple, German chocolate, carrot—taking care to find out people's preferences and keeping a list. Also, those who were sick or suffering trouble knew they could depend on soup and pie from Ruth. She was glad to have been relied on in this way. Such kindness was uncomplicated, easy to give. In the summers, too, she delivered to people in their offices bunches of the dusty purple grapes from the old arbor sagging behind the house. They were delicious, with an old-fashioned sweetness, and Peter hated to see them go to waste. The bees would ruin them if she did not give them away.

He did not think of the grapes as belonging to them, in any case. Everything they had, including the house itself and most of its furnishings, was theirs only provisionally, for as long as they remained at Derry.

Her work in the world had not been equal to Peter's.

She knew that, but she had wanted to be of help to him and to the boys. She had wanted, as she had said often to Dr. Wenning, to be of use in the world.

• • •

Peter and Ruth had lived and worked at Derry for just over fifty years. In the summer of 1960 when they arrived, Peter was just shy of his twenty-seventh birthday, tall and gangly and all Adam's apple and kneecaps and hair flopping in his eyes. His first job at the school had been to teach American history.

The Derry Industrial School, as it was called then, had been founded at the turn of the nineteenth century. Parents who had lost a son to influenza in early childhood had established the school with a bequest to the Maine diocese of the Episcopal Church, and its original purpose had been to educate boys once referred to as unfortunate. The curriculum promised a vocational path, the gift of useful knowledge and practical skills— including the harvesting of lumber—which would arm these boys with a way to make a living in the world.

For decades, Derry boys had gone into the forest with teams of horses and wagons, learning the art of selecting and felling timber. The practice had been in use still when Ruth and Peter had arrived, and even after bulldozers and mechanical equipment were available, the school continued to use the horse teams, the method thought to be more in keeping with the Derry spirit and its pride in self-reliance and discipline, the nostalgic virtues of manly, robust health.

In the early years, Ruth and Peter had gone with the boys and the lumbermen who directed them. In winter, bells were hung on the big draft horses' harnesses, the horses' warm breath clouding the air. There had been a gravely festive quality to those occasions—thermoses of milky sweet coffee and cheese sandwiches on brown bread supplied—not a celebration exactly, Ruth had thought, but something significant. Finally, however, it was no longer affordable to timber the land in this way. A company came now to clear-cut a section every few years, and the school depended on the revenue. Ruth missed the old days. She thought she would never forget the sound of the horses' bells, the trees coming down in the silence of the forest, the great ominous rushing sound and the raw, sour tang in the air. Standing beside Peter in the red hat she'd knitted for herself, Peter wrapped in the red scarf she'd made for him, she had felt deep inside her the collision of tree with earth.

The language of the school's mission had changed over the years, of course. The word *unfortunate* could not be used anymore, though as Peter always said, it was the same truth now as it had been one hundred years before that those who were born poor deserved their poverty no more or less than others deserved the silver spoon. But costs had risen steeply, and the trustees were exerting growing pressure on Peter to redirect the school's focus toward paying students. A capital campaign had begun to transform the beautiful but shabby old brick buildings and to *up-market*, a term Peter disliked, the school's image. More and more, especially in the last few years, Peter had been left alone to importune privately his own contacts—old friends they were, by now—to raise the money to protect the boys who needed scholarships. His job had become a continual fight for principle and for the funds to sustain that principle, and Ruth had watched him suffer over it.

Now, after fifty years at the school, nearly forty as headmaster, Peter was, Ruth knew, too much a part of the school's history to be fired, too well loved by too many. The school's financial future was at present too uncertain for the risk of such change. Yet the uneasy compromise in which Derry now found itself, neither New England prep school for wealthy boys nor home for the indigent, could not last long. And the very rich and the very poor were rarely good bedfellows, Ruth thought, no matter what notions Peter cherished about empathy and civic duty.

Peter was now seventy-six years old, Ruth just a couple of months behind him.

He had so far resisted retiring, but it was only a matter of time, Ruth knew, before something unpleasant happened. She felt that time fast approaching.

And then where would they go?

What would Peter, who had worked every day, his whole adult life, for this school, *do* with himself?

He was old—they were *both* old—and she saw that the boys were not as impressed by him as they had been back in the day. He still loped around the classroom firing questions at the students, though now hobbled by his bad knees and much changed in appearance from his younger self, worn down by age and disease. But his enthusiasm was more performance than it once had been, she knew. He'd been uncannily good with names when he was younger—amazing really, Ruth had thought—but more often now he relied on old-fashioned endearments: Sport, Champ, Buster, Pal. Peter's reputation—a thing separate from Peter himself, she thought, like the story of a great king—held him aloft in the minds of most boys. But one day last year she had seen a boy walking behind Peter and imitating him, swinging his arms ape-like and lurching like Quasimodo. The impression had not been inaccurate, and Ruth had felt sick with pain and anger. It had taken all her restraint not to go up and grab the boy by the arm and slap his cheek.

That night, she and Peter had quarreled—her fault, as usual. She had picked a fight over something inconsequential, her anger easier to bear than her grief.

She hated that he gave off a whiff of injury, like a weakened animal being tracked in the woods. She hated the complicated misery of her pity.

Still he wouldn't agree to retire.

He could not even talk about it.

And she, because she loved him, could not talk about it, either.

After her lunch, she went outside to weed the flower bed in front of the house. It was warm for September, the air still and the birds quiet in the trees. It was as if the storms to the west were attracting all the energy in the atmosphere, creating around them a perimeter of unnatural calm. She realized that she had spoken to no one all morning. The telephone had not rung.

When she struggled to her feet at last following two hours on her knees, her back was so stiff she could scarcely stand upright.

It seemed an indulgence in the daylight hours, but she went indoors and ran a hot bath anyway. She had time before dinner, she thought. The day's long silence had made her uneasy, and the evening ahead would be tiring. There was no harm in a quick bath.

Yet she soaked in the tub for a long while, trickling water over the chilled atolls of her knees. Big, doleful things her kneecaps appeared from that perspective, her chin held just above the water. Six feet tall once, her legs powerful from years of regular walking, she had lost height as she had aged. After going through menopause, she had shrunk a quarter-inch or more every year, and she had grown heavier, too, pounds now apparently impossible to shed. When she folded laundry, she hurried to put away her underclothes, so distressingly large.

Addressing her image in the mirror directly was all right; it was odd, how one could look without seeing. But it was unpleasant to accidentally glimpse her reflection in mirrors or store windows, like a creature stumbling into civilization from the wilderness. *Hulking* was the word that came to mind

Her old friend Dr. Wenning, a doctor and a professor of psychiatry for whom Ruth had worked part-time while Peter was at Yale, had despaired over Ruth's posture.

Ruth, her back rounded, had sat at a wobbly three-legged table, typing Dr. Wenning's lecture and patient notes from yellow sheets covered with her illegible scrawl.

Do not *slump* so, Ruth! Dr. Wenning would cry. In her habitual cowl-necked sweater, her white hair a bird's nest, Dr. Wenning would frown at Ruth. Chin jutting, shoulders back, she presented her chest.

Like a figurehead on a ship, Ruth, she said. Breasts forward. *Thus.*

Dr. Wenning had been barely five feet tall. The effect had been Napoleonic, ridiculous.

Ruth had laughed.

Go ahead, Dr. Wenning had said, shaking a finger. But your height is not an *affliction*, Ruth. Biologically speaking, it is a survival advantage. Embrace your height!

On days when Ruth felt disquieted, as she had been today—the tiresome, noisy vacuuming, the tornado warnings, the lonely afternoon and long evening's duties that always accompanied the first day of the school year still ahead of her—Ruth missed Dr. Wenning.

It had been thirty years since she had died, Ruth sitting beside her bed in the hospital in New Haven, where Dr. Wenning had practiced medicine for so many decades, treating with Teutonic calm and courtesy the hysterical, the suicidal, the dangerous, the brokenhearted.

My friends, Dr. Wenning had always called them.

Ruth had stayed at the hospital for three days during which Dr. Wenning had not regained consciousness.

Perched on a hard chair, inching closer to the window as the sun moved across the sky, Ruth had reread *Middlemarch*, plucked for its heft from the bookshelf at home before she'd left. Occasionally, she went downstairs to call Peter from the pay telephone on the first floor across from the hospital's cafeteria, where the smells in the hall of toast and egg salad and hamburgers, the cheerful sounds of conversation and the clinking of silverware, warred with the underlying odors of sickness, the dramas of birth and death taking place nearby but out of sight.

Carrie Brown

Trays of bland meals had been delivered with depressing, even cruel regularity, to Dr. Wenning's room. Ruth had felt outraged by these trays, the callousness of their disregard; clearly it could be seen that Dr. Wenning—eyes closed, whey-faced and bloated—would never eat again. Exhausted, terrified, Ruth had had no appetite, and she had hurried to put the untouched trays outside the door, clattering the dishes angrily as she did so. *Why* did they continue to bring them?

For two days, Dr. Wenning had moved restlessly in the bed, though never opening her eyes, her mouth working in ways that made Ruth's throat constrict with helplessness.

Dr. Wenning had suffered her first bout of breast cancer years before, had survived one mastectomy and then another. She had known that this would be the end.

I know very well what will happen to me, Dr. Wenning had said, addressing her cowed young physician on her last visit to his office, Ruth sitting beside her, obedient as a nun.

It is pretty easy, Dr. Wenning had said. She had smiled at the young doctor, but his ears had gone red.

You give me enough morphine to sink a naval carrier, Dr. Wenning said. No stinginess in that regard. We are not, after all, worried about my *addiction*.

Do you hear me, Ruth? She had reached over to clutch Ruth's arm and had gripped it lightly, as if to emphasize Ruth's presence there for the doctor, someone who would hold him accountable.

Then her tone had softened. Ah, she had said lightly, almost gaily. What a nuisance I am to you. I hate it when my patients are physicians. Sorry!

She'd shaken her head, as if he and she were in agreement about their mutual obstinacy, their presumption, the necessary ego of those who took the Hippocratic oath.

Dr. Wenning had hefted her purse to her lap. But you understand me, I know, she said. And Ruth here knows what I want. So . . . it is okay? We are of one mind.

She had patted Ruth's arm, as if Ruth had made this speech.

Afterward, breathless as they left the doctor's office, she had apologized.

I had to scare him a little bit, she said. It was not too bad, though? I tried to be gentle.

Ruth realized she had never seen Dr. Wenning be anything *but* gentle, though she could be brisk with people she called bureaucrats and tyrants. A line from Shakespeare had come to Ruth; most of the time, Dr. Wenning's tone would *sing the savageness out of a bear.*

On the third morning of Ruth's vigil at the hospital, something seemed to ease inside Dr. Wenning's body, and she had quieted. Ruth, staring at her, felt distance enfolding between them, though their positions never moved. The intervals between Dr. Wenning's breaths became farther and farther apart.

Throughout the day, glancing up from *Middlemarch*, Ruth started forward in her chair only to see—after a long moment—Dr. Wenning's sad, flat chest rise again.

Late on the evening of the third day, Ruth was awoken by a nurse's hand on her shoulder.

She jumped up.

All traces of Dr. Wenning, everything Ruth had known

about her, had disappeared. Ruth cried out, her book falling to the floor.

In an instant that Ruth realized she had missed, Dr. Wenning had left her. The thing on the bed—the face hollow beneath the cheekbones, the nose a bloodless beak, the hand curled on the sheet—was almost unrecognizable.

She discovered then, though she had imagined it otherwise, that it would have been impossible to mistake sleep for death.

Night had fallen. Through the open window, Ruth heard the sound of wind in the treetops, the noise of traffic. Other nurses came into the room; how had they been summoned? One of them—there, there, she said; I've seen much worse—ushered Ruth from the room, as if now there was something mysterious to be done to Dr. Wenning that was too private, too obscene to be witnessed.

Ruth went downstairs, her legs wavering beneath her.

The cafeteria had been closed, the lights out. Through a round window in a door behind the lunch counter, she could see into the lighted kitchen, where someone was still at work, his white paper hat moving back and forth across the porthole window.

Inside the phone booth, she turned her back to the empty hallway, pressed her handkerchief to her face. When Peter answered the phone, she couldn't speak.

Oh, Ruth, Peter said at last. I'm sorry.

The sympathy in his voice had made her cry.

He had not been able to come with her. That had been before he'd been made headmaster. He was only a teacher then, and it had not been easy for him to leave the school. There weren't enough teachers as it was, and when one of them quit or was sick or had to be away, the burden fell to the others, and the boys could be unruly and needed a strong hand. Resentment flared up quickly among colleagues who thought they spotted a shirker in their midst.

And Dr. Wenning had been no relation, after all, though she had been mother, father, sister . . . everything, really, to Ruth.

Outside the phone booth, someone had tapped a knuckle impatiently on the glass.

Ruth had made angry gestures of dismissal at the intruder, turned away her wet face.

Ruth had felt forlorn in the weeks following Dr. Wenning's death.

One night, after another silent dinner, Peter had put down his fork.

She is still with you, Ruth, he said.

He had meant to console her. She knew that. But she thought his certainty fatuous—how on earth could he be so sure?—and she had snapped at him and told him so, though of course she regretted it later.

It made her feel hideous, being cruel to Peter, even when that cruelty arose—as she came to understand that it usually did, as was the case for most people, of course—out of pain.

She did not exactly wish that she had Peter's faith in God—you couldn't *try* to believe in something; you either did or did not—but she envied it. And his faith had only grown stronger over the years, though by what mechanism he could not say. He was, Ruth sometimes thought, remarkably inarticulate about the things that seemed most important. In their early years, she had argued with him about God, even though then, as always, he had failed to rise to the attack.

It's just a *story*, she said once. All that about the world being made in seven days, the Garden of Eden, the serpent who speaks, the stone before the mouth of the cave, the water turning into wine, blah blah blah.

He had shrugged. Think of it as a metaphor, he suggested.

Well, I just *can't*, Ruth had snapped. And dead is dead.

Yet she also felt grateful for Peter's faith, the way his conviction occasionally made it possible for her to trust, even temporarily, his version of things, a world where one was never really alone. And it *was* true that it made her feel less lonely to remember things about Dr. Wenning, to picture her. She would try to reconstruct Dr. Wenning's face: blue eyes bulging behind the thick lenses of her glasses, the splatter of black moles like pepper on her neck, the unlikely softness of her plump hands, like little pillows. She tried to remember exactly how Dr. Wenning had looked sitting across from her in their favorite Italian restaurant in New Haven, Dr. Wenning wearing her big clip-on earrings, chunky square amethysts made of resin, and a red checkered napkin tucked under her chin. The chandeliers with their ivory silk shades had cast a pink light over the room, over the white bowls of spaghetti with vodka sauce that Ruth and Dr. Wenning always ordered.

The comfort these memories held for Ruth—the moments when she could actually conjure forth Dr. Wenning's elusive, vanished presence, the sound of her voice—was fleeting but piercing, a joy, though a joy strangely akin to pain. How close those two states often seemed, Ruth felt. How odd that one cried tears of *joy* as well as sorrow.

Every year on the first night of the school year it was the same. Dinner in the dining hall, Peter's address to the boys at the chapel, then drinks and something to eat at Ruth and Peter's house afterward for the faculty, who came in shifts so as not to neglect the boys on their first night.

Tonight she would go to dinner and to Peter's talk, as she did every year. And she didn't mind giving the party. She would never *not* have given it, in any case. Yet always when the school year began, she felt a little dread at what lay ahead. Cocoa nights with the boys, dinners with the trustees, retirement parties, school-wide picnics . . . she did her best on these occasions, but she was not naturally good at such things.

As she said to Peter, it was absurd for a basically shy and uncomfortable person to be in charge of making *other* people feel comfortable. A loner—though a *lonely* loner, as she knew herself to be—she had never found the public side of things, of being Peter's wife, to be easy. What she *had* liked was to work. It was never a problem for Ruth to work. Hobnobbing with the high and mighty, as she said, was simply not her thing. And she was better with the boys than with the adults, anyway.

In the bathtub now, she lifted one foot and with her big toe turned on the faucet to run a trickle of hot water into the tub. She would likely forget someone's name tonight, she thought, or the names of their children, as she seemed to do more frequently.

They'd had no children of their own, a grief between her and Peter, though this was never mentioned anymore. Sometimes in the old days she saw that Peter had been caught off guard, noticing her with someone's toddler in her lap. He had turned his eyes away from hers then, keeping a distance. It would have been too much for a look to pass between them. And children inevitably had seemed to like her, finding her at public events at the school as if they'd been watching for her, swinging on her arms when they saw her or crawling familiarly into her lap, where they leaned against her, gazing out defiantly at their embarrassed parents.

Aware of the weight of them against her, the intimate smells of other people's houses in the children's fine hair and on their skin, Ruth had tried to stay still on these occasions, like the careful servant of a dignified child emperor who has consented to be comforted, but with whom one must not take liberties.

She and Peter weren't so sad about it anymore; they could smile over a child's head now, Ruth's hand tentatively touching the child's shoulder, the child turning to lay a palm against Ruth's cheek or her breast. Ruth had to close her eyes at these moments, the heat of the little hand against her skin.

They'd had the school, she and Peter. All the boys.

They'd had other people's children.

In the years when Peter was first headmaster, Ruth had given gifts on birthdays and at Christmas to the children of the faculty. She chose these gifts—rocking horses, dollhouses, enormous teddy bears—on twice-annual shopping trips to Boston, trips she undertook alone, staying in a hotel and eating solitary meals at the hotel's restaurant.

Peter thought the trips were a kind of holiday for her and encouraged her to go. She didn't want to tell him how sad they made her sometimes, all those toys. She hated how pathetic she'd felt in the hotel's dining rooms as she gulped her wine, cut up a lamb chop, forked in mashed potatoes against the trembling of her mouth. She would cry if she did not have to chew and swallow.

Worst of all was that she eventually came to understand that the gifts were considered—by some—extravagant. Her efforts were not appreciated; they conveyed an attitude of noblesse oblige on her part. Nothing could have been further from the truth. She and Peter could ill afford such generosity, though she realized that others had no way of knowing this, perhaps. But people who were badly paid were sometimes quick to become bitter, she understood. People felt obligated to repay her kindness somehow, she realized, or it was a burden to them to write a note of thanks. She had felt hurt by this—she had wanted to please—but it had been with mingled disappointment and relief that she'd finally given up the practice.

Now she only sent cards at Christmas, a photograph of Derry taken by Peter—Derry in snow, Derry in autumn, deer at Derry, boys cavorting at Derry, sunset at Derry—and signed with love from Dr. and Mrs. van Dusen.

Over the years, as the children grew up, she crossed out the

Dr. and Mrs. and wrote instead in her big sloping script, Peter and Ruth. She had kept an album of all the Christmas cards they'd had made of Peter's photographs.

In a few years they would be eighty, she and Peter. Some of the children who had been born while Peter was headmaster were now in college. Some of them were married, with children of their own. Ruth had lost track of them all, though many had stayed in touch with the van Dusens out of loyalty and affection, proudly sending cards at Christmas with photographs of their spouses and children, beautiful little strangers.

She nearly drifted off to sleep in the bathtub, but finally the water was too cold to be comfortable. She stood up unsteadily in the tub, reached for a towel and wrapped herself up in it.

In the bedroom, she looked at the clock. It was nearly five p.m.

She called Peter at his office—it was odd that he had failed to check in during the day, as he usually did—but there was no answer. Nor did his secretary pick up his phone.

Ruth sat down on the bed and dialed his cell phone number, but he didn't answer that, either.

Well, it was the first day, she thought. They were all busy.

She put on a slip and her navy blue dress. Standing at her bureau, she found in her jewelry box a large gold sunburst pin Peter had given her. He did not trouble about his own clothes— she had to throw away shirts and trousers that became disreputable, frayed along the collars or cuffs—but for a man of thrift, he was an impulsive shopper, and he had what Ruth thought was a disconcerting taste for dramatic costume jewelry. Occasionally the things he chose for her—soapstone dolphins on black cords, hunks of turquoise wrapped in thick silver bands—were so conspicuous that Ruth knew people felt compelled to compliment her on them, even if they were ugly, which they sometimes were.

He would notice the sunburst tonight and be pleased.

She carried her shoes from the closet and set them down by the bed, a show of her good intentions. She would be ready on time.

She would not even pull the bedspread away from the pillow, she thought. But she longed to close her eyes for a few minutes.

She lay down carefully on her back so as to minimize wrinkles, tugging the fabric of the dress smooth under her bottom. Her body was hot from the bath, and the bedspread felt warm beneath her, the sunlight having moved slowly across the empty bed all afternoon.

She woke with the alarm of those who know they have overslept.

Smoky, golden haze filled the window between the curtains, and the carillon bells were ringing.

She sat up abruptly. The smell of burning leaves reached her through the open window. Two beautiful old oak trees had come down across the entrance road to the school in thunderstorms the week before. There were only four men left on the physical plant crew, and two of them too old to be doing such work safely, she thought. It had taken them days to cut up the trees and haul away the wood, everyone aware that the students were arriving soon, that haste was needed. They must be burning the brush behind the old garages this evening.

They had been sad to see them go, those trees, she and Peter. Somehow one just hated to see them on the ground like that.

She looked at the digital clock beside the bed, but its face was blank. She realized that the power had gone out while she'd been asleep. The mirror over the bureau was empty and dark.

What time was it?

She had been dreaming, she remembered then, and the scene of her dream came to her. There had been a canyon with high, ochre-colored walls and, in a valley below, an enormous solitary building like a warehouse, the many windows illuminated by a sunset. Hawks had circled in a cold, high, desert twilight. In the dream she had been standing above the canyon, looking down into it, the landscape somewhere in the west, Utah or Nevada, she thought. She had never lived in that part of the country. Yet the feeling in the dream had been that she was returning after many years to somewhere she had once known well, a place now deserted. A memory of it had stirred in her somehow, even as she was dreaming, the canyon's echoing emptiness and the towering sky familiar.

As if in answer to the bright, precise vividness of this vision, her head began to ache.

Ruth had suffered from nightmares for many years, though over time they had come less and less often. She hardly ever had one anymore.

Perhaps, as Dr. Wenning had once proposed, the balance of

her life had finally shifted, the weight of her years of happiness with Peter asserting itself against the unhappiness of her childhood. Usually now her dreams, like this one—like most people's, she assumed, the events and settings distinct but without sense—were simply mysterious. Yet though the dreams resisted interpretation—she had no idea what this one *meant*—they had a strong feeling to them. These feelings, difficult for her to put into words, nagged at her for hours, sometimes for days, after waking. This dream, stubbornly visual, would stay with her, she thought.

She had long ago stopped telling Peter about her dreams. His lack of interest—raising his eyebrows at her in the mirror by way of response as he brushed his teeth in the mornings—had been poorly concealed. She had been a little hurt by this, even as she had understood it. Still, one wanted to tell *someone* . . .

What would Dr. Wenning have said about this dream, she wondered now. The silent, eerily familiar landscape, the hawks making their slow rotation high in the sky, the windows in the building flaming red and then washed black as the sun dropped below the horizon . . . what did it mean that one's mind produced such images? And how strange, Ruth thought, to appear to remember in a dream a place her mind had *invented*.

Yet to a person whose own past was a mystery, everything was a clue . . . and nothing. It didn't do to make too much of such things.

Ruth's friendship with Dr. Wenning was, she knew, the second luckiest event in her life after her love for Peter. For the four years while Peter was at Yale working on his degree, Ruth had ridden her bicycle every Saturday afternoon across New Haven to the suite of rooms near the Green where Dr. Wenning maintained her private practice.

There Ruth organized Dr. Wenning's books—there were usually heaps of them open on the floor and tables when Ruth arrived—typed up her notes, washed the dishes in the little kitchen, and pushed the carpet sweeper over the Oriental rugs. Sometimes she made tiny cups of the strong coffee Dr. Wenning liked and brought them to her while she worked at her desk, placing them by her elbow. Dr. Wenning, though she did not look up from her work, would reach out to touch Ruth's arm in gratitude.

Ruth had never known someone to concentrate like Dr. Wenning.

In the high-ceilinged apartment with its air of bygone grandeur, Ruth felt removed from the world, suspended above it. From the windows, she watched cars and pedestrians appear below through the leaves of the trees the way she imagined glimpsing the earth through clouds from an airplane. The unnatural quiet—the steam rising from the electric kettle on a tea cart in Dr. Wenning's study, the sherry glasses occasionally trembling on their papier-mâché tray, the gears of the mantel clock brushing and whirring—had made Ruth, usually so reticent, feel strangely voluble.

She had wanted to tell Dr. Wenning everything.

Yet Dr. Wenning herself seemed to invite confession. With her high, thick waist and firm belly and wide blue eyes, she gave the impression of being able to absorb all manner of tragedy, like the Chinese brother in the tale who swallows the ocean.

Ruth learned that Dr. Wenning had been born in Germany in 1919. She had been in America on a teaching fellowship when the United States entered the war. The head of the psychiatry department at the hospital in New Haven, also a Jew, had helped protect her from internment in the United States or exchange with the Third Reich, but most of her family had died in the camps, only an elder brother surviving.

By 1954, the year Ruth met Dr. Wenning, she had been teaching for many years at Yale, one of the first women on the faculty and distinguished for her research on trauma and memory.

There had been love in Ruth's young life by then; she had loved Peter at first sight. But her love for Dr. Wenning was different: a slow love, a love that came at her in waves, each larger and more powerful than the one before.

So, Dr. Wenning would say at the end of those Saturday afternoons, rising from her desk just as the light began to change and appearing in her office door to smile upon Ruth.

Enough of our ceaseless labors for one day, she would say. Tell me what amazing thing you have dreamed last night, Ruth.

They sat at opposite ends of the enormous sofa in Dr. Wenning's inner office, mugs of tea or milky Nescafé in their hands. Sometimes Dr. Wenning poured sherry for them.

Come, Dr. Wenning always said, patting the sofa cushions and making herself comfortable, as if she had all the time in the world.

I want all the details, she said. Do not be stingy with your narration, Ruth. You are an *Olympic* dreamer. I am very much interested.

Not until years later, long after Ruth and Peter had left New Haven, did Ruth fully recognize the kindness of Dr. Wenning's attention to her during those years. She must have been terribly busy, Ruth realized, and terribly tired, carrying with her not only her own sad history but also the woes of so many other people. Yet she had made Ruth feel proud of her dreams, of the minute details she seemed able to remember.

Ruth would relate her dreams, and Dr. Wenning would rub her chin, listening.

Remarkable, she would say, as if Ruth had performed a surprising feat of memorization or mental agility, like being able to recite the alphabet backwards, which Ruth actually could do effortlessly. Once she performed this trick for Dr. Wenning, to Dr. Wenning's apparent delight.

Your mind, Ruth! Dr. Wenning had tapped her own temple with a finger. It is really quite beautiful. Even the horrors of these dreams of yours—the specificity of them is remarkable. Artistic, of course, given your temperament.

She had leaned over and patted Ruth's knee where she sat curled up at the end of the sofa.

These dreams will not trouble you forever, I think, she had said.

Look at you, Ruth. You were built for happiness. A picture of happiness.

Yet Ruth did not always feel happy. In the months before her marriage to Peter, she suffered another spell of aching curiosity about the blank document that was her past. Her mother's identity was completely unknown to her and her father's was uncertain; who and where had she come from? The urgency of these spells had waxed and waned over the years. Sometimes it was as if she couldn't think about anything else. At other times, she felt oddly released from the mystery of her past, as if its importance to her had simply floated away. Who cared, after all, who Ruth's parents had been?

Yet as the date for the wedding approached, learning something—*anything*, she thought—had felt to her of increasing significance.

Doesn't it matter to you? she asked Peter.

No, he said. I love *you*.

Then, at her expression, he said, Yes! Yes, of course, it does.

Finally, at Dr. Wenning's suggestion, Ruth sent off formally typed inquiries—she struggled over the language of these letters, crumpling up sheet after sheet of paper—to the prison where her father's life had ended and to the courthouse where the trial had been held. Finally a reply had come to her, brief and impersonal, from a government office. The prison facility had closed. Its records had been destroyed in a fire.

Dr. Wenning threw up her hands at this news, an eloquent drama of exasperation.

Well, *of course* they were lost, she said. *And* in a fire. In the roman à clef that is your life, Ruth, of course there must be a fire that destroys the secret.

There had been nothing in the transcript of the court proceedings, which Ruth already possessed, beyond what she already knew: that her father had called himself, even to her, by a name she thought was probably not his own, that he had been as impenetrable to her in life as in death. Still, she had said to Dr. Wenning, I wish I knew *something* else about him. About my mother.

Dr. Wenning had nodded. But perhaps, my dear, she said, you would not like the truth so very much more than the mystery. Better to have the mystery and make the story what you like.

Ruth looked away. I want a happy ending, she said finally.

From behind her desk, Dr. Wenning had gazed at her.

A happy ending, Ruth, she said—forgive me—is a bullshit construction of the entertainment industry. First you are born and then you die. If you are lucky, you are happy some of the time. Sometimes, if you are *very* lucky, you laugh a lot along the way.

Also, she began, but then she paused.

She waved at the room around them, and Ruth understood that she meant not just the bookshelves and the ornate crown molding and the paintings on the walls, but the world beyond those walls, Ruth's life with Peter, their future.

Perhaps, Dr. Wenning said, you already have a happy ending.

The bedroom in the silent house at Derry was full now of shadows.

Ruth felt around on the floor for her shoes, pushed herself up from the bed. Surely dinner had already begun. Peter would wonder what had happened to her.

She went into the bathroom. In the mirror over the sink, the late afternoon's light slanting through the window struck one side of her face—chin, high cheekbone, temple—brightening the silver of her hair. Two toothbrushes in an enamel mug on the sink's edge, a cracked oval of pale green soap in a scallop shell, a damp washcloth draped on the glinting tap . . . these, too, were illuminated.

How beautiful such ordinary objects appeared, she thought, like the humble objects in Vermeer's paintings—table, ewer, drape of fabric—mysteriously elevated to the level of sacrament. She loved Vermeer's work, its artful familiarity.

The light behind her shifted, the room darkening another degree. The tableau on the sink's edge faded, a dying away of the light.

Ruth bent to the basin, splashed water on her face, cupped her hands and drank. Brushing her teeth, she grimaced into the mirror.

She was late. She would have to hurry.

In the bedroom, she found her watch on the dresser, held her wrist against her bosom to strap it on. It was just past six, after all. She had not slept as long as she'd thought, despite the endless, forlorn feeling of the dream.

She and Peter had lived in the headmaster's house at the edge of the school's campus since Peter's appointment to the job forty years before. A settled-looking white clapboard Colonial with a circular drive before it, the house was in need now of a coat of paint. A shutter from an upstairs window had fallen earlier that summer; Peter had carried it to the garage and set it up on sawhorses, intending to repair it himself, but he had no time and, in truth, no skill, either, for such things. He had, as always, only his good intentions. They had argued about his getting up on a ladder, anyway.

The power in the house frequently went out. A high wind could do it, or nothing at all. She'd have to go down the basement before she left and check the old fuse box.

The house lay down a tree-lined gravel lane less than half a mile from the campus. The road ran for miles through empty forest, a rural route designated only by a number, before the paved surface resumed in the next county. Little traffic passed from either direction, and they had no neighbors. Except for the carillon bells, or on afternoons when the wind carried the sound of the boys' shouts from the playing fields, it was a quiet place.

The Appalachian Trail ran nearby. On the far side of the road across from their house, a gap had been cut and a gate installed in the old stone wall. A signpost for the trail and a historical marker identifying the school's campus were mounted nearby on a metal post. The trail followed the road for several hundred yards before veering back into the forest.

Sometimes hikers with their big walking sticks went silently past, Ruth just happening to look out a window or step outside in time to see them, their heavy packs and determined stride giving them the air of pilgrims. She did not think they looked happy, these loners desperate to escape the world, or at least other people. A few times over the years, one of them had crossed the road to ask for water or matches or even food. Their unkempt appearance, the certainty they appeared to possess about their pursuit—they seemed beyond the need for, even disdainful of, ordinary human commerce, as if they were engaged by something far more important—had always made her feel a little foolish, as though her domestic concerns, her artistic ambitions, her longing for rootedness, were character flaws that revealed her fear, the sorely limited scale of her world.

Shortly after they'd moved into the headmaster's house at Derry, she and Peter had walked a bit of the trail, a couple of miles north from the break in the stone wall. The section of forest was dense and dark. Ruth had found it claustrophobic, even ominous. She preferred walking along the shoulder of the road, where there was hardly any traffic but where one felt somehow safer, less alone.

A beautiful stand of birches, like a ring of silver ghosts, had grown up near a tiny, still pond about a twenty-minute walk into the woods.

Peter, who always had his camera with him, had lingered at the spot, fussing with his lenses. The delicate trees stood out wraith-like against the firs. Something about the mysteriousness of the little pond, like an enchanted place in a dark fairy tale, had made Ruth uncomfortable.

Let's go, she'd said finally, impatient.

On his knees, trying for a certain angle, Peter had continued to stare through the camera.

It could be maddening, trying to walk with Peter. He always wanted to take pictures. Sometimes she wanted to snap at him to put the camera down and just *look*, for heaven's sake. What on earth would he do with all these photographs, anyway? But she had given him a fancy digital camera just last Christmas, spending hours with an enthusiastic young man in a camera shop in Boston who had seemed happy to explain all its features, even though she'd understood almost nothing of what he told her.

Peter's delight with the gift had touched her. The computer, too, had been a marvelous development in his life: he had grasped its cataloging uses immediately, and he had endless files for things, including for his photographs. There was a file for pictures of Derry, of course, and for individual events at the school—sporting matches, plays, etc.

There was also a file labeled with her name—RUTH, in capital letters.

What do you keep in there? she'd asked him once.

What? Oh, this and that, he'd said. Information for you, policies and so forth.

She had not wanted to think about that, about a time when she might need to know things he would not be able to tell her himself.

Just a minute, he'd said that day, focusing on the birches.

Ruth had gazed around at the woods, the motionless trees.

Finally, after some further adjustment of the lens, Peter had clambered to his feet.

Okay, he said. I think I got it. He'd put away the lens in his bag, tucking it carefully into one of the many compartments.

Ruth had stared off unhappily into the distance. The place gave her the creeps.

Peter attached the various Velcro flaps and adjusted the bag over his shoulder. What's the matter? he said.

Ruth folded her arms. Oh, I'm just hungry, she said. Let's go home.

It had been near dusk when they passed through the gate and crossed the road toward their house a few minutes later. Relief came over her at the sight of the house's lighted windows, the steps before the front door curved in what had looked to her, from the first time she'd seen it, like a smile. She had wanted, foolishly, to run toward it. She felt as if she'd been lost in the woods for months or even years and had finally found her way home again.

I *love* this house, she'd said impulsively to Peter, and yet all at once she'd been filled with the idea of the indeterminate future when she knew they would have to leave Derry, leave this house she loved.

The idea of the future when one of them would die, the other one soldiering on somewhere . . . it was unimaginable. She couldn't bear the thought.

Yes, it's a good old house, Peter said. I'm glad you're happy here, Ruth.

He had put his arm around her, and she had leaned against him.

I *am* happy, she said.

She'd brushed her cheek against his sleeve. She would not let him see her sadness.

Let's make a fire, Peter had said. What's for dinner?

Now, checking her face quickly in the dim glass of the mirror in the bedroom, she was aware of the well of silence down the carpeted staircase, the stillness in the front hall and through the arched doorway to the living room, where she had already set out trays of drinks and glasses, bowls of nuts and fruit for the party tonight. The busy world of the school seemed far away.

Sometimes she appreciated the house's location, their relative isolation. She would not have liked being in the thick of things all the time. But sometimes it was lonely, too. She would have liked working in an office, she had thought over the years, though probably her notions of office life—convivial lunches, familiar jokes, and surprise birthday parties—were silly and unrealistic. The faculty at Derry did a lot of squabbling, she knew, and the school's trustees weren't much better, though there had been many people she had liked over the years, men whose acumen and experience she had admired, more recently women whose understanding of things sometimes seemed to Ruth more complex, more capable of nuance, than the men's.

Earlier that afternoon, pausing in the doorway of the living room to inspect it a last time before going upstairs to the bath, she had noticed that a few early leaves, the lime-yellow fans of the old gingko tree, had already fallen over the terrace outside the French doors. They'd looked lovely, scattered over the old pink bricks. Yet the sight of them had made tears come into her eyes.

She hated that the idea of her own death—or Peter's—came to her so reflexively these days, and often when she saw something beautiful . . . that glowing oval of soap on the sink's edge in the afternoon light a moment ago, the bright color of the gingko's flat-bladed leaves against the brick. She thought about dying too much, she knew. How awful that the world's beauty—one day *truly* to be lost to her—so frequently made her think of leaving the world altogether.

Dr. Wenning would have told her to stop being morbid.

She'd had an ironist's delight in foolish aphorisms. Cheer up, Ruth, she would say. Happiness is a warm puppy.

Ruth had been amused by Dr. Wenning's delight in the 1960's. Except for the Vietnam War, to which she had been early and adamantly opposed, Dr. Wenning had liked everything about the decade's easy sloganeering.

Make love, not war. So simple, she said.

She had liked the peace sign, liked the yellow smiley face that one day began to appear everywhere, liked the hippies for what she felt was a beautiful and intrinsic innocence (while strongly disapproving of drugs, whose effects she said people simply did not understand).

They want to make a better world, those hippie children, she'd said, and they think they can do it. Good for them.

She'd loved the names of the bands: The Monkees. Herman's Hermits. Jefferson Airplane. The Lovin' Spoonful.

People are either on the bus or off the bus, she had told Ruth.

Ruth had rolled her eyes.

Remember the bus? Get on the bus, Ruth, Dr. Wenning had liked to say, when she felt Ruth complained too much about her worries.

Stop fussing all the time about where the bus is going, or whether it will run off the edge of a cliff. Eventually, you are going to go over the cliff, Ruth, no matter what you do. Try to enjoy the ride meanwhile.

But what if I just *can't* seem to enjoy it? Ruth said.

Then I give you drugs, Dr. Wenning said. But I don't think that's what you need.

Are you sure? Ruth had asked.

Pretty sure, Dr. Wenning said. Trust me. I'm the doctor.

Now Ruth gave her hair a few quick strokes with the brush. No one would care what she looked like tonight; she just needed to hurry.

Still, she looked at herself—her strange and familiar self—in the mirror. The words of the Psalm came to her: *Surely goodness and mercy shall follow me all the days of my life.*

She'd always had what Peter called an irrational ability to pick and choose from among the tenets of faith.

God, perhaps. Heaven and hell, no.

Noah's ark? Of course not.

The loaves and fishes . . . well, she liked the idea. Same with the Red Sea parting. The specificity of these images felt persuasive to her.

You know what I like? she had said to Peter once. I like that *surely*. *Surely* goodness and mercy. It's a question, don't you think?

Peter, who had been getting ready for bed, had sat down next to her, pulling on one of the white T-shirts in which he slept.

Ruth, you are ever the ardent doubter, he had replied. Yes, I suppose it is. A question.

A *doubt*, Ruth had said, hitting him on the arm.

All right, he had agreed. A doubt.

Yet what good did doubt do you? Ruth thought now. She adjusted her dress, twitching at the skirt.

Time to go, she thought. No time for metaphysics.

• • •

She went downstairs, one hand on the banister. From a drawer in the kitchen she took a flashlight and opened the door to the rickety stairs leading to the basement, dark and dank as a cave. The battery in the flashlight was weak. *Why* did their flashlights never work properly?

In the basement she picked her way hesitantly through the welter of boxes and cobwebs, the crumbling hills of damp rot. It was cold down there, something rancid-smelling somewhere.

At the fuse box, she trained the flashlight over the circuits with their faded labels of masking tape and flipped the breaker.

For a moment there was nothing. After a pause, she felt the house shudder, heard it buzz back to life above her head.

She climbed the stairs, her hand on the cool, smooth old wooden railing. Peter was certainly worrying about her now.

In the front hall, she stopped to look in the mirror one last time. There was a smudge across her cheek. She licked her finger and rubbed at it.

Then, from upstairs, she heard a sound. Footsteps?

She went to the bottom of the stairs and listened. Peter? she called. Is that you?

But there was no answer.

She must have been imagining it.

Five minutes later, on the lawn below the school's dining hall, she stopped to take off her shoes. They were her good shoes, seldom worn and uncomfortable, and she could not run in them. Still, she hoped no one looked out a window and saw her, the old headmaster's wife, undignified in her stocking feet, carrying her shoes and hurrying up the hillside.

Early-evening light fell over the empty lawns and against the buildings. The Virginia creeper covering the brick was two stories high in some places and darkly lustrous. Birds streamed across the sky, flying straight at the walls and disappearing into them as if diving into water. She never tired of watching this. Here and there sections of the foliage shivered, where birds nesting in it settled for the night. Walking along the paths in the evening, Ruth liked it when the walls beside her rustled in the darkness. It was as if the buildings themselves were alive, big creatures made of brick and mortar, stirring under their green skin.

The school buildings appeared completely deserted, but as she climbed the hill, a muffled, orchestral din from the open windows of the dining hall reached her, the sounds of striking silverware and clattering dishes, the boys' voices carrying over the silent evening, the cacophony strange, almost otherworldly.

Invisible diners, Ruth thought, condemned forever to their invisible supper.

The air had a porcelain calm, no sign of the storms predicted earlier, the tornadoes gathering their evil intentions somewhere. She beheld the scene ahead of her: the ring of buildings at the top of the hill, the streetlamps scattered along the curving drive, their white lights penumbral in the early-evening haze. The maze of shadows from the great trees lay across the velvet hillside.

She hated to go inside and leave it all. She wanted to lie down in the air full of sweet, grassy ripeness and watch the stars come out.

The day was cooling, at last, but her haste had made her warm. Vibrating clouds of gnats assembled and then dispersed above the grass, specks before her eyes. She raised her arm to her damp forehead, moved her shoes to her other hand.

The carillon bells rang the hour.

A moment later, in the silence following the ringing of the bells, she realized that the sounds coming from the dining hall had ceased abruptly.

She paused on the grass. It was not her hearing, she thought, yet there was no sound at all: no knife scraping against a plate, no glass chiming against glass, no human voice. The silence felt like a hood had been dropped over her head.

Two swallows, dipping and swerving, approached, crossing the lawn before her, startling her with their nearness. They veered away toward the horizon of the black woods. Her skin had gone cold, as if a damp cloth had been passed over her bare arms.

Then a bird's sweet little note hung for a moment in the silence. It repeated in a questioning tone and then once more, plaintively.

Something had happened to make them all go quiet like that in the dining hall.

She loved the beautiful old room in which the boys and teachers took their meals, the dark oak beams across the high ceiling, and the bands of light from the tall windows crossing overhead. In the oceanic darkness below, forty round tables with their white tablecloths floated in the shadows, and two hundred boys bowed their heads over their plates. Steam rose from the regiment of tarnished coffee urns along the wall, the radiators ticking and hissing, the air above them rippling. From the kitchen came the yeasty odors of milk and meat and cooked vegetables and, behind those, the sour fumes of bleach and laundry starch and drain water from the dish room.

In the winter, Ruth cut boughs of evergreens and holly and decorated the mantel over the vast fireplace. In spring, she used daffodils and wands of forsythia for the tables.

The sad, sweet bird's note sounded again on the hillside, hanging in the air, a question.

As she neared the flight of granite steps that led up to the building, the approaching siren of an ambulance coming up the main road reached her. She ran up the stairs, trying to hook her shoes on her feet as she went.

In the long hallway—cool compared with the afternoon's warmth outside—the eyes in the old portraits lining the walls

seemed to stare down at her, all of them men in Episcopal vest-
ments, the white of a clerical collar at every neck like a cold dab
of snow against the field of black pigment.

At the far end of the hallway, a group of boys, heads together,
stood in silence at the doorway to the dining hall. They turned
toward her as she approached.

She tried to calm her voice. What happened? she said,
reaching them.

It's Dr. McClaren, one of the boys said. He fainted.

She put her hand to her heart.

It had not been Peter.

The ambulance is coming, she said. There was an unpleasant lump in her throat, a knot of fear now dissolving.

She patted one of the boys on the arm.

Not to worry, she said, and went past them into the dining
hall.

She saw Ed McClaren on the floor between the tables, surrounded by a semicircle of worried onlookers. He was at least a
decade younger than she and Peter, Ruth thought. Florid, with
a fold of stomach over his belt, he was divorced. What else did
she know about him? He had been at the school for only a year,
a post-retirement job from a small college somewhere in the
South. He taught physics and coached the wrestlers.

His eyes were open, but his skin was a ghastly shade, his
lips colorless.

Peter was on one knee beside him, a hand on his shoulder.
When Ruth stepped forward, Peter glanced up at her over the
top of his glasses.

He would wonder where she had been, she knew, but there

was no reproach in his expression. He was, as always, slow to blame, quick to forgive. If anything, he was inclined too often to take upon himself the faults of others.

Once, meanly, she had accused him of playing the martyr.

He had agreed with her, apologized for it. He had a need to comfort the world.

Well, there were worse things.

Now they exchanged a grave look.

Not this time, Ruth said to him with her eyes.

Sometime, of course, his gaze said back. But not now.

Ten years before, Peter had been diagnosed with the late onset of a genetic syndrome that produced, among other effects, immoderate height.

Already a tall man—six feet by the time he was fifteen, six feet four inches by the time he graduated from college— he was now nearly six feet seven inches tall. Ruth knew that eyes inevitably were drawn to him in a room, to the head and heavy-lidded eyes, the thick, soft white hair, the long arms and developing hunchback.

His face, she thought, looked more and more like some- thing carved from rock and trying to return to its original state, the brow jutting, and the jaw pronounced. This, too, the coars- ening of his handsome features, was part of the syndrome. He had been an extraordinarily good-looking man when young. Something remaining in his expression—a basic good nature, Ruth thought—invariably made people feel that he understood them and would take their side. He had a way of drawing confidences from the boys and from teachers without ever saying much himself.

Ruth heard commotion behind them. A paramedic team toting boxes and equipment appeared beside her at the edge of the circle gathered around Ed. An older man with a comically bushy mustache and salt-and-pepper hair, and a young woman, muscled as a boxer, her hair in a high, tight ponytail, moved in with calm dispatch.

Hi there, the young woman said, pulling out a stethoscope. Let's have a little room here, folks. Thank you.

People shuffled out of the way.

I'm fine, Ed said, his voice soft, as if apologizing for the trouble he'd created. Then, as if someone had jumped hard onto his stomach, he turned his head to the side and vomited violently onto the floor.

The crowd leaped away.

Peter glanced back up at Ruth.

She felt a cold hand run up her legs, a buzzing in her ears.

I'll go get the mop, she said quietly.

She pushed open the swinging door into the kitchen, where a radio was playing. The head cook—a huge black man, a former MP in Vietnam—glanced up at her from the big sink.

I need the mop and bucket, Clarence, Ruth said.

He shook his head. That's no good, he said.

A thin young man in a soiled white apron—Ruth recognized him but could not remember his name; it was difficult to keep kitchen help, and he was a newcomer—went away into the dish room and came back pushing the wheeled mop bucket filled with suds.

Her eyes watered against the astringency of the cleaning fluid, but she was grateful for its sharp smell.

I'll take care of that, Clarence said, coming forward.

It's all right, Ruth said. You have enough to do in here. Thank you, though.

In the dining room, the paramedics had unfolded a stretcher onto which they now hoisted Ed without ceremony.

Tears had left tracks on his face. I can't breathe, he said suddenly, his voice panicked.

The young woman paramedic put her hand on his arm and turned her face to speak rapidly—a series of unintelligible words—into a crackling radio mounted on her shoulder.

You're fine, she said, snapping an oxygen mask over his face. Blood pressure's good, pulse is fine. You're going to be fine, sir. You diabetic, by any chance? Smoker?

Ed nodded—Ruth knew he was a heavy smoker—his eyes pleading.

The paramedics moved swiftly now, pushing the stretcher, teachers and boys shoving away the tables and chairs with a horrendous noise to clear a path. The paramedics' radio squeaked and buzzed. The young woman, one hand at the stretcher's head, repeated a series of numbers into it.

In seconds they were gone.

Ruth plunged the mop into the bucket and swabbed the floor. The whole evening, the whole day, she felt had been drawing toward this. Yet she knew it was irrational; *nothing* had happened today. Absolutely nothing.

Around her the boys and teachers pulled the tables back into place. She wrung out the mop, grateful again for the ammoniac smell of the cleaner. Well, it was no trouble to mop. One could manage that.

All their years here, she thought, hers and Peter's . . . this was the life they had led.

She felt an absurd surprise at this recognition. How ridiculous, that this fact should appear to have crept up on her, ambushed her. Of course, this had been their life.

There would be nothing else beyond this for them, for her and Peter, she realized.

She turned the crank to wring the mop again. Her strange dream from earlier, in which she had been alone in that desolate and beautiful place that somehow had felt so much like home, came back to her. Her eyes prickled.

Oh, she was too sensitive; this was Ed McClaren's awful moment, not her own. As Dr. Wenning had always said, sensitive people were the worst tyrants.

Peter appeared at her elbow.

He took the mop from her—automatic, his chivalry—but then he held it absently, as if he'd forgotten what to do with it.

I sent Andy to the hospital with them, he said.

Andy Whitmore, Peter's oldest colleague, teacher of Greek and Latin, reed-thin and a master of calm and civility; he would be of comfort to Ed, Ruth thought. And perhaps there would be someone else they could call, too. Surely there was someone in Ed's life . . .

Peter's face looked gray, blue pouches beneath his eyes.

Poor man, Ruth said. Then she said, Are you all right?

Peter put the mop in the bucket. I'd like to get the boys back, he said. Better to have them finish up dinner. Do you mind taking Ed's table?

Peter always distributed the teachers among the boys at dinner on the first night. These groups would then reconvene periodically over the year for dinner and to debate various questions Peter devised, usually ethical dilemmas: Whom would you save first in a fire, a baby or an old person? Is it right to steal goods acquired unfairly by another in order to help someone else? When is lying acceptable? Sometimes Ruth and Peter lay in bed and tried to dream up new, impossible predicaments; it was challenging to create a roster of original dilemmas so that a boy never faced the same question twice.

Of course, she said. Then she added, I fell asleep at home. I'm sorry I was late.

Peter didn't seem to hear her.

He turned away from her. Please return to your seats, he said, raising his voice. The boys stood around in murmuring groups.

It's all right, Peter called. Back to your tables, please. Finish up, and then there's cake and coffee. Dr. McClaren is in good hands.

He made shepherding motions with his arms, smiling.

Come along, he said, touching the boys' shoulders as he moved through the room, firm but gentle.

Everything's all right now. Good boys.

At the table where Ed McClaren had been presiding, an overweight boy—no chin, no neck, no shoulders to speak of, his eyes an unnerving green, like those of a malevolent Irish silkie, Ruth thought—had already restored what Ruth suspected had been an unrelenting siege over the group. He barely glanced at Ruth when she appeared, unwilling—perhaps actually *unable*, she thought—to interrupt what she could tell immediately was a screed about the upcoming presidential election. Ruth and Peter were longtime devoted Democrats. Ruth, especially, would not hear a word against Barack Obama.

The other boys, including a younger child with beautiful brown skin and black eyes and hair, his posture erect, sat at the table in stoic silence. The boy's beauty was striking. The child looked like royalty, his silence majestic. Nearly all the African American boys at the school were there by Peter's hand; he found them through his connections at public schools in the state and secured funding from private sources for their tuition. He fretted endlessly that there weren't enough of them. The school was predominantly white, and it wasn't easy for the black boys.

Ruth stood at the table, waiting. Sometimes her height alone had the effect of silencing miscreant boys, but the fat boy continued speaking as if Ruth were not even there. The plates had not been cleared away. He took up eating, apparently where he had left off. He waved his fork, food dripping onto the tablecloth.

Negotiating is for cowards, he said in a tone that suggested someone was arguing with him. You don't *negotiate* if you want to win.

Ruth pulled out her chair abruptly. Across the table, the beautiful boy avoided her gaze, looked down at his plate, his shoulders straight.

She cleared her throat.

Well, she began, interrupting the monologist.

Someone, she said . . . tell me about your summer. What interesting things have you been doing?

Her dream from the afternoon pressed against her again, a brief, insistent demand. She had a flash of the canyon's rose-colored walls, the impression of great silence. The room of chattering boys fell back. Then the dream slid away, and the room around her was restored.

She turned quickly to look over her shoulder at Peter—she had a strange, keen sense of missing him, as if she were departing for a long trip—but he was bent toward the boy beside him, his head inclined, listening, as he always did, intently.

They finished the meal, somehow. Coffee and cake were brought out, and then suddenly conversation died away. When she turned around, Peter had gotten to his feet across the room. He looked even more stooped than usual, she noticed, a result of the scoliosis the doctors had warned them about, part of the syndrome.

It was time now for him to retire, she thought. *Why* was he putting them through this? They might still go off and do something together, go somewhere, before it was too late. They hadn't much money, she knew, but surely there was enough. She had been foolish, allowing Peter to handle all that—*making* him handle all that—as if she were a child.

At the last board meeting in May, Alec Brown, a trustee who'd been on the board for years and who had been a good friend to Peter, had taken Ruth aside in the main room of the library while people had drinks there before dinner.

No one will ever fill Peter's shoes, Ruth, Alec had said. You know that.

They had laughed about that for a minute—Peter's feet, size fourteen, were notorious—but Ruth had known there was more coming.

Alec's tone had been light, but then he had put a hand on her arm. See what you can do, Ruth, he said.

She had looked at his hand, then at his face.

Around them she had taken in the sound of merry conversation, ice clinking in glasses. Someone had pulled the long drapes against the glare of the setting sun, and the room was pleasantly cool, the windows open behind the curtains, and a breeze moving.

What if he just wanted to stay and teach? Ruth had taken a gulp of her drink, looked at Alec. He might agree to that, she said.

Alec had not met her eyes.

How about a trip somewhere? he said. It could be hard on a new guy, having Peter around. Hard on Peter, too.

He'd made an apologetic face. And, of course, you'll have to leave the house, he said. There's that.

I know, she said. But the truth was that she kept forgetting that fact.

Now she watched Peter, standing by his seat across the dining room. He was waiting for the boys to quiet, she knew.

Then, smiling, he made a sudden gesture with both hands, a benediction. Off with you.

The boys pushed back their chairs with a joyful sound.

Ruth folded her napkin. Beside her, the fat boy shoveled in cake. He had managed to put away two pieces, she saw, stacking the empty plates beside him like an emperor piling up picked-over carcasses of quail.

By the fireplace, Peter had his back to her again, talking with a handful of boys clustered around him.

It was difficult to resist the crowd moving her along. She allowed herself to be borne out the doors of the dining hall and down the waxed floors of the hallway toward the front entrance.

Jim McNulty, who taught history with Peter, went past her, squeezing her arm as he moved by. Balding, with a monk's white tonsure and sad eyes, a medievalist by training, he had been Peter's first hire at the school years and years ago. They hadn't seen him over the summer—he had a place up on the coast, a cabin where he went for a couple of months every year. The sight of him now made her feel glad, the familiarity of him—an old friend, devoted to Peter—a comfort.

Jimmy, she said. I'm glad to see you. Poor Ed.

I know, he said. He shook his head. Awful.

Then he looked closely at her. Everything all right, darling? Peter's been all right?

Yes, yes! she said, surprised.

Did she look unwell? she wondered. Did Peter?

We're fine, she said. See you tonight?

He blew her a kiss, but then he was gone before she could say more.

· · ·

Ruth loved listening to the boys' choir at Derry, though she had to fight back tears when they sang "Soldier's Hallelujah" or "Once in Royal David's City" or even "Polly Wolly Doodle." She knew it was idiotic, weeping over "Polly Wolly Doodle" or "Jim Along Josie," but she couldn't help it. Tonight they would sing the school song after Peter's address. That, too, might unmoor her. It had been a day of feeling unmoored.

There had been so much to love about their lives at Derry. And now it felt as if it was slipping from their grasp.

For many years she'd worked shifts at the school's tutoring center, where her enthusiasm for grammar and punctuation had helped buoy her spirits during sessions with glum boys and their awful essays about Petrarch or their pets or global warming. She brought chocolate chip cookies on the afternoons she worked.

The cookies went some distance toward cheering up the recalcitrant.

Her favorite job over the years had been working in the school's infirmary, a duty that made her feel competent and kindly and brought out a fussy, bossy Florence Nightingale streak in her. She liked bustling around, fixing glasses of ginger ale with bent straws, cutting the crusts off toast triangles, tucking a flower or two into a vase on a tray. It had not been difficult for her to be patient with boys who were sick. She played gin rummy or Russian Bank with them, read to them for hours from *Treasure Island* or from Sherlock Holmes. She took temperatures, chattering away cheerfully while the boys held the thermometers in their mouths, lips closed, eyes on her face. It was funny, she thought, how her habitual shyness disappeared at those times.

Over the years she had often been asked to take the night shift at the infirmary, when they were short-staffed. She never minded the hours sitting in the moonlight in a chair in a boy's room, watching him sleep. Sometimes she dozed, her chin on her chest, but mostly she found herself wakeful, gazing for so long at a boy's features as he slept that his face seemed to pass through a thousand expressions as she watched, his eyelids moving, his lips opening and closing, a fist coming up to brush an ear or graze a cheek.

The infirmary's west windows looked out over the lake. If the night was warm, she opened the window and listened to the water, the chorus of frogs, the little lapping sounds against the shore, or, if the dam was overflowing, the steady sound of water going over the sluice. These were times of absolute peace for her. There was nothing else she ought to be doing, nowhere else more necessary for her to be. Somewhere, she knew, other people were doing more important things, but when the moonlight fell into the room, she felt herself and the sleeping child joined together in a powerful embrace, and she watched over her charge as if guarding a prince.

At those times she felt, she imagined, some measure of what it might have been like to love a child of her own.

She did not leave the boy, whoever she was watching, until his eyes opened in the morning.

Then she'd smile and stand up, smoothing down her skirt.

Welcome back, she'd say.

•   •   •

She'd always liked listening to Peter's speech on the first night of the year. She had never grown immune to the cheering nature of his remarks, the sense he conveyed to the boys that they were beginning—that the whole community was beginning together—a great adventure. Yet now as she left the dining hall, the open doors of the main building ahead of her and a glimpse of the night sky through them, she felt desperate to get outside.

This day could not end quickly enough, she thought.

She stepped outside onto the building's landing above the flight of steps. The night sky, a red band at the horizon, opened up, star filled.

A knot of boys, shouting and grappling and roughhousing, their shirttails untucked and their ties loosened, passed her.

Hi, Mrs. van Dusen, someone said.

Hi there, she said. Careful!

She hung back against a column. The boys went past her down the steps and out into the crowd, disappearing into the evening's darkness, headed toward the chapel.

The night air was a relief against her skin, as if she'd plunged her arms and face into a pool of cool water. It was always overheated in the dining hall, and her haste earlier in the evening, everything that had happened with Ed, had made her feel dirty. She liked being outside at night anyway, the vertiginous assertion of scale that always followed. Sometimes, she thought, it was a perfect relief to be an infinitesimal presence on the face of the planet.

She watched the boys passing her, aware as always of the extremes among them. Some of them were as beautiful as

Greek statues, marble youths of classical antiquity with lambs borne across their shoulders. Another, unhappy group moved sullenly among these athletes and scholars, their manner simultaneously pained and aggressive, as if they understood how poorly they compared to their beautiful brethren and suffered for it.

She put her palm against the column on the landing and lifted her gaze. Tatters of night clouds floated near the moon. The stars seemed to be clustered high up in the darkest part of the sky. Something about their distant position was a reminder of the scope of the universe. Tonight, she knew, Peter would ask the boys to pray for Ed McClaren. He would tell them how lucky they were, every day the gift of an education laid at their feet, a hot dinner prepared for them at night, pancakes for breakfast, doughnuts on Fridays. A cheer would go up at the mention of the famous doughnuts.

Peter gave the same speech every year, absolutely earnest, and he meant every bit of it.

She knew he got on people's nerves sometimes. He was mulishly tolerant, tiresomely reasonable and conciliatory. There was not much irony in Peter, and some people—bad people, she thought—just plain hated sincerity. But the school would never find anyone who loved it as much as Peter had, someone who loved it without care for his own regard. Tonight he would mention the beauty of the campus, the lovely old buildings and the playing fields planted in grass so green and soft you wanted to lie down and rest your cheek there. For Peter, the bloom of romance—the goodness of the school's initial purpose, the grief of the parents who had lost their child so long ago and who had wanted, in the wake of that loss, to help other boys—had never left his impression of the place. Ruth knew that some of the boys, especially the scholarship boys plucked from whatever misfortune had shaped their lives, would see it tonight as Peter asked them to see it. They would feel their luck, along with their shyness and their worry about being in a new place among strangers, just as she and Peter had felt their luck when they had arrived so many years ago.

It was for those boys especially that Peter worked so hard.

When she had weeded the flower bed this afternoon, the sunlight had been warm on the back of her neck and against her shoulder. But tonight in the air's coolness she could feel the winter ahead. She had been thinking, as she always did at this time of year, of the poem by Keats, his season of mists and mellow fruitfulness. Ever since she'd been taught this work in college, fragments of its lines had come to her as fall approached. *Bless with fruit the vines that round the thatch-eves run . . . while barred clouds bloom the soft-dying day . . . then in a wailful choir the small gnats mourn among the river sallows . . .*

One didn't want to hurry toward one's end, she thought, and yet one longed nonetheless for the days to unfold. Kneeling at the edge of the driveway and pulling weeds earlier in the day, she'd felt that brief flare of pure contentment. The storms would skirt them. The evening's party would be a success. Another year was about to begin. She wanted now to recapture that feeling, that respite in the middle of the afternoon when she had not worried. But it was as Keats had written. One could never get completely away from melancholy. The beginning of things always contained their end.

• • •

She began to make her way down the steps and was almost at the bottom when three boys, a chase in progress, dodged past her. Howls of encouragement went up from the others. The boy in the lead, freckle-skinned, hair close-cropped, long grasshopper arms and legs, went down the steps three at a time, knocking into her as he went past. Ruth stumbled forward, snatched at the air. She grazed the head of the boy before her, his hair in her fingers for an instant, soft as silk.

Sorry, Mrs. van Dusen! someone called.

She righted herself on the steps, flapping helplessly, trying for comic effect.

It's all right! she called. Don't mind me!

On the sidewalk, boys streamed toward the chapel, chattering and laughing, bumping shoulders.

She reached the bottom and stepped onto the grass, the heels of her good shoes sinking into the turf.

The forest surrounding the school had become a black mass on the horizon, darker than the sky. The main building with its high position on the campus had a vantage over hundreds of acres, the forest of alder, chestnut, honey locust, maple, oak, and pine. At night in the winter, especially once snow had fallen, the school's lighted windows and illuminated colonnades, its cloak of Virginia creeper stirring against the old brick, created an illusion that Ruth found almost theatrically romantic. Wood was still burned in the fireplaces, and on cold mornings smoke hung in drifts in the low places, herds of white-tailed deer moving out from among the trees to venture across the playing fields. Somehow, Ruth thought, the wilderness beyond the lighted compound of the school's buildings made everything that had been acquired over the school's history—paintings and books, dishes and lamps and desks and ladder-back chairs and upholstered sofas and faded fringed throw pillows—seem especially valuable, like the intimate belongings of a pharaoh arranged in the chambers of his tomb. Whenever she walked down the halls, the eyes of the headmasters who had preceded Peter gazing out at her from the cracked pigment of their por-traits, she was aware that her own and Peter's place in this con-tinuum was, after all, brief.

Now someone spoke her name.

She had been standing on the grass and blinking up into the streetlights, white moths orbiting through the galaxies of insects. For a moment, when she turned around, she couldn't see anything, the space from which someone had spoken to her a pure darkness.

Then an enormous, familiar boy with shaggy hair surged toward her—Mrs. van Dusen! he said again. He gave her a bear hug and loped away.

Welcome back! she said.

Her sweater had slipped off one shoulder, and she pulled it back. What was that giant boy's name? She couldn't seem to remember anyone's name tonight.

When she turned to look up at the top of the steps, Peter stepped out onto the lighted landing among the boys, appear-ing there as if she had called his name. He hesitated between the columns and then began to descend stiffly, going sideways one step at a time in the midst of the throng.

The signs of Peter's illness had begun with his eyes, a degeneration of his peripheral vision. Tests had been run. Meanwhile, he had not been allowed to drive, and Ruth had chauffeured him around for a few days, including to the follow-up appointment at their general practitioner's office. The doctor had been a young man; neither she nor Peter had seen him before. In the brightly lit examining room, he had laid out the symptoms of Peter's condition.

The full lips, he'd said, glancing from the chart in his hand to Peter's face and then back to his folder, speaking as if to students who were taking notes.

Large eye sockets, he said. Eyes slightly recessed. Dominant brow, frontal bossing, prominent jaw . . . Can I see your hand, please? he'd asked.

Peter's hands, like everything about him, were large, his fingers long and slender.

Peter held out his hands, palms up.

Arachnodactyly, the doctor said. Like the spider. He did not seem to notice Ruth's growing perturbation.

Bossing? Ruth said. She stared at the doctor. What's that?

The doctor appeared not to have heard her. Sweat a lot? he asked Peter.

Peter nodded. In the heat, he said. Exercising, he added. He cleared his throat.

The doctor turned finally to Ruth. Snoring? Getting worse?

Ruth clasped her hands together in her lap. She did not trust herself to speak, afraid her voice would tremble.

Haven't you noticed, the doctor said—he looked back and forth between Ruth and Peter—that he's getting taller? His shoes getting tighter?

Ruth had felt stricken. She *had* thought Peter was getting taller somehow, but it seemed so unlikely. He'd lost some weight, and she'd attributed the odd effect of his apparently increased height to that change in his appearance. But he'd complained about his shoes, and just the week before she'd replaced both his ancient wingtips and a pair of sneakers.

The syndrome, it turned out, was a form of gigantism. Marfan syndrome, the doctor had continued, an uncommon genetic disease, an inherited defect of connective tissue. It was relatively rare, though less so than one might think, he said.

I've never seen it before, actually, he admitted, but there was no reason for them to worry about it much in a man of Peter's age.

Other things, he implied, unsmiling, would probably finish Peter first.

Peter had taken the news with what Ruth considered freakish calm.

In truth, though, there was little to be done. He had regular echocardiograms, as there could be trouble with deterioration of the walls of the aorta, an enlargement of the heart. (How terrible and ironic, Ruth had thought, if Peter should die because his heart was too big.) But so far he'd been fine. Other than new prescriptions for his glasses—at least every year and sometimes more often—there wasn't anything else to do in terms of treatment, they'd been told.

The doctor had put more drops in Peter's eyes that day and sent him off with a pair of folding cardboard sunglasses, which he had obediently put on. They were much too large, even for his big head, and he had looked ridiculous.

In the car on the way home, Ruth had glanced at him in the passenger seat. When they left town and the road passed into the woods, the light was like that of the old newsreels that used to play in movie houses when she and Peter were young, flickering and premonitory, disconcerting. But Peter had seemed serene, sitting quietly in the passenger seat, as if not only his vision had been compromised but also his ability to speak or even think.

He was not a fighter, Ruth had thought then. His strengths were endurance, not belligerence; obedience and compromise, not resistance. If he were told he would soon die, he would accept it without self-pity or complaint. For Peter there would be no raging against the dying of the light.

Long ago, when they'd been very young, everything for her a kind of now-or-never drama, she had told him once that she hated him, that she never wanted to see him again.

He had accepted it—had believed her, because it was not in his nature to deceive himself and so he could not imagine Ruth doing so—and had turned sadly away. It had been for them a nearly fatal submission.

Now she watched him come down the steps of the main building, looking over the crowd of boys and teachers milling around on the pavement below. How was it that they had been married for so long, over half a century?

He would never see her, she thought, but she waved anyway.

Surprisingly, his gaze found her. He lifted a hand and came toward her.

• • •

Peter had left the house early that morning, having been awake and restless, she knew, since before five a.m. For years in their marriage it had been Ruth who'd had trouble sleeping. Now she couldn't seem to sleep enough. Peter, however, seemed more and more often to be awake in the middle of the night. Occasionally, he went downstairs and had a glass of milk and some cookies; she was aware sometimes, waking in the middle of the night herself, of the smell of Oreos on his breath.

Last night, coming briefly out of sleep in the darkness, she had sensed him awake beside her.

She had rolled over to face him. What's the matter?

His eyes had been open. He had reached over to pat her hair, his big hand resting heavily on her head.

But she hadn't been able to stay awake. Before she'd heard his answer, she was gone again, tugged back down into sleep.

When she'd opened her eyes this morning, he'd been gone, the bedroom full of explosive light.

Is anything wrong? she had asked him a few days before. Is everything all right at school?

Never better, he had said, but he'd busied himself with something or other, and she'd thought he was withholding.

She knew that she was sometimes unhelpful when difficulties presented themselves at the school. She was made easily angry on his behalf, full of righteous indignation and frustration, suggestions about what he should or shouldn't do. She'd had to remind herself—especially when she was younger and less patient—just to listen sometimes, not to weary him with tirades, however sympathetic their origins.

Once, complaining to Dr. Wenning about Peter's tendency toward ponderousness, his quiet method of reaching decisions—How can I help him if he doesn't tell me anything? she had protested—Dr. Wenning had said to her: Not everyone likes to talk so much as you and I do, Ruth. Maybe a little silence is nice sometimes. Good for the marriage.

Peter made his way toward her now, moving against the tide of boys, parting them as he came. Some of them came up only to his waist. He held his hands over their heads, elbows up, like someone pushing through deep water.

When he bent to kiss her, she put her hand on his cheek. Under her fingertips she felt a patch of bristles, a place he'd missed, shaving.

You've had a long day, she said. You all right?

Then a boy, practically bouncing with urgency, was beside them. Dr. van Dusen? he said. Can we—

Peter turned from her, his hand falling from her arm. In a moment he was gone from her side, pulled back into the crowd.

She stood for a minute, waiting.

The bell in the chapel began to ring. Everybody would want Peter for one thing or another tonight, she thought. No point in waiting.

She turned away and went on without him.

She walked alone down the path toward the chapel. The world, so solemn and aloof in the growing darkness, looked like a painting or an engraving, she thought. The big motionless shapes of the oak trees with their heavy crowns standing at a distance on the lawn; beyond the trees, the palisade of wrought-iron streetlamps. Along the road, a row of parked cars, silver-backed in the moonlight. The light at the horizon had faded, and overhead now the sky was a deep, humbling blue.

Ruth had studied languages at Smith. In the Old High German she knew, the word for *blue* was *blau*, which meant *shining*.

It was a shining kind of night.

The world was everywhere a mess, she thought, countries all over the globe being torn to pieces, it seemed, by flood or fire or poverty or hate. And sometimes she had so many complaints about even her own small safe corner of it. But how dazzling it could be.

At the end of the path where the trees parted, the white steeple of the chapel stood out against the sky. At the steeple's top, the weathervane's bronze ship pointed her bow west.

Once, years ago, Ruth had won a five-dollar bet with Peter about weathervanes: the ship faces the oncoming wind, she'd insisted. It doesn't follow it.

She had known this as she knew so many things: from reading. She read voraciously, novels and histories, dozens of self-help guides—though Dr. Wenning had disparaged such material—nonfiction on diverse subjects: world hunger, astrophysics, nineteenth-century European art. Over the issue of the weathervane, she had been her worst self, triumphantly pushing the open volume of the encyclopedia across the dining room table at Peter and jabbing the page with her index finger.

She had made him get up and give her the money right then and there, even though they'd been eating dinner at the time. That had been part of her problem, she knew; she'd never made any money of her own in her life. Gloria Steinem had been two years ahead of Ruth at Smith. Beside someone like Gloria, Ruth felt the paucity of her experience, her meager achievement. Over the years, she'd done every sort of job imaginable at the school, answering the phones, playing the piano to accompany the choir—though inexpertly, it was true— even teaching French. But because she was Peter's wife, and because he was the headmaster, and because that's how things were then, it had been assumed that she would never be paid for any of it. That was how women had been treated—*wives* had been treated—in those days. Today no one would tolerate such an arrangement, she knew, and everyone was better for it.

As she had watched Peter cross the room that night to find his jacket and his billfold, lifting the coat from the chair and patting the pockets, her absurd victory had felt pyrrhic, of course.

I've got some work to do before the morning, he'd said after that, and he had taken himself off to his study upstairs.

She'd been angry with herself, ashamed. Why had she needed to prove to Peter, of all people, that she knew which way a weathervane faced? He had never doubted her intelligence, never once been anything but grateful for her presence at his side, the way she had put her head down and worked alongside him. Yet she had cared so much about being *right* all the time, because that's what happened when you felt that you were a powerless person, just someone's *wife*. She'd never told Peter she'd wanted to be paid for what she'd done at the school, and in the end it wasn't about the money, anyway. But perhaps it would have helped her feel less useless sometimes, if she'd ever had a paycheck with her name on it.

She looked up now at the white steeple of the chapel, its confident ascent. The young women hired today to teach at the school were accomplished and ambitious, half of them with doctorates—one of them had *two* doctorates, Peter had told her—even though it was only high school. All of them were busy with their careers and often children, too. It was difficult not to feel a little silly, a little superfluous, when she compared herself with these young women.

She thought about the amateurish paintings she'd made over the years, the failed play and the failed novel she'd written, the hours spent practicing the piano in hopes of being good enough to play professionally one day, even just with the ragtag local orchestra in Bangor. All those *years*, she thought now, when she had struggled so hard to be accomplished in this or that. She'd never had quite enough talent, in the end, or maybe it was patience. Few people did, she knew. Still, she couldn't pretend it hadn't hurt sometimes, knowing that.

For a while she had wanted passionately to be a playwright. She'd written a play set in the nineteenth century about a Japanese geisha, but she couldn't seem to drag her mind sufficiently away from *Madame Butterfly*, which she loved, to make the work original. Then she'd tried a novel about a star-crossed mixed-race couple in the antebellum South that owed a good deal to *Romeo and Juliet*. Peter had faithfully read both the play and the novel, but she'd known they weren't any good.

This is really pretty darn sad, Ruth, he'd said, rubbing his head in a distressed way after turning the last page of her novel. Did both of those young people have to die in that fire?

She'd taken up plein air painting for a while, signing up once for a weeklong course on an island off the coast about two hours from Derry. Peter had framed one of her paintings from that course—a seascape—as well as one she'd done at Derry. She'd enjoyed the hours executing them, but she wasn't an idiot. She could see that she had no real talent.

She still played the piano from time to time, but mostly she'd given up on the rest of it. And she did not really regret having abandoned these pursuits—except occasionally, she thought now, on evenings such as this one. The world felt to her on this night full of mysterious, blazing beauty and also fear and tragedy. The unsettled day, its little portents, her sense of dread and loneliness . . . and yet also the stars, and the deep blue of the night sky, the white silhouette of the chapel's spire. She wanted to be able to *answer* the world somehow, to *say* something about how extraordinary it was, how extraordinary it was being alive. And how complicated it was, as well.

For how did it happen that sometimes the goodness of things—the beautiful world, her love for Peter, her gratitude for the life she had led, as opposed to the life she *might* have led, without Peter—made her feel like weeping?

She had no answer for any of this.

After that foolish business over the weathervane, she had apologized to Peter. She'd perfected that in their marriage, saying she was sorry.

She had gone to his study later that evening after their quarrel, bearing a tray with cake and a pot of coffee.

Knock, knock, she'd said, pushing open the door with her shoulder, entering the room, tray first.

Peter had not turned around from his desk, looking down studiously at the papers on his blotter, as if he had not heard her come into the room.

She'd set the tray on the table in front of the fireplace, poured the coffee.

Next to the word *pedant*? she'd said finally. In the dictionary?

Outside the study window, rain from the gutter had made a distinct, dripping sound. Peter had not spoken.

A little picture of me, she'd said. Boring mistress of the crossword.

Peter had taken off his glasses, rubbed his eyes.

She'd hated herself then. Who could *stand* to live with her?

I come bearing cake, she'd said instead, busying herself with the plates.

Finally he had swiveled around in his chair to face her. She had made an apple walnut cake, his favorite. She could whip up one of these and get it in the oven and have it out in under an hour.

He'd taken the plate when she handed it to him. He never could resist food. It was wonderful to cook for him, his delight boundless. You had to watch out for him when he was hungry— he was capable of knocking her practically off her feet when he needed to eat—but he was always so *grateful* to be fed.

She'd given him a fork, put a napkin on his knee.

Then she'd perched on the ottoman by his chair, knees together, chin on her fist, watching him.

It's a little crumbly, she said. I left it a couple of minutes too long in the oven. Sorry.

She meant, sorry for being such an awful bitch, but she didn't say that. She said *god damn it* and occasionally *shit,* but neither of them used the f-word. They just didn't do that.

He'd eaten the cake, hunched over. She knew he was not above acting a little pathetic when he wanted to extract an apology. This is delicious, he'd said at last. Thank you.

She'd leaned forward from the ottoman and put her arms around his neck, her forehead on his shoulder. God damn it, she'd said then. Stop enjoying that cake so much.

When she let go of him, sitting back and wiping the wetness off her cheeks, he'd looked at her from under his bristly eyebrows. The look had been sly, pleased. He was happy to have aroused her pity, if that's what it took.

Later that same night, before they went to sleep, she had trimmed his eyebrows. She'd made him sit down on the seat of the toilet, his big face upturned, long legs sticking out of his boxer shorts, while she wielded a tiny pair of sewing scissors over his eyes in the bright light from the fixture above the bathroom sink.

You look like a bad old hog, she said, nipping and tweezing. A big wild old pig.

Eyes closed, he had smiled, reached for her, running his palm up the inside of her thigh.

She'd swatted him away. I've got a pair of scissors here, she said.

When she finished, she looked down at him.

His face had been calm, untroubled. The lines across his forehead and around his eyes and mouth were the kind of lines that people who smiled a lot tended to get; they made him look good-humored.

She, on the other hand, had awful grooves between her eyebrows, as if she'd spent her whole life frowning, as if everything that had come before her had required her careful inspection, had misbehaved and refused to stand still properly.

She leaned down and put her lips against his forehead. She loved the way Peter smelled, of wood smoke from the fireplace and of Drysol, the old-fashioned deodorant he stubbornly preferred—it was hard to find these days—and of his whiskey from before dinner.

Better? he'd said. Less piggy?

She'd kissed him again.

A thing of beauty, she'd said, is a joy forever.

At the entrance to the chapel now, she hesitated, letting people move past her. She looked up the path, but there was no sign of Peter in the group of boys and teachers coming down the hill. People greeted her, embraced her, kissed her on the cheek, marching forth with unrecognizable faces out of the shining night.

She smiled brightly. Hello! she said. Hello, hello!

She caught a glimpse of Charlie Finney, the school's new vice president. He'd come to Derry just three years ago. He was a big, fit young man, highly competitive on the tennis court—he had quickly abandoned Peter for younger, spryer opponents—

and with a weightlifter's exaggeratedly developed chest. He had a high, intelligent-looking forehead, receding blond hair, a long pointy nose. He reminded Ruth of an Irish setter. His wife, Kitty, seemed like a cheerful person, busy with their three rambunctious young boys, all of them thick-legged, curly-headed people like Kitty, always in a kind of sweaty state, it seemed to Ruth.

A few times Ruth had run into Kitty on campus, and she had seemed eager to talk with Ruth, but one little boy or another was always dashing off or bonking his brother on the head or something—Ruth watched them, marveling—and mostly the women's interactions had ended with Ruth waving an awkward good-bye at Kitty's apologetic retreat.

Once, in the post office, Kitty had looked imploringly at Ruth, meanwhile trying to restrain a squirming toddler from running into the parking lot after his brothers.

I'd love to have you over for tea one day, Kitty said, just to hear about all your time here, Ruth. You know so much about this place, and you've done so much . . . but the house is always such a mess, and Charlie hates it when . . .

She had trailed off.

Stop it, Nicky, she'd said sharply to the child thrashing in her arms. Then, to Ruth, she had turned an embarrassed face, damp eyes. Sorry, she'd said.

Ruth felt surprised. Peter was regularly acknowledged for his contributions to the school, but it wasn't often that people took note of her work. Yet she could not think about this; she wanted so much to reach out and touch the head of the child in Kitty's arms. What a crop of perfect curls he had, like a cherub's.

You can come to our house, Ruth said. Bring the boys. Anytime.

I'd love that, Kitty had said. But they're such a wrecking crew . . .

Heavens. Nothing to wreck, Ruth began, but a howl had gone up from one of the other boys.

Oh, god—Kitty had dashed away.

Just telephone, Ruth had called after her. Anytime.

But Ruth had never heard from Kitty. She had imagined that Kitty was—as any young mother would be, of course—too busy for tea with an old lady.

Charlie had been clever about the school's investments, Peter said. He was knowledgeable about secondary school curricular reform and accreditation matters and so forth. Yet Ruth disliked him. She did not in general trust people who spent too much time working on their own bodies, she told Peter—though not without a twinge of self-consciousness over her added pounds—and every time she saw Charlie on campus he always seemed to be emerging from the gym, a towel around his neck, or heading off on his bicycle in some silly-looking outfit that made him look like Spider-Man.

Charlie Finney was ambitious, Ruth had said.

Nothing wrong with that, Peter said. *I* was ambitious.

But Ruth thought Charlie was manipulative and disingenuous, as well as ambitious. She imagined that he wanted Peter's job, and she had no doubt that he thought he could do it far better than Peter, though he was too calculating to say so outright, too well mannered, too political, to reveal himself in that way.

He sometimes called Peter *Pater.* Ruth hated this.

It's so patronizing, she'd told Peter. And so . . . *stupid*!

Peter had shrugged. I think he means it fondly, he said.

Oh, *Peter.* Ruth had gazed at him. Honestly, she'd said. I know you're not such an innocent. Can't you see he means to dethrone you?

Well, it isn't much of a throne, Peter had said. It's just an old swivel chair and a couple of drawers full of paper clips.

You're just putting on an act, she told him. I don't know why you do that.

Peter had run Derry brilliantly for all these years. He had the respect of his peers at other schools, had chaired national committees, had overseen many improvements at Derry, all the while working hard to find the boys for whom an education would matter most. People loved him.

But Charlie Finney just wanted to turn Derry into a fancy prep school, Ruth thought. He wanted to live in the headmaster's house, and he wanted to get rid of as many of Peter's poverty cases, as she'd heard Charlie call them, as possible. There was no question about it; Charlie Finney wanted to be king of the hill. He did not care about the scholarship boys, the children for whom the school had been founded. He talked often and with great seriousness about sustainability—which, as Ruth said to Peter, was just a way for people to avoid having to have principles and do the necessary work to live by them. And he was always cracking his knuckles, a habit that got on her nerves.

He brushed her cheek now, not a kiss exactly. Something that would look to others like a kiss, she thought.

You look absolutely lovely tonight, Ruth, he said. What a pretty pin.

Oh, stop, she said. Despite his politicking and his obsequiousness, she found that she occasionally enjoyed sparring with him. He got her dander up, as Peter said.

But sometimes she also felt a little sorry for him. No one would ever love Charlie Finney the way Peter was loved. Charlie Finney had never sacrificed himself for anything or anybody, she thought. People loved Peter because, in the end, he did not believe himself better than anyone else. He believed in the inevitable virtue and happiness of a community if all members were treated with respect and kindness.

Yet despite her suspicions about Charlie and his motives, she wanted him to reassure her now. He had probably spent more time today with Peter than anyone else. What had Jimmy meant earlier, asking her if she was all right, if Peter was all right?

Did things go all right today, Charlie? she asked.

Where *was* Peter now? she wondered.

But Charlie had turned away to speak to someone else, and he didn't answer her. She felt embarrassed.

How dare he act so important, she thought.

People passed her on their way into the chapel.

Yes, yes! she said. Drinks at our house, as usual. You know where to find us. Good to see you. Had a nice summer? Welcome back.

The line dwindled, boys shuffling ahead and disappearing into the dimness. Still she waited on the threshold. Inside the chapel, candles had been lit in the sconces and on the windowsills. She looked in the door. Watery cones of light flickered up the cool, white walls. She stood for a minute, letting her eyes adjust, and then finally she moved forward into the dimness to take a seat at the end of a pew. The boy beside her was apple-cheeked, with a wild mop of brown curls, his knee going up and down in a maddening way. A pair of sideburns crept down his cheeks like fuzzy orange caterpillars. This was the new style, she had noticed at dinner.

She tilted her head back against the pew. Earlier this summer she had finally cut her hair short, after years of wearing it long. She still enjoyed the feel of her new head, how light it seemed, her hair a fluffy silver cap. The wood under her neck felt silky and cool.

Why didn't I do this before? she'd asked Peter, sitting at her dressing table on the evening of the day she'd had it cut.

She'd turned her chin this way and that, examining herself in the mirror.

I always wait too long to do things, she'd said. Like changing with the fashions.

She'd glanced at Peter, who had been sitting up in bed, glasses on his nose, eyes on the page of *Time* he was reading.

Or is it too much like a crone? she said. Too much ancient vestal virgin?

From the pillows, Peter had put down the magazine.

You look beautiful, he said. It was what he always said.

Pale-skinned and freckled, with a redhead's bruised-looking lips, Ruth recognized herself in portraits of Queen Elizabeth I, the same terrified, haughty look. All her life, she knew, people had mistaken her shyness for disdain. Her unusual height, her big feet, clownishly long—pontoon boats, Peter called them—

all this had made her self-conscious. And she knew she was capable of serious missteps about clothing, as well. It had always been difficult for her to judge about hemlines. The 1970's particularly, when long skirts had been in fashion, had been a terrible era for her. In photographs from that period she thought she looked like someone who'd been abducted and taken into a cult.

In her younger years, though, when she had not been so heavy . . . well, perhaps then she had been *almost* beautiful.

The evening she and Peter had made love for the first time, two teenagers hidden in the sand dunes on a blanket, Ruth had opened her eyes to the night sky when Peter collapsed against her. She had felt triumph, alongside her own marveling. A hundred yards away from them, the waves had broken onto the shore. Ruth, the weight of Peter against her, had filled her hands with sand, sensing the depth of the earth beneath them. *She* had made that sound come from him. She had made him bury his face in her hair, say her name again and again.

But once you got to be the age they were now, you stopped thinking about being beautiful. Still, it had been good of him to say her hair looked nice.

In the chapel now, breathing the cool, entombed air, surrounded by the smells of smoke and wax, she tried to quiet her mind, but she could not settle herself. For a couple of years an emergency room nurse had offered a yoga class in the basement of the library in Wyeth. Ruth had gone every week until the instructor moved away, and no one could be found to lead the class anymore.

She took in a deep yoga breath through her nose, exhaled quietly.

Peter had approved of the yoga.

Good, he'd said, when she'd reported that she'd signed up. Maybe it'll help you relax.

I don't deserve him, Ruth had said once to Dr. Wenning. I'm nothing but trouble for him, always complaining about him, and he's the nicest man on the planet.

Then why does he stay with you? Dr. Wenning had folded her arms, looking bored. She'd disapproved of this line of reasoning from Ruth.

He's a big boy, your Peter, Dr. Wenning said. He could leave if he wanted to, go find somebody else. Gina Lollobrigida, for instance.

Gina Lollobrigida, Ruth had learned, was Dr. Wenning's idea of a bombshell.

Will it be forever? Dr. Wenning had held up her hands, shrugging. Nothing is promised, Ruth, she said.

Anyway, I think it is the balancing of the scales, Dr. Wenning had said finally to Ruth's worried silence. Not everyone gets a good husband. You know that. Some people get a schmuck, a nincompoop. You got a lousy childhood. Worse even than lousy.

Ruth started to object. Dr. Wenning's own young life had been terrible beyond all imagining—

True, true—Dr. Wenning held up a hand, interrupting her—some have it even worse than you. But, still, the gods are attentive. They gave you a prince of a husband. Try just to enjoy him.

• • •

Ruth had been present for Peter's annual welcome address to the school every year since he had become headmaster at Derry. He'd been so handsome and sexy in those early days. Ruth had always understood exactly what girls meant when they said a fellow was so good-looking it made you weak in the knees. For years, she had sat through this occasion in the chapel, hands folded in her lap. She'd looked like the portrait of the headmaster's good wife, but sometimes her mind had strayed. She'd thought of other things.

Sometimes Peter naked. Sometimes sex.

Or sometimes she'd run over the preparations for the cocktail party. Quiches defrosted? Cheese and crackers? Olives, lemons, extra beer in the second refrigerator in the pantry, cocktail napkins, flowers for the front hall and the dining room table . . . over the years, she had learned how to do this, how to be a hostess.

She remembered the first time Peter had given this speech. Though the trustees had held a formal search for the position, the head of the board had told her privately that it had never been a contest. Peter had had the job from the moment he'd applied.

He's an impressive fellow, your Peter, the man had said. We're lucky to have him.

When Peter had risen from the pew to turn and address the boys and the faculty for the first time as their headmaster, the room had gone suddenly silent, everyone instantly attentive. Peter had reached into his jacket pocket and withdrawn his remarks, unfolded the papers on the lectern. But then he had not looked at them again. He had spoken for half an hour, never once glancing at the pages. Watching him, Ruth had felt as if a wand had been run down her body from the top of her head to the soles of her feet, splitting her open. She had been so proud of him.

That night, they had hosted their first cocktail party. Afterward, the kitchen cleaned up, Ruth had felt both exhausted and exhilarated by the evening.

She had climbed into bed beside Peter.

So, she said. Is it something you do with your hands? Or your eyes? How did you make them all be quiet like that, all at once?

In the dark, she had studied Peter's face. He'd been lying on his back beside her, eyes closed, his familiar profile on the pillow: high forehead, big nose, the sensuous cleft of his upper lip, the exaggerated chin. He'd opened his eyes, and then he'd rolled toward her and put his hand on her hip, squeezed once, deliberately.

He doesn't want to talk, she thought. He wants to have sex.

I don't know, he said. It's nothing.

Come on, she said. Really.

He rolled away from her. I don't know, Ruth, he said. Really. It just happened somehow. He rolled back and patted her hip again.

Ruth ignored the squeeze. She wanted to talk.

The silence in the chapel that night had been instantaneous, pure and perfect, as if he'd snapped his fingers. It *meant* something, she felt, that he could do that. And his failure to be aware of his role in the event, even to be interested in it, was connected somehow to his ability to make it happen, she'd thought.

Come on, she said again. Tell me. You must know. It wasn't anything I could see, obviously, but it was like there was—oh, I don't know—*something* in the room.

In the darkness beside her, Peter ran his hand from her waist over her hip and down her thigh.

Maybe it's sort of like the *via negativa,* he said. Understanding a thing by understanding what it is not. For instance, it was not *me.*

She lay beside him on her back, listening to the thrumming of the night's thunderstorm. The sound trailed away in intervals over the hills. When lightning flickered, the bedroom ceiling appeared above her for an instant, a perfect square of blinding whiteness, shocking her with its nearness, bringing the room in close. Other details, as if from the flash of a crime scene camera, had blazed forth, just for a second: finial on the bedpost; length of beaded molding; Peter's wool sweater, charcoal gray, tossed on the chair. A little fear had flickered over her, like a lizard scuttling across her skin.

The *via negativa,* she repeated. Well, maybe. If you say so.

She had closed her eyes again, reached over to find his hand and bring his palm to her mouth.

She knew at that moment—as, she realized, she had not fully understood it before—that one day she and Peter would be parted, and not by her own or by Peter's choice.

Hours seemed to have gone by, but when she turned around again to search the empty doors of the chapel, Peter was standing there, absolutely still.

It was Ed McClaren, she thought. She felt her chest constrict. Ed had died.

Then abruptly Peter strode past her and down the aisle. He turned around when he reached the front of the chapel.

He stood there quietly, but not as if he was waiting, exactly. His belly was slack, his expression oddly empty. His shoulders seemed to have rounded further.

Something was the matter, Ruth thought. She started forward, her hands finding the rail of the pew before her. She stared at him, the big familiar planes of his face, his long legs and soft paunch. She could not see them from where she sat, but she knew the details of his body in her mind: thistledown in his ears, brown spots across the backs of his hands, scars in half-moons over his knees.

Peter seemed to be gazing at something over the heads of the boys facing him.

Though usually the boys quieted instantly when Peter stood before them, tonight they continued to chatter as if they could not see him, as if only *she* could see him.

Ruth glanced behind her. The doors to the chapel had been left open, framing a square of dark blue twilight. A cold feeling began in her hands, ran up her arms, gripping her neck and shoulders.

She turned back and tried to meet Peter's eyes, but she could see he wasn't looking at her . . . or for her, she realized. It was as if he stood at a distance from her, from all of them. He looked sad, his expression soft with sympathy, with regret. How could she tell this from so far away? But she could. She knew she could. He gazed away from her, away from everyone in the room, apparently intent on the open doors as if something might move out there.

Ruth pressed into the back of the pew and braced herself against the vertiginous feeling of tilting downward.

She aimed the thought at him: Make them be quiet. Start talking.

But still Peter didn't speak; he merely gazed up the aisle at the open doors.

She was aware now of the empty campus surrounding the chapel, its silence, all the people—innocent boys, adults with their complicated lives—gathered inside. It was when Ruth became conscious of needing help—please God, thank God—that she felt most persuaded of the reality of God, as if God were at that moment reading her thoughts, watching her in her moment of desperation decide to have faith in him. Now she had an apprehension of a presence outside the white walls. Something had orchestrated the whole day, the whole evening, steering it toward this moment of crisis. Something had built the whole waiting world around them, trees, scented grass stretching away into the darkness, stars. She was afraid.

There was a rippling along the pew, boys jostling one another. The boy beside her bumped hard against her shoulder.

He turned an agonized face to her, color leaping into his cheeks. Sorry, he whispered.

Face blazing, he leaned forward to flash a look of hatred and fury down the row.

Fights were inevitable at the school, often at sporting events. One moment everything was under control—the players spread out over the grass, clouds arranged prettily in the sky. And then the next moment a boy somewhere on the field would have struck out savagely, a stick swinging, a fist. Suddenly a clot of bodies would be angrily grappling and struggling, the referees moving in. These incidents happened so quickly they left Ruth breathless. She felt now, in Peter's strange silence, the potential for chaos among the boys.

She felt the anxiety of the moment pass now into her belly, her bowels. Should she stand up? Could she go rescue him?

Peter cocked his head slightly. He'd been doing that, she'd noticed, tilting his head as if he couldn't quite hear.

The din of the boys around them rose another degree. She glanced behind her again, but the white frame of the doors contained only the pure, deep, shining blue of the night sky. A silhouetted figure crossed the open doorway, a dark form moving from one side of the chapel to the other. Then there was nothing but the empty square of the night, and Peter's silence, and the dangerous restlessness of the boys around her.

3

Peter knew what was about to happen. The boys had filled the chapel between him and the open doors, the square of blue twilight glowing at the end of the aisle. In the past, when the shuffling and throat clearing had died away, a true and deep silence would enter the room, an invisible presence.

In the face of it, the babbling of the private mind, the ceaseless effort of holding up for examination before the conscious self one thing after another, the whole demanding dumb show of the imagination . . . all of this would cease, the mind as empty as if its contents had been sucked into a vortex. The paradox, Peter thought, was that this state of emptiness was simultaneously a state of acute, almost transcendental engagement.

He'd tried to explain this to Ruth. But her whole history, everything about her childhood, had conditioned her to vigilance, not acceptance. It had always been difficult for her to relax. He was grateful for the calm that had overtaken her later years and that spilled now into all corners of their life: the unmade bed, the haphazard meals of this or that, whatever they could find in the refrigerator or cupboards—bread and cheese, pickles and ham, bottles of wine. He was grateful for her clever mind—my god, she knew something about practically everything; she would have won on *Jeopardy*, he'd always thought—and grateful even for the untidy house.

What did it matter really, that the house was untidy? He had put too much pressure on her about such things over the years, he knew, even as he had disliked himself for worrying what others would think. And she had worked so hard for him, for the boys. She had been the picture of duty.

She was a funny person, too, his Ruth, though not many knew that about her. She had always made him laugh, so witty and smart. And she was beautiful, though he knew she had never thought so. Gorgeous big breasts and big sweet mouth and melting eyes and long legs . . . his *beautiful* Ruth. He had a sudden memory of her on the tennis court—she was a terrible tennis player—running crazily from one side of the court to the other as he lobbed balls at her, her face red as a beet, her big feet pounding away in her big sneakers, her big hands swinging her racquet wildly as if she were being attacked by bees. She had looked great in tennis shorts, all those freckles on her legs. She'd tried awfully hard at it. He'd loved her for that, her determination to get out there and play with him—to keep him in shape, as she said—despite having no talent for it.

My god! I am so *terrible* at this! she would cry in frustration, watching a ball she'd hit sail off into the trees. And then the next one would follow, equally wide of the mark. Sometimes she had made him laugh so hard he'd have to stop, doubled over, and rest his hands on his knees. She didn't mean to be comical. She just was. Once she'd thrown her racquet at him.

She could get fighting mad, too, his Ruth. You didn't want to cross her.

Usually he did not need to speak or raise a hand to ask for silence in the chapel on this first night. Ruth had asked him that one time how he managed it, and he'd been truthful when he'd said he didn't know. He didn't believe he was in control of it, actually. The boys familiar with the ritual fell quiet of their own accord, knowing it was expected of them. The younger ones, glancing around, alert to something happening in the room, eventually grew silent, too.

That shared silence was magical for Peter.

Tonight, however, the boys did not seem to see him standing there. They turned around and exchanged fake punches with the fellows behind them, or tapped the shoulders of the boys in front and then withdrew their hands, gazing innocently toward the ceiling. He watched all this but felt unmoved by it, as if standing at a great distance. Laughter broke out here and there. He saw teachers lean forward, frowning at the miscreants.

Peter waited for the horseplay to stop, for conversation to cease. He didn't know what else to do. He could not see Ruth in the darkness of the chapel. He wondered if she had gone home, perhaps, to get ready for the party afterward. He was sorry that he'd been pulled away from her earlier. He'd wanted to take her arm, walk with her down to the chapel. He'd missed her today. He felt that more often these days, sometimes at odd moments: he *missed* her beside him. Like any man, he admired a beautiful woman, had stolen his share of looks at centerfolds over the years. But really the only woman he'd ever wanted was Ruth.

He'd felt it from the moment she'd showed up at his house when they were twelve years old, his father the town physician who had taken her in when she was alone.

At the far end of the aisle, the square of blue twilight glowed steadily.

Peter understood that his extreme height, the pronounced size of his big head, wielded a kind of drama; just standing up in front of them could make the boys be quiet in the classroom, though his size rarely seemed to intimidate little children. When he stood on the sidelines at athletic events, there always seemed to be one or two urchins, the children of faculty members, hanging on to his arms like monkeys and walking up his sides in their grass-covered sneakers.

He was sorry, but not as sorry as Ruth imagined perhaps,

not to have had children of his own. He was mostly sorry for Ruth; it was really Ruth to whom children were drawn. It had been hard for him to bear the longing in her eyes sometimes.

He'd tried to give her so many children, in a way. All these decades of boys.

They'd been enough for him, but perhaps not for her. Still, she had not complained. They had not spoken of it, really.

That, too, had been a mistake, perhaps.

He knew in general that he could put his height to good use. He had seen how it worked in the classroom. His stature, his athleticism . . . these had helped him be a good teacher. During graduate school, he'd left Ruth alone in New Haven for three months while he'd served briefly on a commission for training seminarians in rural ministries as schoolteachers. As the panel's youngest member, recommended by a history professor at Yale, he'd been farmed out to the least hospitable sorts of locales, tiny towns in Minnesota and Wisconsin near the Canadian border, places that might have taxed older, less vigorous men. During those cold, dark days spent observing from the back of one-room schoolhouses, his knees jutting up above the tops of the low desks, he had discovered in himself, alongside a love of God, an instinct for how to teach and a rambunctious style. In the classrooms at Derry, though he wasn't in them so much anymore, Peter behaved as if every answer, no matter how lackluster or hesitant, was a revelation. He loved to see the boys' eyes light up at his pleasure.

He disliked formality. He wanted the boys to call him Peter. He insisted on that. Everyone at Derry, in fact, whether they worked in the kitchen or drove one of the big mowers that roved over the playing fields or taught Shakespeare or physics or Greek, called him Peter. He hated standing on ceremony.

From the open doors came a blissful rush of cool air toward him, as if the grass outside, the trees with their drooping, fragrant burden of summer leaves, had given up the last of the day's warmth. The knee that troubled him the most, his right knee, sent out a sudden throb of pain. The discomfort rose, flared and then ran up his leg, touching a finger to the base of his spine. He felt sweat on his forehead. He shifted, tightening his calves, releasing them. The pain dimmed a little, wandered off. Peter realized that he'd been holding his breath. His chest felt sore and tight, as if he might have broken a rib.

But it was not his heart; he thought it was not his heart. He felt it thudding along uninvolved, uninterested in the strange tumult of feelings he was experiencing. This sorrow. This bewilderment. This anger.

He had given his first day speech to the boys at Derry for years—the same talk, more or less, about responsibility and opportunity—and he'd long ago done away with notes for it. The point of the evening was less what he said anyway, though he'd been proud of his words at one time, the sentences carefully crafted. Ruth had helped him; she had always been the better writer. He'd never thought much of that play or that novel she'd worked on, though—too depressing, though he never would have told her so. He had tried to be enthusiastic.

It was the experience of this moment, when the school community gathered under one roof in the darkness and the silence that Peter wanted to give the boys. It worked like an inoculation, he thought, protecting them against the worst of what might happen to them over the year, the various crimes perpetrated both by and against them. Right now, the new boys were at the fragile peak of their bravado, having made it through the parting from their families, the confusing business of the first day, without public tears. But some of them were precariously close to breaking down, Peter knew. He searched the audience and tried to fix his attention on them, the new boys, fourteen- and fifteen-year-olds not yet free of their child-hood selves, required to sit in the first rows. He counted on their faces to restore his equanimity, his sense of purpose.

A few days ago, just out of the shower one morning, Ruth had stood on tiptoe beside him, a towel knotted under her arms. She had kissed him as he'd straightened his tie in front of the mirror. Outside the window, a bird had been warbling, a long stream of entreaties, of fulsome nonsense.

Peter had made a goofy face at her in the mirror. He had not wanted to tell her how strange he'd felt lately, how unin-volved, somehow, in what was happening. He'd felt it power-fully the moment he'd opened his eyes this morning, as if he were watching the world through wavering old glass.

He was depressed, perhaps. They said it just came on peo-ple sometimes, like any sickness. Perhaps it was an inevitable part of the syndrome.

It had nothing to do with Ruth. He was sure about that.

It was something else, some hand reaching toward him from elsewhere, groping around for him, trying to *tell* him something. He had looked down at the cleavage of her breasts under the towel, the little accordion fan of wrinkles there, but he had not felt aroused, a further dismay. Ruth's breasts, her glorious freckled breasts, had always aroused him.

And poor Ed McClaren today, that god-awful scene in the dining hall . . . he hoped the man would be all right.

But he knew, somehow, that he would not be.

The new boys usually seemed poignant to Peter, full of promise and worry and false gaiety. He was struck every fall by the difference a summer made in the appearance of returning boys who, in three months' time, had acquired shoulders and facial hair and an adult bearing. All day today he'd roamed around, shaking hands, greeting returning students, meeting the new boys, surprising and pleasing a few by knowing their names. Facebook was a great tool for that; he loved Facebook. Here and there he carried into a dorm room on behalf of a flummoxed new boy and his pleased parents a box or a suitcase or a complicated tangle of computer equipment trailing cords.

He had, just like his old self, conducted bits of business with the faculty members with whom he crossed paths, coming back to his desk between these periods of sociability and encountering the messages of phone calls that needed to be returned.

But he'd said the wrong thing to a few people today, irritably chiding Mark Simmons, the art teacher, for forgoing a tie, though Mark had steadfastly refused to adopt this required convention for his entire career at Derry, and twice interrupting (boorishly, he thought now) during a presentation to the new boys about the library with irrelevant and probably incorrect observations about the school's wireless service. He had just wanted to hear himself speak, to reassure himself that he was—what? *Present,* somehow. Yet he had forgotten names, had failed to remember details about certain changes in the calendar agreed upon earlier in long, tiresome meetings.

Worse than these lapses, though, the sort of forgivable lapses perhaps typical of a man nearing eighty, he had been aware that he was chasing all day after the optimism that had once been, had always been before, so effortless.

Several times today he had crossed paths with Charlie Finney—Charlie had used that nickname Ruth so hated, *Pater,* and had saluted him with what seemed a false smile—and Peter had felt for the first time a real fear in Charlie's presence, an anger so rare that he almost didn't recognize it.

How dare you, he had thought. How *dare* you take that tone with me?

Now, facing the assembled school, he recognized that his performance today had been exactly that, a performance calculated to create the appearance of his own involvement. At his desk, during the few moments of quiet throughout the day, he had not talked on the phone or read through the papers stacked up and awaiting his attention. He had stared around the paneled walls at the portraits of his predecessors, the whiskered gentlemen and clean-shaven clerics who had led the Derry School since its creation in 1902. He had stared out the window. He had extended his foot, as if testing for solid ground, into the sharp parallelogram of sunlight that fell over the carpet. The sun's heat had blazed against his ankle, almost burning him. He had not wanted to move when the time had come for his next appointment.

He had loved this place so much. He had worked so hard for it. And he knew it was being gradually taken from him.

He was just like everyone else, of course. He would die, and the grass would grow right over his grave.

Somehow, he realized, he had begun speaking. He had arrived at the part of his speech about the eye being on the sparrow, the paragraph he'd constructed carefully to be read as both a comfort and a warning: they were *seen*, these boys. No one would be overlooked.

He did not remember having started, though, and the shock of disorientation he felt made him stop. His mouth had been moving, and words had been coming out of him, all of it issuing as if from an automatic reflex. He remembered a scientific experiment from his youth—or was it from one of the science labs he'd observed at Derry? An electrical impulse made a frog twitch. The brain was not involved.

Peter felt the mass of people before him shrink slightly, shiver, and then fix like a tiny, faraway image calcifying under a microscope. Where was Ruth? Had she actually gone home without him?

In the awkward silence that now filled the chapel, an explosive snort of laughter came from somewhere in the darkness of the pews. Someone, one of the boys, had not been able to bear the tension of the moment. A contagious ripple, the possibility of horrible affront, ran through the boys in that area—

Peter saw a section of the pews writhe like something about to strike—and then died away. He knew then that he must just get to the end somehow.

Ruth? Where was Ruth? He looked for her again, but he did not see her. Fear began in him now in earnest, a headache as shocking as ice applied to his temples. Sweat ran down his face, into his shirt collar.

He'd lost Ruth on the way to the chapel. She hadn't waited for him.

With a strange effort, as if tuning himself to the right frequency, he began speaking again, heard his own voice, heard relieved laughter from the audience—he had told the joke about the cow and the horse and the pig. Nearly there, nearly there, he thought distractedly, and then, thank God, he was at the end of it.

He smiled—where did that smile come from? A rictus, the frog jumps—but what he felt, he knew, was grief.

He could not make out a single face in the darkness. He felt none of what he usually felt on this occasion, the thing he had been so glad for Ruth to feel at last, the thing that came into the room every year because of the silence . . . no, the thing that *was* the silence, a moment of extraordinary communion, Peter believed, a rare blessed moment that made him feel both unimportant and yet also part of the infinite, important largeness of the world.

But it had not come this year. It had packed up its bags and gone away, he thought, like an old man with a hunched-over back and a battered suitcase walking alone down the road in the darkness, away from Derry, away from the boys, away from Ruth, away from Peter.

He had been left behind.

Afterward, outside the chapel, someone was speaking to him. Peter knew he knew who it was, but for the life of him he could not remember the man's name. He remembered Ed McClaren, and that something had happened to him.

He saw Ruth come up behind the interlocutor, her eyes wide, questions all over her face: What is *wrong* with you? her look said. You're frightening me!

He could not tell her how strange he felt. He could not sort it out.

I left something on my desk, he told her abruptly, afraid to say more, afraid that he could not get the words out properly, that his mouth wouldn't work. I'll see you later.

Ruth will take care of you at the house, he then said with concentrated politeness to the man before him; he knew the extreme formality of his tone was wrong, but he didn't know what else to say. Who was it? Jesus, he couldn't remember. A coil of fear shot into his stomach, up his esophagus, into his mouth. It tasted like blood, as if his tongue or his gums were bleeding.

I'll be along, he said, and hurried away.

He had hurt Ruth, had frightened her, but he had frightened himself more. Still, he had not wanted her to watch whatever was happening to him.

And he did not want any of these people—these strangers—

at his house tonight. It felt outrageous to him, the prospect of their intrusion into whatever terrible and important thing was happening to him. It was as if they were planning to turn up at his funeral, corks flying, arms slung over one another's shoulders, bawdy songs belted out into the night. Of course it wasn't like that at all. He *knew* that. They were only doing what they were expected to do, what *he* expected them to do: to come and be convivial for an hour or so, to shake hands with the new teachers and settle their first-year jitters with a few funny stories, a few insider tips, a few drinks, reassure one another that they were glad to be there.

He was not himself, he thought. It had all become too difficult, his job. He was no good at it anymore.

Instead of going to his office, he continued alone along the brick path that wound under lampposts between the buildings. The Virginia creeper covering the facades like a second skin shivered in the night breeze. The leaves had just begun to turn from green to a glowing, complex crimson, like an oxidized penny. The vines encased most of the main buildings on campus. A few years ago, he'd presided over contentious meetings about the creeper, and whether it was destroying the masonry. Peter thought it gave the campus an air of enchantment. At night, with lit windows peeping out from the foliage, the buildings appeared to be made entirely of green leaves, a fantastical effect: two stories, three, in places, of living foliage. Birds nested in it, feeding all fall and winter on the hard purple berries.

As he walked now, the walls beside him stirred as though something secret ran beneath their surface.

He crossed one of the colonnades, preparing to take the

long way through campus to his house. He only needed a walk, perhaps, some fresh air, something to settle him. This part of the campus, the administration and classroom buildings, was deserted. By now the work in the kitchens was over, the remains of dinner in the dining hall cleared away, the giant dishwashers churning, emitting gassy fumes of bleach into the darkness of the tiled pantries with their wet floors and sour-smelling drains. On the playing fields, the grass would be cold to the touch now, stiffening in the night air.

He turned off the colonnade, began to descend the steps. The breeze did not reach the inner courtyard, and the vine-covered walls around him were still, black leaves hanging quietly. Something was slipping away from him.

But not the things themselves, or the place, the lovely world of Derry, the beautiful, material world of his own life, he thought. Not his beloved Ruth, with her sad start in this life and all her bravery in the face of it, her funny stories and her straightforward way of looking at the world. She had entertained him so much over the years. He had almost lost her once, by his own cowardice and fear, but it had all worked out, in the end.

There was no one else like her.

But something *was* leaving him. He moved close to the wall of the building, stared up at the facade of motionless greenery, as if he could detect and prevent the departure of this thing, whatever it was. As he did so, a desperate fluttering in the leaves just over his head startled him. He stepped back as the shape of something dark flew from the foliage, the wings of an alarmed bird almost brushing his face.

He felt a powerful grief, as if a dear companion had stepped across the divide and turned to raise a hand before disappearing.

4

At the house, Ruth turned on the lamps in the living room with shaking hands, and then went immediately into the kitchen. The cheese puffs took only a few minutes in a hot oven. She turned it on, aware of the unwashed plate from her sandwich earlier in the day, left in the sink.

In the face of Peter's bewildering behavior at the chapel, she had felt mortified, humiliated, aware of people's eyes on her, and she had rushed away, pretending haste in order to get ready for the party. She hadn't fooled anyone, she thought now.

It was his age, they would speculate. He was too old to be doing this job. He was losing his mind. He was no good anymore. He had lost his touch.

But it was not that which troubled her. For a moment she had to put her face into her hands. She stood very still in the kitchen, breathing in the smell of her own palms. The way he had spoken to her, as if she were someone he disliked, as if she were a stranger.

She struggled to fit the oven mitts over her shaking hands. Something was terribly the matter with Peter. She shouldn't have let him go off by himself like that. But he had been so certain, so cold. And there were all these people coming! She had to get ready.

She had walked alone to the house, quickly, almost running, stumbling in her good shoes. The others would follow along eventually, she thought, but she imagined they were keeping a respectful distance now. Or perhaps none of them would come at all. For a second she saw them, standing outside the chapel on the path, a few people appointed to get the boys to their houses, the rest of them plotting, considering: How could Peter be removed from his job? How could they get rid of him?

She jumped when Charlie Finney spoke quietly to her from the doorway.

Do you need any help in here, Ruth? he said. He sounded tentative. She was unused to that tone in him. Or she distrusted it.

Stop it, she thought. Do not feel sorry for me.

She would not turn around from the window over the sink. She looked at the reflection of him in the glass, a dark wavering shape, his balding head shining oddly.

You gave me a fright, Charlie, she said, coming in like that.

She knew she sounded angry. She turned away from the window, opened the oven door, and clattered the baking sheets unnecessarily.

He stepped into the kitchen.

I'm sorry, he said. But people are in the living room. Should I bring in some ice?

Oh. Yes, she said. Ice. Bring in ice. By all means.

She closed the oven door but did not turn around, afraid of her blazing cheeks. She thought she might weep, if she looked at him.

There was silence behind her. Then she heard his footsteps move across the kitchen, heard him open the freezer, ice clinking into the bucket. He must have brought it with him, people in the living room standing around awkwardly, waiting for her to appear. The hostess. She looked down at the stained and scarred countertop. A strip of the laminate edging had fallen off. She and Peter had tried to glue it several times, but it never wanted to stay. The raw seam looked filthy.

The house was shabby. She knew it was, and humiliation flooded her. Some of it was her neglect. She just didn't care too much about that sort of thing, fancy decorating and so forth. If it was comfortable, she was happy enough. But some of it—most of it, really—was that there had never been enough money. She'd been foolish, all these years, to work for nothing. She was a Smith graduate, for heaven's sake! And what had she done with that education?

Nothing.

Worked for free for all these years, worked so that people like Charlie Finney could have it all, in the end.

Peter had never taken enough money for himself, putting so much of it back into the school, into the students and even the faculty and staff and their troubles, writing checks in his big block letters to help pay the tuition of local boys from Wyeth, boys whose letters of application to the school broke his heart. She did not know how much of his paycheck he had returned to the school over the years, but she had a sudden apprehension that it was much more than she'd known, much more than was reasonable or wise.

This was why he'd never wanted to talk about retiring, she realized. There *was* no money. He had spent it all on other people.

In the windowsill above the kitchen sink, his plants were crowded in their old clay pots, some of them filmed with white mold. A spider plant sent out its tentacles, little baby spider plants, a crazy thing.

Peter loved that plant, tossing the tiny spiders with a finger so that they bounced a little. He touched them the way one would chuck an infant under the chin.

He would have been, she knew, a wonderful father.

Outside the window, the night sky had thickened, drawn in closer, clouds moving in beneath the moon and stars. She remembered the radio forecast from earlier in the day, the storms to the west.

Peter liked to watch the Weather Channel on television, sitting forward in his chair, elbows on his knees, a drink in his hands.

Holy smokes, he would say, shaking his head. Look at the size of that mess.

Charlie spoke behind her.

It's been a rough day, Ruth, he said. First, the business with Ed . . . I think it shook up Peter. It shook up everyone. It shook *me* up! He gave a nervous laugh. Not a good start to the . . .

Then he hesitated. Ruth, has Peter been . . . you know, he said. Has he been all right? Has he been under any stress?

Ruth whirled around. Charlie blanched.

Stress? she said. *Stress?* Don't condescend to me, Charlie Finney. You know as well as I do how hard he works, how little help he gets. He is a *good man*, she said fiercely.

She had put up her fists, bunched inside the oven mitts, as if to shake them at him. She looked absurd, she realized. She dropped her hands.

She went on, though, helpless to stop herself. You with your fancy-pants marketing and websites and snazzy videos and *e-blasts* and—she struggled for the vocabulary—*blogs*. Your *blogs*, she said. Your important relationships with people at all those other fancy schools. Your texting and tweetering . . . and whatnot. *Peter* just wants to *help* people, those who deserve it, children who *need* him. Not those who already have enough money to get anything they want in this world.

Charlie held up his hands. Ruth, he began—his face had gone from white to red.

He was embarrassed, not angry, she thought, but she couldn't stop.

I know, she cried. I *know*. It's the rich who will help pay for those who cannot afford it. I *understand* that. I understand trickle-down just fine, thank you. *Peter* understands it, for god's sake. He's been making it work for thirty-five years, civilly and man-to-man, finding people who also wanted to help those who are unfortunate. One of you could lift a finger to *help* him here, she said. He's doing it all alone.

She wanted to weep.

Charlie was looking at her, his expression unreadable.

You're trying to change this place, she said then. It has been *a good place*.

She hit the table with her hand, still in its oven mitt. The sound was muffled. She ripped off the mitts, snapped them savagely against the table's edge.

You don't know what it's been like here, she said.

She looked at Charlie, clutching the ice bucket against his chest. She thought for a minute of his three children, all of them big strong boys like Charlie himself. A fortune, he had, in those children. Lucky man.

You just don't know, Charlie, she said. She gestured around at the old table, the two mismatched chairs, the old pots and pans hanging on a pegboard. There was a stain, she noticed, in one corner of the ceiling.

A long silence unfolded between them.

Charlie cleared his throat. Ruth, he said. I'm sorry. It's just that—we're a little worried about him. Worried about you.

She turned away abruptly, waving her hand. I'm fine, she said. I'll be out in a minute with the cheese puffs. Go ahead.

She winced. How stupid she sounded. Cheese puffs.

I'm sorry, he repeated. Take your time.

She stared out the window. She could tell the storm was moving in, could feel the huge movement of the big trees outside. She heard the hinge of the swinging door behind Charlie as he left, the silence in the room that told her he was gone. She turned around from the sink. Automatically, she bent to look in the oven door. Peter had replaced the oven lightbulb the week before, and she looked now at the cheese puffs, growing brown inside. On the kitchen table, on the lazy Susan, were Peter's various medications, her calcium pills, her multivitamins, her reading glasses, his reading glasses, a sticky plastic honey bear, a pair of salt and pepper shakers made in the shapes of light-houses. They'd been a gift from someone, one of the boys.

Then she heard a noise at the back door, a scraping and breathing sound.

She always left the back door open unless it was too cold outside, the screen door closed against bugs. On the back porch they kept their mud boots and some tools, a shovel and a hoe, the rakes, a basket she used when weeding, the axe.

There was nothing of value there—not that anyone would ever try to steal anything, she knew. Somewhere they had a key to the front door of their house, but they'd never locked it, not in her memory. She didn't even know where the key was.

She looked at the bright oven window, its heat and glow. From the living room and the front hallway she could hear the muted sound of conversation. People had come after all, she thought. But they sounded like people speaking after a funeral, a little careful about the volume, an awkward laugh escaping here and there. Life goes on.

Where was Peter? What was he doing? What was happening to him?

She heard the sound again, someone—something—outside the back door.

She looked at the telephone, hanging on the wall, but before she could reach for it, a voice—a cultivated, polite voice, quiet—said, Hello? Ma'am?

She turned slowly toward the door, aware that while she could not see him, whoever he was, standing in the darkness, he could see *her* perfectly, her navy blue dress and the big gold sunburst like a target on her chest, the lighted window of the oven and her cheese puffs rising inside, the pathetic, domestic clutter on the kitchen table, the jungle overtaking the window-sill. She heard the noise of the wind rising outside, a moaning.

They had come such a long way, she thought, she and Peter. Over the difficult terrain of the early years, over the long and sometimes fraught expanse of their middle age, into the plateau of old age . . . What would come next? When she had imagined it, she had thought of attractive country inns and beach vacations, the kinds of places she and Peter had stayed sometimes over the years, Peter doing recruiting business for the school here and there, the vacation house of a wealthy trustee loaned to them for repayment of hard service.

The voice from the darkness spoke again: Please help me.

Who is it? she said. She reached out for the edge of the table. Who is there?

I've been on the trail, the voice said. Hiking the trail. I need help. With my dog. It's my dog.

Why did he not open the door, she thought? Why did he not come in?

Please, the voice said, and now there was a little command in it, less of a plea. The voice was young, though. She need not be frightened, she thought. It was only a hiker, some young fellow, a nature enthusiast, shy, too shy to come in, with a sick dog, an injured companion.

She moved slowly toward the door.

There was a whining sound from outside, but she could not tell if it was human or animal.

I'm coming, she said. Her hands were clumsy on the door handle.

The young man standing on the porch was wild-haired, dreadlocks down to his waist, a mossy beard over his chin. His face was dirty, his knapsack rising behind him on a metal frame like a horrible hunchback. He held a gun pointed at her chest, at the starburst there. At his feet lay a dog, some sort of beagle, old and grizzled, with a gray muzzle. The dog's eyes were closed, its belly heaving.

She remembered, from long ago in her childhood, another gun. In all these intervening years she had not seen a single other gun, yet the black eye of it seemed now so familiar, as if she had been waiting for all these decades for it to reappear, to reassert itself. It was as if she had known that one day it would, just as she had come to anticipate her nightmares and their familiar landscapes.

She closed her eyes, opened them again. The man was still there.

My dog is old and sick, he said. You have a car. That's your car in the driveway, I know because I've waited for you. Give me your car keys.

She did not reply for a minute, her voice stuck in her throat, as if he had wedged the gun into her windpipe.

They had shot her father that day, the day they finally found him, but they had not killed him.

I need to get him to a vet, the man said, louder, as if she were hard of hearing. Get me your keys.

She was stunned by his filth, by the depth and extent of it, his clothes like something that had been buried and then

THE LAST FIRST DAY

unearthed, by the wealth of objects hanging from his backpack, pots and hanks of cloth and rope, a tattered paperback somehow threaded by fishing line, stuffed animals, one of them a purple spotted giraffe, one of them a fish, she thought, with big, fleshy lips.

As she stood there, he reached with one hand, still pointing the gun at her, and swung one of the stuffed animals toward her, shaking it, as if it were speaking.

Please help me, he said, without moving his lips, his voice high and childish-sounding, like a ventriloquist's voice. His eyes slid away from hers.

I am desperately ill and need the attention of a doctor, he said in the voice of the creature he held, and she saw now that it was not a fish, but a dog, his ears worn away, a grotesquerie.

Over the years, Ruth had met several of Dr. Wenning's patients. She'd kept only a few private patients, by the end, people she had met at the extreme exigency of their need, after they'd been arrested or admitted to the hospital, but who had responded well to drugs and treatment, and whose stories had moved her particularly. Her manner with them, when she came out of her inner office to greet them, Ruth primly engaged in filing or typing, had been respectful, friendly, and intimate . . . as if she were glad to see them.

Yes. My old friends, she had called them. Why else would I spend time with them?

There had been no mistaking these people, these desperately ill people, for other, normal people, Ruth had seen. Passing them in the street, you could see in an instant that there was something terribly wrong with them. Her own father, she'd realized, had been an anomaly—apparently perfectly sane, even gentle with her, but all the while his hidden life piling up behind him, like heaps of debris shoved helter-skelter into a closet, her father leaning against the door—legs crossed, casual as you please—to keep it from spilling open. Mental illness, Dr. Wenning had said, took just as many forms as physical illness.

The man before her, she realized, was one of these sad victims.

He whipped away the stuffed animal behind his back, returned his hand to the gun, and shook it at her. In his normal voice, he said, I'll shoot you if you don't give me your keys. His eyes, when he turned them to her again, were full of desperation.

I have to go inside, she said. I have to get the car keys from my purse.

He made a sound of anguish, as if the options before him were unbearable.

She realized that a smell drifted off of him, a sickening smell of filth and human sweat. She stepped back, and he gave out a high cry, a squeak. At his feet, the dog stirred.

The vet's office is on Main Street, she said.

You turn right here, out of the house, and just follow the road straight into Wyeth. It's about three miles. They won't be open now, but they put a telephone number on the door, for emergencies. It's a building with a brown roof, like a Swiss chalet. You can't miss it. You can call them from there.

Give me your cell phone, he said, suddenly completely lucid-sounding. It was shocking, hearing the words *cell phone* come from him, as if someone from the eighteenth century in doublet and ruff had stepped forward and started talking about Internet access and automobiles.

She wondered if he'd been putting her on, the voice part of whatever the wretched pathology was from which he suffered.

But he said to her then, in a malevolent whisper: Hurry.

In the kitchen, her legs wavered.

I'm looking for them, she said to him, gazing around frantically. There was her purse, on Peter's chair.

Oh, Peter, she thought.

She shook out the contents of her purse, all of it falling to the tabletop, checkbook and wallet, compact and notebook—when had she last used a compact, she thought?—a litter of pens and pencils, an old hairbrush, white hairs threaded through its bristles. The keys, on a ring with a red rubber Buddha that stuck out its tongue when you pressed its stomach—a joke gift from Peter, because Ruth could never find her car keys in her bag — landed with a jingle.

How quickly her life seemed to be moving toward its end, she thought then. After so many years of glorious tedium, of day after day in the kitchen, of mowing the lawn and climbing the steps to this building on campus or that one, cheering the boys on from the sidelines, making love with Peter or quarreling with him, sitting at boring dinners with trustees who sometimes couldn't be bothered to remember her name, after car tune-ups and dentist appointments, crowns on her teeth and new glasses for Peter and more daffodil bulbs in the garden . . . now it was all speeding up. That was how it would be, she thought. He would shoot her, and then he would take the car.

Oh, Peter, she thought.

On the porch, she held out the keys. The man had not moved, the gun still pointing at her, as if she'd been a retinal image on his eye, present even when she wasn't there.

Cell phone? he said.

I don't have one, she said. It was the truth. Peter had one, of course, but she'd never really needed one.

He looked at her, suspicious.

I know, she said. She felt stupidly embarrassed. But I just don't.

He took the keys from her. Then Ruth watched, horribly mesmerized, as he kissed the barrel of the gun and laid it on the porch floor. He knelt beside it, and for an awful moment, she thought he would shoot her, then shoot the dog, then shoot himself. Why? Why, she thought? There was no logic to it! But he only scooped up the dog in his arms, and then stepped backward off the porch.

She waited. A moment later, she heard the car's engine start, her old Subaru. She hoped there was gas in it.

She went back inside the kitchen. The smell of the cheese puffs came to her, powerfully—she smelled sage and Parmesan cheese and egg—and she ducked quickly to peer in the oven window, saw that they would burn in another minute.

A moment later, Charlie Finney was in the kitchen and had her by the arm. She thought that someone had seen the man with the dog, that Charlie had burst in to save her. Charlie! she said, but he put his arm around her shoulders as if to comfort her and led her out of the kitchen.

In the front hall, there was great confusion. Ruth stood still. People moved around her as if she had turned to stone or salt and could no longer see or hear them. They came and went, opening and closing doors. At first, she began to turn away from them all gathered in the hallway, as if to go back into the kitchen, to begin the day all over again.

Where had she been? She had been in the kitchen, eating a ham sandwich for lunch, Schumann's "Tangled Dreams" playing, then the tornado warning on the radio. She had been in the bathtub, soaking her tired back. Asleep on the bed, on the sun-warmed bedspread. The clock had stopped. The lights had gone out.

In the cracked silver surface of the mirror over the table across the hall, she caught a glimpse of a figure —herself, still a stranger with her newly short hair. Her face was white, her eyes wide open, dark. But she knew there was no going back, no undoing what Charlie Finney was saying to her.

Ruth, he said. Ruth, it's Peter.

The lilies on the table that she'd arranged earlier that afternoon, a blaze of orange trumpets, seemed now to be turning toward her, listening. People crossed around her, back and forth, the closet door opening and closing. Someone handed her a raincoat. Her purse.

Here's your purse, Ruth, someone said.

Someone else took away the raincoat; she won't need that.

Here, Ruth, I'll hold the umbrella. Come this way, Ruth. All right? Oh, my god. Where did this storm come from?

It just blew in, someone said, didn't it? They weren't calling for it . . .

Is she all right? Let's just get her there.

I can't believe it, someone said. Two in one day. And *Peter.*

She was gratified, hearing that tone, the clear grief in it. It was Charlie Finney speaking. She turned to gaze at him.

He looked undone. *Ruth?* he said. His voice shook. Let me help you.

Outside the house, her car was gone, as if it had never been there. Standing in the gravel driveway, she staggered against the wind, so powerful it nearly knocked her over. A fierce joy seized her: the wetness against her face, the storm's upwelling sound, the big trees creaking and swaying overhead, tattered leaves flying through the air, a strong, green, grassy smell. The light was otherworldly, a strange shine on everything, rocks and grass gleaming, glittering below the darkness bearing down from overhead.

Scattered drops fell, striking hard. The rain was nearly there.

God, she loved weather, she thought; she always had. Peter, too, hunched over the radar maps on his computer, or the two of them on the beach, holding hands, watching storms roll in across the Atlantic.

Holy cow, Peter would say. Holy smokes. Look at that, Ruth. Look at the size of that thing.

They'd felt it, that wild joy.

Except it was *not* joy she felt now. Instead something like slime was spreading over her, disgusting, horrifying. She suppressed a shiver, convulsed, swallowed, tried to contain it.

She was having a *memory* of happiness, she realized, not

the thing itself. *Once* she had loved weather. Now no more for joy.

She'd known it was going to happen, hadn't she? All day, she'd known it.

Overhead, the trees' branches lashed against the dark sky. It was funny, she had said to Peter once, pencil poised over her crossword, that the meaning of the word *lash*—stroke, whip, shake—was so oddly contrary to its synonyms: tie, bind, fasten. She remembered this moment of puzzling discovery, because at the time Peter had looked up and recited, in its entirety, a poem by Alexander Pope.

She had stared at him, astonished. *Peter* didn't know any poems. *She* was the one who knew all the poetry, had smugly quoted things to him over the years.

It's the only one I know, he had said. We were taught it in English class.

He'd begun again, as if she'd said he couldn't do it twice: *True ease in writing comes from art, not chance, As those move easiest who have learned to dance* ...

She couldn't remember any more of it now, but it had had the word *lash* in it somewhere.

Peter had said the whole thing and then shrugged, returning to the newspaper.

She had been baking a cake that morning. She remembered that moment now, the smell of the cake, a lemon pound cake, and her sense of satisfaction at having gotten it in the oven so early in the day. She wasn't usually that organized. It had been a Sunday, and Peter had not gone to work . . . but they'd had something to do later, something unpleasant, so the day had been clouded by her awareness of that duty awaiting them, that interruption to their rare, lazy domesticity, that thing that had sat there glumly ahead, like a toad.

What had it been? Oh, yes. God, of course. A funeral. Peter's old secretary, Ellen.

The rain was moments away. She could feel it. Lifting her head, she could smell it, too, a fox catching a scent.

For a moment she stood alone on the driveway, no one touching her. Then a car appeared. She waited, like a queen who had never done a thing for herself, while someone opened the car door for her. She got in and obediently fastened her seat belt. Somehow the car moved forward—who on earth was driving?

There was a sudden cracking noise overhead, and she ducked involuntarily, crying out: a branch struck the roof of the car as it pulled past the stone pillars.

It was Charlie Finney, at the wheel. Peter's enemy, her enemy.

No, she thought. Let it be said at the end that she was truthful; she had no real reason to accuse him. Why not think of him as Peter's friend, her friend?

Pater, he'd called Peter.

Perhaps he'd had no father, she thought, as she herself had had no mother, no father.

Poor Charlie Finney, she thought.

She left her hands in place in her lap, but she turned her face away from Charlie now: she wanted to be alone. A flash of lightning—a shuddering exposure—and the field across the street flared into view for an instant, the gap in the stone wall through which the hiker and his dog must have come, minutes before. The tops of the trees were bent over nearly parallel to the ground. Lightning flared again, illuminating a darkly shining horizon. She felt as if she were crouched down inside the mouth of a cave, peering out at the last sight of the world.

Then a second crash sounded, thunder this time, and the noise of something enormous dividing in the air. The rain began. The windshield before her face dissolved.

5

Over the years when Ruth had been at her most anxious, her most upset, Dr. Wenning always said to her: Ruth, Ruth. Sometimes you just have to be patient, wait it out. Put on the teakettle. Iron some clothes. Bake a cake. Read another book, why don't you?

For a few years, Ruth and Peter had owned a dog, a homely, wrinkle-faced, rusty-bearded mutt adopted from the pound in Wyeth, devoted to them. He had come with his name— Hercules. When he'd died, she and Peter had been broken-hearted. Dr. Wenning used to say: take that big pooch of yours and put him on his leash and go for a long, long walk. You will feel better afterward.

Play a little piano, Dr. Wenning would say. How about you try the violin?

A mediocre but enthusiastic cellist, Dr. Wenning complained often about Ruth's failure to study the piano more seriously. It showed, she said, a lack of imagination and discipline, that Ruth had never become a better musician.

Then, seeing Ruth's face, she would say: Oh, my dear. It will pass, today's sadness, tomorrow's sadness, the next day's. Something else will happen. Just wait.

In the sunny living room of the new house—she always thought of it as "the new house"—Ruth folded the laundry on the dining room table—blond wood, Scandinavian design, completely modern—enjoying the scent of the clean clothes, the softness of Peter's worn old shirts, even her big old white underpants. In the bathroom, she picked up his wet towels from the floor, hers as well, and carried them outside and hung them in the sun on the railing of the deck overlooking the lake.

They never would be tidy people.

It had been a stroke that had felled Peter, but a small one, after all.

It was luck, only pure luck, that a boy—a homesick boy, escaped from his dorm and wandering the campus in the dark trying to reach his parents on his cell phone, looking for a hot spot where he could get a signal—had found Peter, collapsed in the courtyard. The boy had had the good sense to call 911 immediately, to stay with Peter, who later remembered the boy kneeling beside him, remembered the feeling of being unable to speak, though he could see and make eye contact, remembered trying to smile, remembered lifting his hand and the boy taking it, holding on.

Charlie Finney stepped in, as Ruth had known he would, to take over at Derry.

It had been absurdly easy, after all, for them to walk away. They had owned virtually nothing, so there had been nothing to take with them. She thought they'd probably had a bonfire after she and Peter vacated the headmaster's house. She bet Charlie Finney had burned everything, every worn old sheet and patched bedspread, figured out how to buy himself some nice new furniture, a snazzy gas oven, a stainless-steel fridge.

She and Peter had a few clothes, a few books, a few personal mementoes. Really, when they packed it all up, she realized the degree to which they'd been like penitents on the devotional road. Most of what might have been their savings, as Ruth had suspected, Peter had put back into the school.

In the rehab hospital, in the days before he regained his speech, Peter could communicate only by writing.

Are you okay? he wrote on a pad.

She took the pad from him, bent over it. Yes, she wrote. No, she wrote. Then she crossed out no and underlined the word *yes*. She pushed the pad back to him.

Are you angry about the money? he wrote.

Yes, she wrote. Then she sighed. NO, she printed in big capital letters. She circled it and then turned the pad around so he could read it.

He read what she had written, put his hand, the one he could lift, over his eyes.

She leaned forward, touched her forehead to his.

. . .

The community of Derry, past and present, took up a collection on their behalf, cash and pledged amounts. The contributions bought Ruth and Peter a tiny house—this sun-filled A-frame at the edge of a lake in the Adirondacks—the property offered to them at a deep discount by a board member in gratitude for Peter's years of generosity, his years of service, his years of love. Contributions came in from every graduating class over Peter's years as headmaster. Many classes had one hundred percent participation.

There had been an enormous party for them. A white tent had been set up on the big lawn, strings of lights wound everywhere, a dance floor in the center. A twelve-piece band had been hired to play. The whole thing had cost a fortune, Ruth had thought at the time, disapproving, eyeing the ice sculptures and the shrimp by the kilo, oysters on platters everywhere, an open bar. Who on earth had paid for all this?

But what could they do?

Ruth and Peter—leaning on a cane—had stood as if in a receiving line at a wedding, greeting people as they came through. So many people, all of them embracing Peter and embracing Ruth, thanking him, thanking *her*, many of them wiping away tears.

We'll miss you both so much, they said, again and again, and Ruth had had to put her fingers over her mouth.

After all, it had not been unnoticed, her work.

Kitty Finney, her hair worn girlishly in a hairband, had come up to Ruth and embraced her.

Where are the boys? Ruth asked.

Babysitter, Kitty said. She had a drink in her hand and she raised it in Ruth's direction. Thank god, she said, grinning.

Then she had impulsively hugged Ruth again.

I won't ever be able to do what you've done here, Ruth, she said. I don't know how you've done it. You did *everything*. You know everybody. Look at all these people, all these people who love you.

Ruth looked past Kitty. People had begun to dance, and she was having trouble hearing what was said to her over the sound of the music. Someone waved to her from the dance floor. She waved back.

Kitty took a gulp of her drink. You and Peter were a team, weren't you? she said.

Ruth turned to her. Kitty's eyes had filled with tears. She took off her headband and pushed her hair back from her face with her hand. Then she resettled her headband. Sorry, she said. Sometimes I'm just overwhelmed. I just know I can't do what you've done.

You'll be fine, Ruth said. Of course you can.

She remembered the sagging grape arbor behind the house, the buzzing fuse box, the lights on in the windows of the house at night, greeting her when she came home. She remembered the birds flying into the walls of the buildings on campus at dusk, the rustling creeper, deer moving out across the frozen fields in winter. She remembered the bells on the horses' harnesses. She remembered pale boys lying in their beds in the infirmary, remembered tooth marks on pencils, smudged erasures on papers. She remembered the boys singing "Nearer My God to Thee."

She remembered her younger self, the woman in the Liberty scarf, cheering on the boys at the track meet, Peter keeping the camera steady on her face on a sunny fall day long ago.

The love between them.

I was lucky, she said now to Kitty. You'll do a wonderful job, you and Charlie.

The evening ended with an announcement that the school had drawn up plans for a new library to be named in Peter's honor.

Ruth, in the dress she'd bought for the occasion, had helped Peter cut a ceremonial ribbon.

Her dress was pink, a daring color for her. It had a ruffle around the neck.

I like that dress, Peter had said when they'd been getting ready earlier that evening. The ruffle makes you look like a cupcake.

A *delicious* cupcake! he'd said quickly, seeing her expression.

She'd hit him on the arm, but only gently. She was still careful around him, watchful. The first time he'd had an orgasm after the stroke, she'd ended up in tears.

It's all *right*, he'd said, holding her to him while she cried.

It's fine, Ruth, he'd said. Really, I'm fine.

The months while Peter was recovering, their daily routine so different from the one they'd maintained at Derry, possessed a loneliness that reminded Ruth of their years in New Haven, when Peter had been so busy with his graduate studies. Ruth had worked all kinds of jobs in those years, trying to earn money, but still she had sometimes felt as though she was standing still, while Peter moved on ahead of her. They were each sometimes tired, or bored, or restless . . . but often, it seemed, not at the same time, Peter collapsing with exhaustion just as Ruth found a movie she wanted to go see, or Ruth succumbing to a cold or the flu when Peter had a break between classes. They made love at odd hours—in the middle of the night, or just before dawn, or hastily, when Peter came home for lunch, kissing hungrily in the hall afterward, Peter shrugging into his coat, Ruth handing him a paper sack with an apple and a slapped-together sandwich.

The last winter that they lived in New Haven, Dr. Wenning had slipped on the ice in the parking lot of the hospital and suffered a bad sprain to an ankle. She'd needed help, and so Ruth had packed a suitcase and gone to stay with her for a few weeks, sleeping uncomfortably on the tiny overstuffed sofa in the study at Dr. Wenning's apartment.

Ruth did the laundry, which included washing by hand Dr. Wenning's yellowed old slips and heavily fortified brassieres, hanging them to dry on a complicated hanger contraption over the bathtub. She cooked scrambled eggs or baked beans for their supper. During the day, she drove Dr. Wenning to work and carried her bags and briefcase, fetched liverwurst-and-pickle sandwiches for them at lunchtime from the deli down the street. While Dr. Wenning taught her classes or saw patients, Ruth read. *Madame Bovary.* Turgenev's *Fathers and Sons. Our Mutual Friend* by Dickens. Chekhov's *The Cherry Orchard.* Sometimes Ruth was able to meet Peter between his classes at a tiny breakfast and lunch place near campus, where they ordered coffee and sat in a booth, kissing like lovers who had been parted for months.

Every night, she called Peter to say she missed him.

She felt sorry for Dr. Wenning, shuffling around in her slippers, her ankle the size and color of an eggplant, but Dr. Wenning seemed to have little self-pity. Only once, gripping the kitchen table, leaning over as if she could not catch her breath, she had said, My god, Ruth. I don't know what I'd do without you.

Ruth had felt embarrassed, heartsick. What *would* Dr. Wenning do without her?

One night, she had been awoken by Dr. Wenning, standing in the doorway of the office on her crutches.

I am afraid we have to go to the hospital, Ruth, Dr. Wenning said.

She had been wearing a frayed old robe, dark blue, with wide lapels and a heavy tasseled cord. Her hair—snow white as long as Ruth had known her—was wild. Without her glasses, she looked vulnerable, tired, an old queen aroused from sleep by urgent matters of state.

Ruth had struggled upright on the couch. What's the matter? she said.

Mr. Mitzotakis is in a bad way, Dr. Wenning said. She turned, and then she turned back. The oranges in the refrigerator, she said. Bring those, please.

On the way to the hospital, Ruth had glanced at Dr. Wenning, sitting in the passenger seat beside her. From her filing for Dr. Wenning, Ruth remembered that Mr. Mitzotakis, one of Dr. Wenning's patients, owned a plumbing business.

Is Mr. Mitzotakis all right? Ruth said.

Dr. Wenning gazed out the window. Snow fell, lightly and beautifully, through the arc of the streetlights. Ruth was not an experienced driver, and the icy road made her nervous. Her hands were cold inside her mittens.

Mr. Mitzotakis has attempted to fly from the second-story rooftop of his garage, Dr. Wenning said finally.

Oh, Ruth said. She had not expected that.

He didn't get very far, Dr. Wenning said.

The car, Dr. Wenning's old ocean liner of an Oldsmobile, began to drift, as if it were light as a feather, across the center-line of the road. Ruth held her breath until she was able to pull the car back into the proper lane. The tires spun beneath them on the snow, making a high, whining sound. Ruth clutched the wheel. Sweat broke out across her forehead under her hat, making her head itch.

Mr. Mitzotakis had broken both of his legs, one in several places, as well as his left arm and several ribs. He had a concussion. At the hospital, the grim-faced nurse in charge of him, her gray hair tucked in a net under her cap, told Dr. Wenning that shrubs planted along one wall of the garage—those, and the accumulated feet of snow—had apparently cushioned his fall.

You know he was wearing this big wing contraption? the nurse said. She circled her finger in the air by her ear, rolled her eyes. Cuckoo, she said. Then she eyed Ruth.

He doesn't seem to like women, she said, warning Dr. Wenning. He's been *very* rude.

Ruth stood there, holding their coats and Dr. Wenning's bag. She had offered to help Dr. Wenning into her white doctor's jacket, but Dr. Wenning had shaken her head. She wore an old tweed blazer, her familiar cowl-neck sweater.

Ruth's fingers found the soft black velvet collar of Dr. Wenning's winter coat in her arms.

Wings? she thought.

Dr. Wenning rubbed her hands together, cracked her knuckles, a sound that made Ruth cringe. Dr. Wenning usually did that when she was angry.

He likes women fine, Dr. Wenning said. Just not certain women.

The nurse shrugged—bored rather than offended, Ruth thought—and raised the top sheet of paper on the chart. Bad lacerations, the nurse reported. From the bushes. They sewed up the worst spot, on his back. And he's probably going to lose the eye.

Which? Dr. Wenning stared down the hallway, her hands folded across her belly.

The nurse consulted the chart. The right one, she said.

Dr. Wenning's chin dropped slightly. She made a sound of disapproval. Too bad, she said. He has a severe astigmatism in the left. The right eye was perfect.

The conversation that followed—Dr. Wenning's questions, the nurse's answers—was mostly unintelligible to Ruth. She understood that they were talking about medications, dosages. She understood that Mr. Mitzotakis had been severely depressed.

The nurse snapped shut the chart.

He's pretty doped up, she said, but he won't stop talking. You want to knock him out altogether?

She cocked her head toward the curtain, behind which Mr. Mitzotakis lay.

Listen to him, she said. He's still at it.

There was a pen in the lapel pocket of Dr. Wenning's blazer. Ruth watched Dr. Wenning take the pen out of her lapel and slip it, where it could not be seen, into a lower coat pocket.

Please wait here, Ruth, Dr. Wenning said. You brought the oranges?

Ruth handed her the bag. Dr. Wenning gave Ruth her crutches.

From where she stood outside the curtain, Ruth could hear the sound of Mr. Mitzotakis moaning and, between the moans, a kind of hectic chanting. Ruth looked away quickly when Dr. Wenning parted the curtain. She did not want to see Mr. Mitzotakis. Once or twice when she had been working at Dr. Wenning's office on a Saturday, he had come in for an appointment. A stout, middle-aged man, he was swarthy, with unattractively pockmarked skin. But he was also intelligent-looking, proud; his chest had seemed to Ruth somehow oddly inflated. He wore thick glasses, and his hair was slick and wavy—dyed, Ruth had guessed. He had bowed to her in an old-fashioned way.

Ruth heard the sound of chair legs scraping the floor.

Petros, she heard Dr. Wenning say. Petros, can you look at me?

There was a silence. Then Dr. Wenning said, You are in a bad way here, my friend.

Ruth stood still outside the curtain.

Mr. Mitzotakis began to whisper, a sound somehow more terrible than the frantic chanting that had preceded it. He had been praying, Ruth understood then, in Greek. Doctors and nurses passed Ruth in the hall, but they made no sign that they noticed her standing there, wide-eyed, holding the coats. Curtains were swept aside and then whisked closed. Orderlies pushed rattling metal carts loaded with bottles and jars and boxes down the tumultuous corridor, the floor shining as if sluiced with water. The double doors at the end of the long hallway swung open, and she turned toward them, toward the rush of cold air. Outside was the December night, the red light of an ambulance parked at the curb, headlights illuminating a filthy gray snowbank, the smell of exhaust.

She did not want to be there, in that hospital, with Mr. Mitzotakis.

She thought she understood why a man would jump off his garage roof, wearing a pair of wings. She did not want to understand it, but she did.

She wanted to call Peter, but it was the middle of the night.

Overhead, the lights in the hallway seemed to flare and then dim. She looked around for a chair. She needed to put her head between her knees or she would pass out, she thought.

From somewhere she smelled cigarette smoke. She turned, her eye drawn against her will to the gap in the curtains.

Dr. Wenning was lighting a cigarette. Ruth had never before seen her smoke. Dr. Wenning exhaled a cloud, and then she passed the cigarette to Mr. Mitzotakis, leaning over the bed to hold it to his lips.

Now we will both be in trouble here, Dr. Wenning said. Don't forget I did this for you, Petros.

Mr. Mitzotakis was wrapped in gauze like a mummy, both legs suspended in plaster casts. His face was the color of sand, his thick hair disarranged. He moved his head from side to side, stopping only to drag on the cigarette Dr. Wenning held for him. One side of his face was badly mangled.

Then he groped in the air with his unbandaged hand. Ruth saw Dr. Wenning reach out and catch it.

She held it between her own.

So, they did not work, your marvelous wings, Dr. Wenning said, her tone quiet. She was looking not at Mr. Mitzotakis's face but down at the bedclothes, her head bowed. Still, it is a beautiful and sad story, she said, the story of the daring and loving and clever Daedalus. Nothing wrong with Daedalus, Petros.

Mr. Mitzotakis turned his face aside. Ruth saw his chest heave with suppressed emotion.

Well, we had agreed already that the wings would not work, Dr. Wenning went on, as if she had not noticed that he was crying. Of course they would not. Remember that, Petros. This is not the issue. It is not that the wings do not work, that you are a man, and a man cannot *fly*. But you thought perhaps you could die this way, and now not only are you *not* dead, but you are very, very badly injured. That must feel . . . I am trying to imagine it, she said.

Mr. Mitzotakis turned his face to her. The eye that was not swollen shut was at half-mast, like a drunk's.

Ruth felt her legs tremble.

Dr. Wenning brought her lips down to his hand, kissed his knuckles.

You are one of the most brilliant men I know, Petros, she said. I would like to see these wings of yours sometime. They are wonderful, I am sure. You didn't ruin them, I hope, subjecting them to such an endeavor?

Then she sat up. I have brought you something, she said. Along with these evil smokes. She dropped the cigarette into a cup of water by the bedside.

My god, they must be busy tonight, she said. No one has come in here to shout at us.

She reached down to the bag at her feet and withdrew one of the oranges. She began to peel it, leaning on the bed with her elbows, like a girl resting on a windowsill. The scent was bright and clean; an orchard entered the little enclosure behind the curtain. Ruth could not take her eyes from the gap.

Dr. Wenning offered a section to Mr. Mitzotakis; he opened his mouth.

He swallowed, said something in a low tone. Dr. Wenning continued to peel the orange. He said something else. Dr. Wenning nodded. She brushed the peel into a little pile on the bedclothes, fed him another section, then another. She peeled a second orange.

More words passed between them, but Ruth could not hear them all clearly. Finally she looked away.

She felt very, very tired.

. . .

So many years later, as she and Peter patiently did his stroke recovery exercises together—blowing dish soap bubbles from a child's bubble wand to strengthen the muscles in his face, walking slowly up and down and up and down the stairs, riding the stationary bicycles side by side at the local YMCA— Ruth thought often of this night with Dr. Wenning and Mr. Mitzotakis.

She remembered the scent of the cigarette smoke, the feel of the thin predawn air, the light snow flying past horizontally when the doors at the end of the hallway had opened to the cold darkness outside. She remembered the sound of Dr. Wenning's voice, how she had sat so calmly with the fact of Mr. Mitzotakis's wish to die.

She remembered the oranges, their color and scent.

In the car on the way back to Dr. Wenning's house later that night, Ruth had said, He's a plumber, Mr. Mitzotakis?

A plumber . . . and a sculptor, Dr. Wenning had answered. I think it is useful to him as an artist, knowing how to build things with pipe.

She had looked up through the windshield, squinting at the falling snow.

Ruth had thought about the story of Daedalus and Icarus, the son who had flown too near the sun.

He has a son? Ruth said.

Dr. Wenning agreed. *Had* a son, she said.

The son . . . died, Ruth said.

Dr. Wenning nodded again. That is correct, she said. Killed himself. Petros's wife left him afterward. This is not uncommon. It takes great strength to keep a marriage together after something like that.

Ruth was quiet. She tried to concentrate on driving. She could feel the snow beneath their tires, the inches of it packed below, the ice beneath that. A car passed them, its snow chains dragging and clanking.

Petros is a dramatic person, Dr. Wenning said. Those wings . . . who could understand that? But the man's sadness? That is very real.

Ruth realized that her chest hurt, as if she were the one who had fallen through the snowy air to the frozen ground below.

Then she remembered something.

Why did you move your pen? she said. You moved your pen, to your other pocket.

Dr. Wenning looked at her sharply. Then she smiled.

Ha, she said.

She reached over and cuffed Ruth lightly on the shoulder. You have such the sharp eyes, Ruth, she said, pleased. Truly? I did not think about it, really. I just wanted to go in there . . . as his friend. No business. I already give him drugs. I wanted to bring only the oranges. And the cigarettes. I knew he would want a cigarette. A man who tries to kill himself and fails should have a smoke, if he wants one.

Later, after Ruth and Peter had moved to Derry, on one of her trips back to New Haven, Ruth had asked Dr. Wenning again about Mr. Mitzotakis.

Ah, the wings, Dr. Wenning said. Yes, I saw them once. Enormous things, black like a bat's wings. Terrifying, hideous, even, but quite beautiful in their way. They were in a museum, in an exhibition. Didn't I tell you?

She'd shaken her head. A passionate man, Petros, she said. He was quite attached to those things.

No pun intended, she said. Of course.

Then, one Christmas, Dr. Wenning sent Ruth Mr. Mitzotakis's obituary notice from the newspaper.

Dr. Wenning had underlined the words *died peacefully in his sleep.*

Ruth had recognized the triumph there. Mr. Mitzotakis had survived.

Ruth liked tidying up the A-frame. She bought a Swiffer—what a marvelous gadget that was—and enjoyed pushing it around the smooth floors, dust collecting neatly on the little cloths. The house was so small it took hardly any time at all to make it spick-and-span, and Ruth felt pleasure—though she recognized it as shallow—at owning material things for the first time in her life: Table. Bureau. Bed. She bought colorful throw pillows for the sofa, enjoyed arranging them this way or that.

They had two plastic Adirondack chairs, side by side, on the deck.

They went grocery shopping together, Peter holding on to the cart. They went to the movies and out for supper. Peter continued to cultivate his old sources for the school, families who dedicated their contributions specifically for scholarships. Charlie Finney called often to speak with Peter, asking for advice, and one day Ruth was surprised to hear Kitty's voice on the telephone.

She called under what Ruth understood finally was a pretense—some silly question about the house. What she really wanted, Ruth realized, was just to talk, to ask about various personalities at the school, about how to deal with the prickly secretary in the admissions office, about what should be done to recognize the years of service of a fellow retiring from the grounds crew, about whether Ruth thought a book club for parents would be a good idea. After that first conversation, Kitty called Ruth nearly as often as Charlie called Peter, and Ruth found herself reporting news of the Finney children to Peter over dinner at night—one of the boys had trouble with his hearing and was being tested—or a bit of gossip Kitty had passed on, or some detail about Kitty's experience with a trustee or a teacher.

Do you know that her favorite book is *Middlemarch*? Ruth told Peter. Just like me. And that she plays the piano?

I wish you were here, Ruth, Kitty said one day. It would be so nice to have your company.

Tears came into Ruth's eyes.

I'll come and visit, Ruth said, when Peter is better.

Ruth had learned a great deal from Dr. Wenning, she thought, folding the laundry on the table, glancing up from time to time to watch Peter, sitting on the deck in the sun, reading. Pain and beauty were so often tangled up together. Joy and sorrow came and went from a life, the balance sometimes shifting one way, sometimes the other, like a car sliding on an icy road. The trick was just to hold on somehow through the difficult stretches.

Haven't you found, Ruth, Dr. Wenning had said once, that sometimes in our lives we are lost in the hinterland, neither here nor there?

Ruth and Dr. Wenning had been sitting at the time in a concert hall at Yale, waiting for the performance to begin. The musicians in the orchestra had been tuning their instruments.

Sometimes we are lost in the wilderness, Dr. Wenning went on. We are far away from the shoreline, the cheerful port where the ships go and come, but also from the busy city, with its lights—Dr. Wenning had waved at the brilliantly lit room around them—and its apples for sale on the sidewalk, and the sound of typewriters going everywhere—clackety, clackety, clackety—everybody talking away.

Ruth had turned in her seat to look at Dr. Wenning. Such a long speech was unusual for her.

The hinterland . . . it is like a desert, Ruth, Dr. Wenning had continued, gazing up at the concert hall's elaborate ceiling, its gilt cornices, its painted stars.

Or sometimes the hinterland is a forest, Dr. Wenning had said, the trees so close together that we cannot see a path between them, only darkness or emptiness everywhere we look. We do not know which way to turn. It is not a place for citizenship, the hinterland. It is no kind of place, and so our instinct is to keep going, keep on walking. Eventually, though, so long, as you do not give up, you find your way *out* of the hinterland. That is the nature of it. It is only a middle ground, a location that separates one place from another.

Someone had touched Ruth on the shoulder, indicating the

seats just beyond them. Ruth had moved her legs out of the way, hoisted Dr. Wenning's big handbag onto her own lap.

Ah, I go on and on, Dr. Wenning had said, when the stranger had passed.

You know me, she had said. How I love a metaphor. I should have been a poet.

But still—she began again as if Ruth had been about to interrupt her—for these voyages, Ruth, she said, these passages through the hinterland, what we need is a companion, a friend at our side.

She had leaned over and patted Ruth's hand.

All right, my dear, she'd said. Now the music begins.

After Dr. Wenning passed away, it was difficult for Ruth to make herself believe that her friend, as Peter suggested, was somehow near her. But sometimes she could manage it: first the curtain in the hospital drawn across the room where Mr. Mitzotakis lay, then the cigarette smoke, then the bright color of the oranges, their scent so sweet and strong, and then the sound of big wingbeats, the feel of air moving against her cheek.

6

A year after Peter's stroke, his speech nearly fully restored—only the right side of his face drooped a bit, his right leg still a little slow and clumsy—they drove to a nearby inn to celebrate his recovery. Peter sat in the passenger seat beside her, dozing.

Getting out of the car at the inn, he gave her his hand so she could help him and smiled his lopsided smile at her.

The inn was just as she had imagined it would be, very pretty, with a wine list and a good menu, nice little shampoos and so on in the bathroom. She unscrewed the caps and sniffed the contents, pleased.

The next afternoon, they borrowed one of the canoes, took it out onto the lake. It was fall, the shoreline reflected in a brilliant rim on the surface of the water. They paddled for an hour or so, not speaking much. When they arrived back at the inn's boathouse to return the canoe, another couple, much younger, was also returning their boat. The woman was attractive, tiny and lovely and neat in the way that Ruth, invariably the tallest woman in the room, her big breasts pulling her shoulders forward, had always envied.

She'd always wanted to be a tiny, skinny blonde.

This woman now was exactly that: blond, her hair expertly colored and cut. She wore a pair of tight black shorts, like the sort bicyclists wear.

When they pulled up to the dock, Peter insisted on climbing out first—ever the gentleman—to steady the canoe for Ruth.

Heart of a lion, Peter, Ruth said to him sometimes, fondly.

Ruth noticed the attractive young woman glance at Peter, the still handsome, rough lines of his face, the silver hair falling boyishly over his forehead.

Peter held out his hand. He was sweating, and there were rings of wet on his gray T-shirt under his arms. His fingers closed around her hand, and she gripped back, holding on. For a minute the canoe wobbled underneath her, and she thought she might fall. She was too heavy these days. It was all that sitting around with Peter, she thought, playing cards with him to help him recover his dexterity. She couldn't play cards without wanting to eat some nuts.

Oh, I'm so *fat*, she had complained the night before, toweling off after a hot bath, glancing at—and then averting her gaze from—her image in the mirror.

Peter had been slowly knotting his tie, frowning and lifting his chin in that way he had.

You're beautiful, he said.

He had never been unfaithful to her, she thought. There had been that painful period long ago, when they were very young, long before they were married, when they hadn't seen each other for a while. She imagined that maybe he had slept with someone else then, maybe even a couple of some-ones, though they hadn't ever discussed it. There might even have been prostitutes, for all she knew. Young men used to do that. It had been more acceptable back then in a way, certain kinds of prostitutes like good-natured old friends or teachers, casual and a little carnal, teaching young men how to relax.

Now, on the dock, Peter pulled, surprisingly strong, and she stood up, the canoe bobbing dangerously beneath her. A moment later she was safe on the dock.

Oopsie daisy! Peter said.

What a funny, old-fashioned expression, she thought. It made the tears come into her eyes.

That was a nice day, she said, as they walked up the leafy path to the inn, the late-afternoon sunlight falling down through the trees.

Yes, it was, he agreed.

She took his arm.

They made love before dinner, that business not so easy as it once was, it was true, but then you didn't really mind so much about that anymore, either. You did the best you could. Yet the old longing was still there between them. When Peter pulled her against him, her back to his belly, when he kissed her neck, ran his hand down her side, following the dip of her waist and the rise of her hip, she still felt that old heat.

At dinner, they shared a nice bottle of wine in the inn's pleasant dining room, curtains drawn against the dark window glass. She ordered fish, as usual, and Peter ordered a steak, and then he fell asleep in bed before the nightly news had finished on the television: the deadly account of casualties from the war in the Middle East; footage of endangered harp seals in the Canadian Gulf of St. Lawrence; the revelation of comical indiscretions on the part of a politician in Washington, his name—unbelievably—Weiner.

Oh, for god's sake, Ruth said, holding the television remote, speaking out loud to no one in the pretty bedroom at the inn, for Peter was snoring beside her.

Oh, their heartbreaking faces, those seals. Their gray whiskers.

The dog's gray muzzle, she remembered. The man's face.

The faces of the many boys from Derry, the beautiful and the not beautiful, the lucky and the unlucky.

Sometimes, when she was alone, she actually spoke aloud to Dr. Wenning. Are you there? she asked the empty air.

For a while that night, Ruth lay awake beside Peter in the dark, looking out the unfamiliar open window into the night sky blazing with stars. There seemed to be more stars than usual here, a conference of them, all gathered together.

She put her hand on Peter's back, spread her fingers against his warm skin and rested it there until she felt his pulse against her palm.

You never knew how much happiness—or how much unhappiness—would be delivered to you in a lifetime, no matter whether you deserved it or not. So there was really nothing to be done, as Dr. Wenning had said, but get on the bus.

Get on the bus, Ruth, she said. Make love, not war. Give strangers a piece of your heart. Sing "Kumbayah."

Ruth had rolled her eyes.

But Dr. Wenning had loved that song. A woman who had lost everyone in her family to the Nazis had loved "Kumbayah."

Do you know what it means, Ruth, that word? Dr. Wenning had asked. It means Come by here.

I would like to say that to God sometimes, Dr. Wenning said. Hey, God. Come by here, please. I need your attention for just a minute.

Ruth stroked Peter's back lightly, softly, with her fingertips. He had the softest skin, Peter, like a baby's. Even his feet, so big and white, were soft.

He made a little noise, a little snore like a hiccup in the quiet of the room, and then all was silent again.

She thought of the stars and the lake and the forest around them, the gentle, brilliant darkness. Surely goodness and mercy, Ruth thought.

Surely goodness and mercy shall follow me.

A few days after Peter's stroke, Ruth's car had been recovered near an entrance to the Appalachian Trail in northern Maine. Someone—the man, presumably—had left a little bier of stones at the signpost, the dog's dead body, legs tucked in neatly, nose curled to tail, beneath the heap.

Of the man himself, there was no trace. He had disappeared into the forest, back to whatever awful dark place he had come from, she assumed.

She started awake occasionally in the middle of the night, the terrible stuffed animal through whom the man had spoken snarling at her. But mostly what she felt about the whole incident was sadness, not fear. Not anymore.

Charlie Finney had driven her home from the hospital that night, after she'd seen Peter and had spoken with the doctors. Peter had been able to smile crookedly at her, to lift his hand and let her hold it. She had gripped his hand hard—probably hard enough to hurt him—and kissed his knuckles, weeping.

He wasn't entirely out of the woods, the doctors had said that night, but they were pretty confident he'd be all right. He'd been lucky.

At the house, Charlie had gotten out to open the car door for her, and she had given him her hand, let him help her. It had stopped raining by then. The storm had blown through, leaving branches littered across the lawn, another shutter down, crashed into the bushes beneath the kitchen window. But there was no worse damage, as far as she could see.

Will you be all right, Ruth? Charlie had asked, and she had kissed his cheek, patted his shoulder.

Go on home, Charlie, she said. Thank you for your help. It's been an awfully long day.

She had turned toward the house. Somehow, the front door had been left open—or perhaps the wind had blown it open— and inside the house was lit up, lights on in the front hall and the living room and in the kitchen, just as if the party were still going on, the drink glasses glinting on the tray, the dishes of nuts, the triumphant heads of the lilies in their vase on the hall table, the speckled brown Comice pears in the blue bowl . . . pears she had arranged earlier that very morning. It seemed a lifetime ago.

She walked toward the bright light, waving over her shoulder at Charlie, knowing it would all be just as she had left it, the impression of her head on the pillow and Peter somewhere nearby, still in the world.

PART II

The First Day

Ruth was twelve years old when she and her father arrived in Wells, Massachusetts, just before dawn on the morning of July 4, 1945. In her memory, they had never lived anywhere for longer than a few months. She did not know how often they had moved in the time before she could remember, through how many streets, in how many cities—over how many fields or across what bodies of water—her infant self might have been carried, wide-eyed and seeing but without knowledge or consequence.

She had been born in Detroit, her father said.

After that?

He shuffled a deck of cards, dealt them each a hand. It would be impossible, he said, for him to recall exactly the sequence of their moves.

Ruth understood that her father had been spared military service during the war because he was her only parent. He was an auctioneer, running farm and home and business sales for people in straitened circumstances, families that had lost their men overseas or whose fathers and husbands had returned too shattered to work. Auctions, Ruth had learned, often followed in the wake of defeat or death. Standing with her father at fences inspecting pastures or barns, or walking with him through dusty, darkened stores or hushed houses, she heard the stories about foreclosure and ruin, the men found swaying from barn rafters. The years before and during the war had been a time of loss and a terrible privation, she understood. The stories behind an auction were rarely happy ones, and her father did not talk about them.

But you are *helping* people, Ruth said, wanting to understand his work in this light.

He hesitated. In a way, he said.

But sometimes, he said, people hated the man who sold everything they'd spent a lifetime working hard to acquire.

A town gets used up, was how he always put it. Time to move on.

Yet she knew that it was not *just* this that made her father come home one night in place after place and announce that they would leave that evening or the next one, that he had a new home for them, a better prospect. There was something wrong in her father's life, in their life together. She understood this, but being so close to it perhaps, she told Peter later, she had not been able to see it clearly. Its presence was felt but invisible, a disturbance in the air like a cloud of tiny insects, buzzing a warning.

There would be work in Massachusetts, her father said. The town of Wells was near both Boston and Providence, close to the sea and to farmland, to country and city, and he had sent away for a local newspaper from there in order to find a place for them to live, to make necessary arrangements. In the car on the long trip from Roanoke, Virginia, where they had been living, to Massachusetts, Ruth studied the map, holding a flashlight over it. Wells did not appear to her to be near anything except the Atlantic Ocean, on the map an expanse of pale blue emptiness.

They drove all night, but the sky was still dark when they pulled onto the street where the house her father had rented was located. He stopped the car under a tree, a deeper darkness, and took off his glasses. He made a sound of fatigue, leaned his head back against the headrest, and closed his eyes.

Are we going in? Ruth asked.

He did not open his eyes. We don't want to disturb people in the middle of the night, he said.

Ruth rolled down the car window. Her father had been smoking cigarettes and drinking coffee to keep awake, and the inside of the car smelled sour. She wanted to get out. She thought she could hear the ocean a few blocks away.

Go ahead, her father said, as if he could read her thoughts. But he didn't move, didn't rummage for a key in his pocket and hand it to her. The dark house with its aluminum awnings over the windows appeared forbidding, like a place where something bad might have happened. Ruth knew that her father understood she wouldn't go in without him. He slept, his bottom lip sucked in, as if he had no lower teeth.

It was rare for Ruth to see her father asleep. In whatever place they were living, if she woke at night and came out of her bedroom she would find him reading, or laying out games of Pyramid on the kitchen table, or she would smell cigarette smoke from the back steps or the porch or the fire escape, where he sat in the dark. Occasionally on weekend afternoons he would lie down on the bed to rest, an arm over his eyes, his feet—still in his shoes—held off the edge of the bed so as not to soil the bedspread. He never put on pajamas at night, as she imagined other fathers did.

She did not have much experience with other families, but she knew that her family—such as it was; it was only ever her and her father—was not like other families.

There was a sudden movement in the side yard of the house in front of which her father had parked the car. Startled, she turned quickly to look, but it was only bedsheets on a clothesline, she saw, the wind inflating their ghostly expanse in the darkness. For a moment, through the open window of the car, the sound of the ocean reached her distinctly, the scent of it present on the breeze.

Nothing moved on the front lawns of the houses. Here and there the yellow eye of a porch light illuminated a circle of colorless grass, the black shape of a shrub, a silver milk box on a stoop. In the tunnel of trees along the street, she watched the leaves shifting overhead, listened to the quiet rustling of their movement. She had been staring all night at the dark road, a procession of taillights and headlights, but somehow now she could not close her eyes. From time to time she heard the distant, rhythmic crash of the surf, waves breaking along an invisible shoreline somewhere nearby.

She gazed at the white line down the macadam. Then she

saw something—a flickering shape—in the dim light at the end
of the street. She sat up straight.

A moment later, the image became clear: it was a boy on
a bicycle, sitting upright and steering with his knees, coming
toward them. He rode like a circus acrobat, no hands on the
silver handlebars, his bicycle weaving down the center of the
street. As he approached, she saw him tossing rolled newspapers onto the front walkways and heard the thud as they landed
against the concrete or in the damp grass. High up within the
cool, bell-shaped darkness of the trees the streetlights shone in
hazy rings.

The idea of the ordinary, settled life of a boy who had a
paper route filled Ruth with longing. She would love to have a
paper route, she thought.

The boy neared their car, his knees pumping and his back
straight. It was still too dark to see his face clearly, but as he
passed under the streetlights she caught the shine of his hair,
the line of his shoulders, the gracefulness of his posture. He
looked to be about her age, she thought. He went past their
car in an instant, but Ruth heard the soft ticking sound of his
bicycle tires against the pitch of the blacktop. He was whistling. The sound seemed close to her ear, as intimate as breath
against her cheek.

She turned in the car in time to see the boy lean into the
curve and veer onto a dark side street. Then he was gone.

Ruth turned around again to face the empty street. She
knew that she and her father had come, as they had done so
many times before, to another place where they would not stay,

where whatever promises her father might make would not be kept. They would be strangers here, as they had been strangers everywhere.

At the far end of the street through the tunnel of trees, patches of watery radiance bloomed low in the sky along the horizon.

She could feel it before her, the repetition of what had come so many times before, the beginning of something inevitably interrupted, ended, when her father came home to say they would be leaving again.

The boy on the bicycle would go home after his papers were delivered, Ruth thought. She imagined him leaning his bicycle against the wall of a garage that smelled of engine oil and fertilizer. He would lift the empty sack from around his neck and swing it over his shoulder. Inside his house, his mother would be cooking breakfast for him, eggs and bacon, perhaps. She would smile when he came through the door. Ruth imagined a bird in a cage, singing. There would be the smell of coffee, and, on the windowsill, a plant in flower, the reflection of its blossom hovering against the dark pane.

Over the years to come Ruth thought often about the strangeness of this unceremonious moment in time when Peter crossed her path without seeing her in the dark car, this moment when they were so close and yet unknown to each other. In a few years, and then for so many years to follow, they would be entwined in the intimacy of marriage. But that morning the distance between them was oceanic. Their meeting—though perhaps it could not even be called a meeting—was utterly brief and accidental. Peter passed her on his bicycle close enough that she might have put out her hand and brushed his leg with her fingertips, but of course she did not.

How haphazard and arbitrary life was, she would think later. And yet didn't it seem, as well, that there was determination to it all, lines being drawn, vectors measured? Peter believed in God, trusting to purposefulness in their lives, in how things worked out. Ruth was less sure, especially about God. Yet how artfully the world was made, she thought, people moving innocently toward each other along invisible paths, surrounded—just like actors on a stage—by scrims of painted scenery, by special effects like snowfall and rain, the impression of dawn light shining through a window, the sound of thunder in the distance. She rode in an airplane only once in her adult life and could not stop looking out the window at the landscape below. The higher the airplane climbed, the less real the world below her seemed. When the world was so big, how could it be that her path, which had wound such a complicated and difficult route, had somehow intersected exactly with Peter's stationary place on the map?

On a January afternoon four years from the day of this first accidental meeting between them—this meeting that was not, actually, a meeting—the Atlantic Ocean was full of white-caps from a winter storm, and Ruth and Peter walked along the beach following the shoreline. They wore heavy coats, wool hats pulled down over their ears. Ruth's hands in her mittens were buried under her armpits. As they walked, Peter explained about the storm moving toward them. It was called an Atlantic clipper, he said. Ruth watched his hands as he tried to illustrate the giant movements of the air around them, the massive front that had formed east of the Canadian Rockies and was headed south down the New England coastline, gathering moisture as it came from warmer air streaming up from the Gulf of Mexico.

Sixteen years old, she and Peter had been walking the beach together for weeks by then, side by side but not touching. Occasionally they had stopped for Peter to heave things into the water—driftwood, shells, an old shoe discarded by the tide. Ruth had stood behind him, admiring him as he threw, the stance of his long legs, the muscles in his arms, his hair whipped by the wind.

Later, Ruth would think that it was the snow falling that day—on the sand and out across the ocean, too, a melding of sky and water—that hid them from the world and made their first kiss possible. In the cold, snow-filled afternoon, it became impossible to tell where the sky ended and the water began. When they stopped finally and turned to each other, Ruth saw snowflakes on Peter's eyelashes. On the sea behind him, the horizon had disappeared. Peter's lips against her cold cheek, her mouth, her neck, were warm. When he took off his gloves to hold her face in his bare hands, she felt the heat of his palms.

On that first early morning, however, as Peter pedaled his bicycle down the street away from her, Ruth knew nothing of what was to come, of course, nothing of the strange way in which she and Peter would finally meet, nor the way in which they would find and lose and then find each other again.

The boy who was Peter simply vanished on his bicycle into

the pre-dawn darkness, and finally Ruth fell asleep, slumped against the armrest in her father's car parked under the trees.

When the sun rose, she woke, blinking. Her father stirred beside her, the sunlight slanting in through the leaves of the trees reaching his face. He groaned, an arm across his eyes. Then he glanced across the seat at Ruth.

All right, he said. He sat up and put on his glasses. Let's get inside.

In daylight the house was revealed to be an undistinguished stucco bungalow with weeds in the flower beds on either side of a short front walk. A lilac bush with dusty leaves leaned over the sidewalk. Ruth stopped to read one of the paper flyers tacked to the trunks of the trees along the street: a fireworks display would be held that evening on the beach. She had forgotten that it was the Fourth of July. Tonight's celebration, she thought, with Germany's recent surrender, would be enormous.

She followed her father up the front path under the branches of an overgrown viburnum that buzzed dangerously when she brushed against it with her suitcase. She hurried along; there must be a bees' nest somewhere nearby.

A key had been mailed to her father, and the house had been rented to them furnished, as was always the case, wherever they lived. Standing in the front hallway, Ruth recognized its nature. Like other places in which they'd lived, this was the house of an old person who had died recently, she thought. That person's children, usually grown daughters who Ruth knew from experience would appear instinctively to disapprove of Ruth and her father, had come through the house and taken away everything of value or sentiment, leaving behind faded slipcovers and stained mattresses, drapes with transparent patches like decaying leaves, dented pots and pans, and a smell of mustiness and closed rooms.

How did her father choose such places? She had no idea. A wall in the living room bore the ghostly rectangular imprint of a picture or a mirror, something that had been lifted free and borne away. Had it been a sailing ship? A landscape of ruins, Carthage or Athens? A photograph of solemn-faced people in dark coats standing before the plate-glass window of a shop or under a weeping willow? She felt she knew the tastes of the house's former occupants, could construct an imagined life for them from the sad details of what they had left behind. She had seen so many other houses like this one.

In a dresser drawer in the room she chose as her bedroom, a dormered alcove whose peeling, garlanded wallpaper was stained brown in the corners, Ruth found a key with an elaborate head like a ram's horns. She put the key in the pocket of her skirt. She struggled to raise the sash and open the window. It would be better if she could smell the ocean, she thought, but she could not make the sash come free.

Over the next few hours, Ruth put away their clothes and made up beds for her and her father. He unpacked their boxes of dishes, washing and drying them all again. He was fastidious about the plates from which he ate, the cups from which he drank. In restaurants he always wiped the rims of glasses with his handkerchief.

Finally, near noon, they left the house to find food, walking toward town on the sidewalk in the shade under the trees. Ruth looked at the houses as they passed. In one, a woman sat before a set of opened French doors at a piano covered with a fringed shawl, leaning forward and making notations with a pencil on sheets of music propped before her. Ruth felt the familiar envy always inspired in her by porch swings and pretty curtains, the sound of a dog barking, a sprinkler spinning a glistening dome over a lawn.

At the first street corner, someone had abandoned a bicycle, and it lay fallen over on the grass. Ruth remembered the newspaper boy from earlier that morning, the happy boy, as she thought of him.

Though it was the Fourth of July holiday, stores on the main street were open. Tables set up on the sidewalk were stacked with goods, shoes in boxes and women's hats, tools and cartons of nails and roof shingles, boxes of canning jars and big pots her father told her were for cooking lobsters, everything on a special sale. One table in the shade of a tree held cages with brightly colored parakeets in them, hopping from perch to perch. Ruth glanced at her father; he had always said no to a dog or a cat, but maybe he would let her have a bird.

He shook his head. Cruel, he said, to keep a bird in a cage.

They went into a place with a lunch counter. The sounds of conversation and clinking dishes, the smell of hamburgers frying, raised Ruth's spirits. She was glad to be around people. She liked this place, she thought, this small town with the sound and smell of the ocean nearby and the air of celebration in the street. She and her father ordered milk shakes and grilled cheese sandwiches. A boy working the soda fountain, his white hat perched like a paper boat on a heap of bristly red curls, his cheeks blazing with red splotches, spooned maraschino cherries into a dish. When her father wasn't looking, the boy quickly pushed it along the counter toward Ruth. He caught her eye and smiled; she smiled back, embarrassed.

The sun was high overhead when they finished eating, the sky a steady blue. Outside on the sidewalk, Ruth felt the pleasant pressure of heat on her head and her bare arms. She and her father walked down the street toward the water, its sparkling line visible beyond the roofs of the buildings. At the bottom of the avenue across a parking lot, a stretch of dunes rose up, thick with prickly beach roses and run through with narrow paths.

Ruth and her father climbed the sand in their slippery shoes. When they crested the dunes, the water ahead of them was enormous and blinding, full of flickering silver. Ruth, who had seen the ocean once before, when she was much younger, was stunned by the size of it, its glare. She looked at the sailboats and the sunbathers, the tiny, dark heads of the swimmers, some women in flowered bathing caps. A heavy-bottomed ferry crossed slowly against the horizon.

After a minute, though, she became aware that people on the sand below had noticed them standing there in their street clothes, her father with his dark suit jacket folded over his arm.

Ruth understood that her father did not like his work. The way he spoke occasionally about the lives laid bare for his inspection and calculation revealed his distaste for the weary, mudspattered livestock and the sad troves of battered possessions, chipped drinking glasses and forks with bent tines, old chenille bedspreads and clumsily sewn quilts, heavy, ugly furniture so admired by its sentimental owners. He was careful in his own dress and habits, reserved and polite, gazing without expression at horses and bony cattle, looking dispassionately at furniture and weighing its value. But Ruth knew he did not like dirt, the insult of other people's smells or hair or skin. She noticed that his habit of waiting for others to speak made people voluble, a little uncertainty mixed in with their deference to him.

At his auctions, when he began to call for bids using that strange song-like chanting, running up and down the numbers in increments of five or ten, pointing to people in the crowd, it was as if someone else emerged from inside him, another person he could summon or stifle at will. People paid attention to this person, Ruth saw, as if their lives depended on him. It was as if he hypnotized them.

When she was young, her father had given her tongue twisters, difficult phrases he could recite without error.

Round the rough and rugged rock the ragged rascal ran.

Once a fellow met a fellow in a field of beans. Said a fellow to a fellow—if a fellow asks a fellow, can a fellow tell a fellow what a fellow means?

These phrases, so problematic, so thorny to repeat, so liable to lead her into foolishness, tripping over her own tongue, seemed later to her like riddles her father offered, enigmatic sayings that were as close as he could come to explaining himself to her.

The ragged rascal.

The meaningless fellow, standing in his field of beans.

. . .

Sometimes her father sat at the table in whatever place they lived, a cigarette held in his mouth, and drew pictures, elaborate floor plans, of houses he would build one day. He wanted a swimming pool and a tennis court. He wanted fireplaces in every bedroom, and window seats, and bathrooms with big bathtubs. He wanted dumbwaiters and butler's pantries with glass-fronted cupboards, a study with paneled walls, a porch with pillars and a portico under which they would park their car. He was going to be rich one day, he said. He was not meant to be a poor man.

He knew little symbols for things on his drawings, like how to depict the shapes of trees and to indicate which way a door would swing. Sometimes Ruth leaned on her elbows and watched him draw: he had a special mechanical pencil and a sheaf of graph paper.

Looking for the right place, Ruth, he said. Got to find the right place.

That evening as the sun began to set, after a supper of baked beans and hot dogs, purchased along with a few other supplies from the grocery, Ruth and her father followed people making their way up the paths in the dunes. Around them the grass lay flattened by the wind. Ruth could hear the ocean ahead of them as they climbed, louder now and sounding nearer than it had earlier in the day. The tide had come in, she saw, when they reached the top of the dunes, and the wind had picked up. Against the sunset, huge horizontal slabs of clouds like black railroad cars stood along the horizon.

Her father spread out his jacket on the sand for her. She was embarrassed that they had no blanket. They sat down among old people in folding aluminum chairs, families with babies and small children arrayed on quilts. She felt people glance at them from time to time, strangers. Ruth looked up and down the beach; would she recognize the boy on the bicycle if she saw him again?

Soon, though, it was too dark to make out anyone's face.

The rockets, set off from a position some distance down the shoreline, made a high whistling sound overhead, exploding in the night sky far out past the advancing white line of the breakers. Showers of sparks rained into the blackness of the sea.

The people all around them cheered and clapped, and Ruth clapped, too.

Her father bent his head and cupped his hands around a match, lit cigarette after cigarette.

At the close of the fireworks show, a band assembled on the dunes played "The Star-Spangled Banner," and everyone stood and sang, including Ruth and her father, the notes lost in the sound of the wind and the waves. Afterward they walked back through the warm streets in the crowd leaving the beach. Some of the men had dressed in uniform that night, to mark the occasion. Ruth did not know if her father was embarrassed not to have gone to war or was glad to have been spared. He carried his jacket now, hooked with one finger over his shoulder, and he did not look at the people around them, offering only an occasional nod in someone's direction.

Away from the commotion of the surf and the fireworks, the streets were quiet, the air in the tunnels of trees sweet-smelling and soft. The velvet lawns and shadowy porches contained a rapt silence. The procession under the streetlights thinned gradually, families turning off and climbing the steps to their own houses. Fathers laden with picnic baskets and blankets and mothers carrying sleeping babies in their arms called good night to their neighbors as they left the stream of people walking home under the stars.

At a cross street, Ruth's father hesitated.

Ruth glanced up at him.

His expression was alert, suspicious, as if in their absence that evening someone had deliberately sought to confuse them, rearranging street signs, moving trees and shrubs, cleverly altering the facades of buildings.

A car drove slowly past them. Then another.

Her father turned and looked back the way they had come. He ground out a cigarette under his shoe.

But it was all right, Ruth saw after a minute. They had only walked past it, she said, pointing. They had just gone too far.

Next door to their house, an elderly man with a deeply wrinkled face, wearing suspenders and a bow tie, and a younger woman Ruth assumed was the man's daughter—something alike in their faces—sat side by side on a porch swing in the shadows. Ruth saw their heads turn, watching as she and her father came back along the sidewalk and then came up the path.

Ruth's father unlocked the front door of their house and held it open for her.

Ruth lifted her hand in greeting to the people watching them from the porch. As she ducked under her father's arm, she saw him nod once in the neighbors' direction before coming in behind her and closing the door.

They would know by that nod, she thought, that he had seen them watching.

The next morning was Sunday. Ruth woke to the sound of a lawn mower in the backyard and, farther away, a descending sequence of church bells. She and her father did not attend church, but wherever they lived, he was scrupulous about keeping the grass mowed. If he brought a kitchen chair outside to sit and smoke a cigarette at night, he always took it back inside before going to bed, locking the door and then putting his shoulder to it for a minute as if to test it against intruders. Later she understood this behavior as part of her father's bizarre carefulness, the fearfulness of people who are themselves a danger to others.

The grass in the backyard of the house was full of clover. The day before, when they'd arrived, Ruth's father had unlocked the kitchen door and stepped onto the concrete patio, testing the stiff crank of the awning and unrolling a faded, striped canvas speckled with mold. He had stepped down into the overgrown grass and scuffed the shiny toe of his shoe through it. She had trailed behind him out to the garage, where he'd wrenched open the doors, allowing a parallelogram of light to fall into the darkness and revealing a lawn mower and a gas can, along with shovels and an axe and a coil of rope.

He'd hefted the gas can.

Enough here to get the job done, he'd said. There'll be ticks in that grass.

Ruth lay now in the unfamiliar bed, listening to the lawn mower drone. The neighborhood was otherwise quiet. She assumed that their neighbors were at church. This had been the case in the other towns where they'd lived.

The lawn mower's sound was solitary and conspicuous. Ruth wished her father had left the grass until later in the day. She hated Sunday mornings. They made her feel as if she and her father—overlooked, oblivious—were the last people on earth, everyone else gone away somewhere, called to important business, she and her father somehow miscreant, the eternal outsiders. She could even imagine that everyone else had died, leaving her and her father alone in the world. She could picture it, even though she didn't want to: grandfathers sagged against newel posts at the foot of staircases, children sprawled on their bellies across beds, mothers crumpled by kitchen tables, a brimming watering can fallen to the floor, water pooling across a carpet.

Ruth rolled over in bed and looked out the unfamiliar window of her new bedroom. The morning was overcast, the sky full of creased clouds. Finally, hungry and thirsty, she went downstairs to the kitchen. The walls were covered halfway up in pale green tiles, the grout between them grimy. Her father had made coffee in their percolator, one of the few possessions he carried from place to place. She stood in front of the stove in her bare feet, eating a piece of bread and butter and heating milk in a pan.

As she stood there, she heard the lawn mower in the backyard sputter in an escalating series of loud knocks and then cut off.

She waited in front of the stove, stirring. It took another minute for the milk in the pan to begin to foam.

Outside, the sound of the lawn mower did not begin again. Nor did her father come back inside.

When the milk was hot, she poured it into the cup and added coffee until it was the color she liked. Then, holding her coffee cup and her book—she was reading *Alice in Wonderland* again—she walked through the airless rooms and pushed open the door to the porch with her hip.

Thirty yards away at the far end of the long yard, her father crouched beside the mower, his back to her.

The day was warm, but he was dressed, as usual, in suit pants and a white dress shirt, the sleeves neatly rolled. He had done a third of the lawn, going back and forth between the house and the stucco garage. There were no flowers in the backyard, just a weedy rose of Sharon against the wall. The doors of the garage stood open, the red gas can on the gravel.

Ruth put down her cup, trying not to spill. Then she sat down on the concrete floor of the porch and extended her legs past the shade of the faded awning into the sunlight.

Her father closed the lid of the mower, stood up, and pulled the cord. The engine failed to catch.

On Ruth's legs, the sunlight felt hot. She watched her father take a handkerchief from his back pocket and wipe his face, looking away across the hedge into the neighbors' yard, the grass there crowded with weedy flower beds and a vegetable plot, a tilting arbor with a heavy grapevine dragging the scaffolding toward the earth. A cat appeared silently, bend-ing itself around the leg of a rusted metal chair beneath the arbor.

Ruth watched as her father turned back to the mower and looked down at it, his face expressionless. When he gave the cord a vicious yank, Ruth flinched.

He had told Ruth that her mother had left them when Ruth was a baby.

She had not been suited for married life, he said, or for the burdens of motherhood. He suggested that his relationship with Ruth's mother had been brief, that their marriage had been a mistake.

She didn't love us, Ruth had said, not looking at him.

No, he had agreed. I guess not.

In whatever town they had lived in over the years, he had hired someone—usually an old lady, a neighbor—to watch Ruth after school or on the weekend if he had to be away. He did not leave her alone. He did not neglect her. He had never struck her. She had never even heard him raise his voice. Yet Ruth knew that a deep trouble ran through her father. Other people, she knew, did not move every few months. Other people had friends and families. Other people had the evidence of their lives all around them: houses full of furniture, gardens whose produce filled their pantries and freezers. Even knowing someone who'd died and been buried in the local cemetery was a kind of belonging to a place.

Other people had mothers who had not abandoned them.

Ruth and her father had often packed up and moved in a day.

Her father had only one old acquaintance, a man called

Jake with dark circles under his eyes . . . like a cartoon character of an ex-con, Ruth told Peter later, trying to describe what her life had been like in those years.

Jake used to show up at intervals, she said. He'd walk up to the front door of whatever house they lived in with the air of a dog who has been abandoned by its owner but has stubbornly managed to find its way home again. He would stand there at the front door, moving his head around strangely as if his collar was too tight, grinning at them.

Ruth would remember about her father that at restaurants he had a fondness for heavy, rich dishes like beef stroganoff and shepherd's pie, though he was disconcertingly thin.

She remembered that he encouraged her to read. That he admired libraries.

He taught her to play backgammon and to use the doubling dice, and also to play poker and Russian Bank.

Yet she had known almost nothing of any significance about him. He had never spoken to her about his own childhood.

Nothing to tell, he'd said, when Ruth had asked.

Her memory of her father was full of holes and silences.

Full of nothingness, she told her friend Dr. Wenning, many years later.

Well, it was a *sickness* in him, Ruth, Dr. Wenning said to her. You understand, Ruth, that it was *his* sickness, not *yours*. He was a man in hiding from the whole world, not just from you. You did not know him—of course you did not—because he did not *want* you to know him.

Maybe he was protecting me in that way? Ruth asked.

If you like to think so. Dr. Wenning shrugged. Maybe.

. . .

Ruth had liked working for Dr. Wenning during the years Peter was in graduate school at Yale. She had typed up Dr. Wenning's notes, dusted the bookshelves, watered the plants on the windowsill. Sometimes Dr. Wenning didn't feel like working when Ruth arrived as usual on Saturday afternoon. Instead, she put on a record for them, Mozart or Bach or her beloved Schubert, and the two of them sat, just listening to the music. From Dr. Wenning, Ruth learned to close her eyes when she listened to music.

She also learned to make the strong black coffee Dr. Wenning liked, and how to brew for the right amount of time a pot of a smoky-flavored tea called Lapsang souchong. Sometimes, at the end of the afternoon, Dr. Wenning poured schnapps or sherry into the two tiny ruby red glasses on the papier-mâché tray. It took several months for Ruth to discover exactly how many people Dr. Wenning had lost in the camps during the war: her parents, two brothers, a sister, her three aunts and three uncles and seven cousins. Countless friends.

Prost, Dr. Wenning taught Ruth to say, raising her little ruby glass.

Your health.

Ruth looked up from *Alice* when she heard the lawn mower's engine finally catch again. She watched her father stuff the handkerchief back into his pocket and turn to pivot the mower toward the house. When he looked up and saw her, sitting on the porch, she lifted her hand.

He waved back, his black hair shining in the sun.

He came toward the house, pushing a neat path.

When he neared the porch, she lifted her feet out of the way and he passed by, his shoulders bowed, a cigarette in the corner of his mouth, one eye squinted against the smoke. Then he turned to go back in the direction of the garage. A fan of grass clippings filled the air, the clover in the grass smelling like honey.

Some of the cuttings settled in Ruth's lap.

Later she realized that the racket of the mower's engine had masked the sound of the black-and-white cars' arriving on the street in front of the house.

There were nine police cars, parked one behind the other, Ruth counted later, fixing irrationally on this detail when she was led out to the street. She imagined how they had glided silently to a stop in front of the house, the men inside them flowing out onto the grass, running toward the house in a crouch, guns drawn.

Her father would not have heard the cars, nor would he have seen the men arrive, some of them in shirtsleeves and fedoras, some in uniform, all of them armed.

Something alerted Ruth, however, as she bent over her book. Had there been a sound? Later, she could never remember. She looked up from under her eyelashes—she would not lift her chin; some instinct had told her to keep her head down—and she saw first the pairs of black shoes coming in through a break in the hedge. Then, as if an invisible finger had tilted her chin helplessly upward, she raised her eyes.

The policemen streamed silently onto the grass, all of them training their guns on her father.

All of them except one, who pointed his weapon at her, the hand holding the gun resting on his other wrist.

She dropped her book and put her hands up.

She put her hands up because that's what they did in the movies.

Her father had taken her to the movies from time to time. She liked Abbott and Costello.

Her father turned the lawn mower at the garage to begin the next stripe back toward the house. When he saw the policemen arranged in the backyard, guns pointed at him, he let go of the mower. It went on without him, mowing a crooked path, and Ruth saw him begin to run, heading for the hedge between the backyard and the alley. Was he intending to jump it? It was too high, she thought, beginning to get to her feet. He would never clear it.

Voices were raised. The gunshots were a sound like the air itself exploding in places.

The policeman pointing the gun at her came toward her at a run. He was shouting something, gesturing with the flat of his hand for her to get down.

She scraped her knee. Lying on her belly, she felt the warm, rough surface of the concrete against her cheek, a roaring sound in her ears like the waves in the ocean from the day before. She felt her heart banging against her ribs, against the concrete porch floor.

Somehow her coffee cup had been knocked over. She felt the damp against her face, smelled the milk and coffee.

The policeman knelt down beside her.

Look right here, Missy, he said. Look at me.

She lifted her gaze, looking up at his face as if there were nothing else in the world to look at, only turning her eyes away from him at the last second, following a volley of gunfire to see her father's body bounce forward as if he had been lifted on invisible wires and then shoved roughly between his shoulder blades. He threw his arms open.

A spray of blood preceded him into the heavy air of the July morning.

That afternoon in the police station, Ruth said again and again that she and her father had been in Wells for only one day. Months later, however, sitting with Dr. and Mrs. van Dusen in their living room, three FBI agents perched uncomfortably on the slipcovered sofa and easy chairs, she learned that searches of the house had been conducted that day anyway, floorboards pried away, a section of the concrete in the garage that appeared freshly spackled broken up with pickaxes.

These efforts had revealed nothing, she was told that day in the van Dusens' living room, not a single bill of the thousands, the tens of thousands her father had allegedly stolen over the years, arranging auctions for desperate farmers and small businessmen and then leaving town before any of the proceeds could be turned over to the anxious men and women trying to clear themselves of debt by divesting themselves of everything they owned.

Her father was alleged to be responsible for two deaths, the FBI agents said: In Ohio, one suspicious farmer had apparently gone to find the auctioneer at a warehouse office one evening and had been shot in the back. In upstate New York, a man who supplied trucks for the sale of clock factory equipment was found drowned in a pond, a wound the size of a hammerhead on his brow.

No bank accounts ever emerged.

It was possible, Ruth understood eventually, that her father had opened accounts and rented post office boxes in various places. It was possible that he had given false names and addresses for all of it. It was even possible that he'd hidden the money somewhere, buried it in a field under a tree he imagined he would one day find his way back to, like a dog recovering a bone. She thought about these things over the years, the possibility of the money sitting in a bank deposit somewhere until after years had gone by, when she assumed that the contents would simply be gathered up and stuffed into a sack and taken . . . where? There must be someone, she supposed, who looked at accounts that were inactive for suspiciously long periods of time. What happened to unclaimed money? Did the banks give it away to orphans or widows, to firemen's funds or to the government?

Sometimes she thought about the strange man Jake, about a little key or the code to a padlock concealed on his person somewhere. Maybe he was the keeper of the secret? Maybe he had taken the money?

But anyway, it wasn't the money that interested her, of course, she told Dr. Wenning.

It was not about the *money*, she said to Peter. It was about never knowing, never knowing *anything at all* about her father or why he had done what the police said he'd done. She assumed he *was* guilty, because the police had said so, but it was awful to contemplate.

She never forgot her father's tongue twisters.

Round the rough and rugged rock the ragged rascal ran.

Once a fellow met a fellow in a field of beans. Can a fellow tell a fellow what a fellow means?

Her father survived his injuries the day he was finally caught in the backyard, but after six months in prison, he hanged himself in his jail cell. Or someone else did it for him, Ruth and Peter—older, more experienced by then—speculated later.

Her father did not contact her directly after being taken away—perhaps he had not been either able or allowed to, she imagined later. At some point it occurred to her that perhaps he had not been her real father, after all, that maybe somehow he had been saddled with her, the baby of an unfortunate acquaintance. The mystery of this possibility—that a man who could steal from people, who could shoot someone in the back or bash in his head with a hammer, could also take in and raise a baby, could care for her—would remain with Ruth, haunting her.

He was not unkind to me, she told Peter.

I *think* he loved me, she told Dr. Wenning once.

No, no. I'm *sure* he did, she said.

But actually, she realized finally, she was never really certain about that, either.

The van Dusens' house was a small, pale gray Victorian. She realized later that it was in the same neighborhood as the rented house in which she and her father had spent their single night in Wells—in fact, they had walked past it on their way to the beach for the fireworks display—but she did not recognize the house when the police car pulled up to the curb at the close of that endless day when her father was captured.

That was the word the police used. *Captured.*

It was explained to her late in the day that a local doctor would take her in for the night. Wells was a small town, and there was nothing else to be done with her immediately. (Surely that had been an oversight, Ruth thought later; hadn't they known all about her?) Someone would come to get her in a day or so, she was told; a permanent place would be found for her. Meanwhile, the van Dusens would look after her.

When she was helped from the police car early that evening, Ruth felt hollowed out. She had thrown up repeatedly into a tiny corner porcelain sink in the ladies' bathroom at the police station.

Now the last light of the day fell in fronds over the grass, over the quiet face of the house, over its deep front porch furnished with brown wicker furniture. Shrubs covered in lacy white blossoms lined the walkway of the house. Green urns spilling yellow flowers flanked the steps to the porch. In a front window, a lamp with a round blue glass shade floated like a planet hovering in the dusk. Ruth had an impression of silence and calm.

I don't understand, she had said again and again at the police station.

That afternoon people had touched her shoulder and bent to offer her things, a glass of water, a handkerchief, once an open box of candy, dark chocolates nestled in frilled paper. She had recoiled as if being offered poison.

A policeman sitting across from her at the table had riffled the pages of a notebook. Other relatives? he said. Anyone else we ought to know about?

What? Ruth had said. It was almost as if she couldn't hear properly.

I think you might have made a mistake, she said once.

One of the policemen had rubbed his hand across his mouth in a distressed way. No, honey, he'd said. Afraid not. No mistake.

He'd asked again about the money, where it might be, what her father might have done with it.

She had looked back and forth among the three men in shirtsleeves who had crowded into the room. Two of them wore guns in holsters strapped over their shoulders.

I've never seen any money, she said.

One of them, leaning against the wall, arms folded, had shaken his head and looked away from her out the window.

Jesus Christ, he said. Jesus H. Christ.

Poor sucker kid.

The policeman holding her arm did not even have a chance to knock. The man who opened the door as they reached the porch was tall and slender, with a neat brown goatee and large, calm blue eyes. He was dressed in a white shirt, the material starched and ironed, and gray cuffed trousers. A crisp crease ran from his shoulder to his elbow, where the sleeves were rolled.

Behind him stretched a softly lit hallway with a shining floor. A blue and white bowl of flowers had been arranged on a table under a tall mirror. Directly ahead rose the stairs, covered in a cherry-colored carpet; a glass lamp with a dark shade illuminated a table on the landing above.

A woman came out of a lighted doorway adjoining the hall, wiping her hands on a dish towel. She was much shorter than her husband, her face round, her pale hair parted cleanly down the center and pulled back tightly in a bun. The skin around her eyes was pale, too, almost translucent. Around her nose and lips, little patches of redness flared, the suggestion of sensitivity. She wore a white blouse and an apron over a patterned skirt.

I'm Dr. van Dusen, the man said. How do you do, Ruth?

His voice was soft. He turned, put a hand on the woman's shoulder. This is my wife, he said. Mrs. van Dusen.

The policeman ruffled Ruth's hair roughly. Thanks, Doc, he said.

Ruth pulled away from his hand, the gesture too familiar.

You'll be all right now, little girl, the policeman said, clearly embarrassed. He shuffled awkwardly on the porch, took off his hat and tucked it under his arm.

We didn't know what else to do with her, he said over Ruth's head. Apparently it'll take someone a couple of days to get here.

It's all right, Dr. van Dusen said.

He opened the door wider. Come in, Ruth, he said. You must be very tired. Mrs. van Dusen will take you upstairs.

Ruth could not bring herself to look at either of them. She understood that the gulf between her and the rest of the world, a gulf she had already felt to be almost insurmountably wide, had now become vast beyond her imagining. She would just walk forward. In her mind there was a vague idea of escape, but not now. Not now, she thought, with so many people looking at her.

Mrs. van Dusen led Ruth up the stairs. At the landing she turned and preceded Ruth into a big bedroom with an expanse of pale green carpet. A large bed with a dark, heavily carved headboard stood against one wall.

Mrs. van Dusen turned down the coverlet away from the pillows on the bed, revealing their immaculate whiteness.

Then she seemed to be at a loss. Finally she indicated the bed, and Ruth understood that she was supposed to sit down. Was she to take off her clothes? Get under the sheets? She had no nightgown, she thought. How could she go to sleep without a nightgown?

Then the absurdity of this struck her—why was she worrying about a nightgown?—and she felt her legs tremble under her.

She sat down on the bed, the mattress billowing away softly beneath her. She had never been in a room so large or so clean. There were photographs in silver frames behind glass on a table topped with a woven cloth, yellow and scarlet threads in a geometric pattern. Roped and tasseled gold cords hung around heavy, dark blue curtains. Ruth stared at it all.

After a moment's hesitation, Mrs. van Dusen knelt beside the bed and began to unlace Ruth's shoes as if she were a child.

I'm sure you need to sleep now, Mrs. van Dusen said.

Ruth looked down at the top of Mrs. van Dusen's head, the part in her hair.

She did not want Mrs. van Dusen taking off her shoes, but she did not know how to stop her.

Mrs. van Dusen slipped Ruth's shoes off her feet. Then, after a moment of hesitation, she raised Ruth's legs to the coverlet.

Ruth lay down obediently.

Dr. van Dusen came into the room carrying a glass of water. He pulled up a small chair beside the bed. Mrs. van Dusen retreated to the doorway where she remained, a worried presence.

From his pocket Dr. van Dusen took a brown vial. He shook two small white pills into one hand and then passed Ruth the glass of water. He opened his palm to her.

She sat up and took the pills, swallowing them with the water, and then lay back down.

She did not know what the pills would do to her. Perhaps everyone intended to kill her, the daughter of a murderer.

She looked up at the ceiling, as white and smooth as Mrs. van Dusen's pale forehead.

How do you feel, Ruth? Dr. van Dusen said.

She did not know how to say: Is my father dead?

Where is my father? she said instead. She had not wanted to ask anyone in the police station that question.

Dr. van Dusen reached over to the bedside table, adjusted the angle of the lampshade to direct the light away from her face.

He was handsome, she thought, watching him. His hair was a thick, golden brown, combed back from a high forehead. The goatee gave him an air of distinction. He was a little different from other men she had known, she sensed. In a book, she realized, his expression would have been described as intelligent.

Do you want to use the bathroom? he asked. Are you cold?

She shook her head, but then she realized that her teeth were chattering.

Ruth lay rigidly on top of the bedspread; Dr. van Dusen reached down and pulled up a blanket folded at the end of the bed, tucking it in around her. He put a hand on her shoulder. His touch seemed to absorb the shaking and he left his palm there. The weight of it was comforting. She made an effort to quiet her body.

You'll feel better soon, he said. What you're feeling now? That's shock.

He looked at his watch and then at her face again. Your father, he said, has been taken to the hospital.

Mrs. van Dusen came back into the room and quietly pulled the curtains.

Sleep now, Dr. van Dusen said. It's all right, Ruth. You can close your eyes. It's safe just to go to sleep.

Ruth could not see them, standing in the hall outside the bedroom door, which had been left ajar, but she could hear their low voices.

She wanted to stay awake, to look again at the room around her. Against one wall was a gleaming dresser of dark wood. She assumed she was in a guest bedroom, but a man's empty white shirt and doctor's long white coat hung on a wooden hanger suspended from one brass handle. A dress-

ing table with an oval mirror stood between the two windows, the rainbow glint of faceted glass jars on its surface. A
small stool with a low upholstered back and a tufted red seat
was drawn up before the dressing table. Two long fissures of
summer-evening light glowed between the long dark curtains.
In the corner of the room was a chaise longue covered in a
printed fabric, a round table beside it stacked with books. She
couldn't quite make out the design of the fabric. She struggled
to prop herself up on one elbow; it felt important to see clearly
where she was. There were little boats with black masts scattered across the fabric. Or were they Chinamen with pointed
hats?

The room seemed as calm and otherworldly as a distant
universe. The weight of her head suddenly felt insupportable,
and she allowed herself to fall back to the pillow. She felt tears
on her face, but before she could wipe them away, she was
asleep.

When she woke later she did not know where she was, nor for
one paralyzing moment, *who* she was. The events of the day—
something terrible was there, behind her thoughts—swarmed
and bulged at the edge of her consciousness, a menace.

Around her, the house—the van Dusens' house, she remembered now—was completely quiet. Night had fallen.

Then everything came back to her. Where was the hospital
where her father had been taken? Should she go find him? But
she did not want to find him. It must be true, everything they
had said about him.

She sat up quickly and put her feet on the floor. Her head seemed to soar away and bump the ceiling and then return to her shoulders. She waited, her heart racing. When her vision steadied, she stood up and walked across the carpet toward the door. Where were her shoes? Someone had taken away her shoes, but she could not stop to look for them. It was necessary that she leave as quickly as possible.

The room tilted, and she staggered. She put out her hand, bruising her knuckles against the dresser.

The bedroom door was ajar. In the upstairs hall, the shaded lamp on the little table was turned on, casting a soft pool of light on the polished wood. Three other doors leading to the landing were closed. A window in the hall overlooked the street, and she could tell from the light outside that it was near dawn. Somehow she had slept all night.

The staircase was ahead, a gleaming banister descending precipitously into the darkness.

Down she went, but her head felt disconnected from her feet. The sensation was like walking down a waterfall.

She paused at the foot of the staircase in the front hall. The front door was ahead, two long panels of glass etched with garlands on either side. When she passed before the long mirror her reflection startled her, and she nearly cried out.

Where would she go? Where in the world could she go now? But she must, she must.

She opened the front door.

A boy—the boy from the day before—was sitting on the lowest step of the porch. Bundled stacks of flat newspapers lay on the pavement in front of him, a pile of rolled papers on the steps beside him.

She could not believe it was the same boy.

A bicycle lay across the front walkway, one wheel canted skyward. The boy's hair, mussed from sleep, stood up in a cowlick in the back. When she'd seen him on the street on his bicycle, she'd thought his hair was the color of haystacks. Now, under the porch light, she thought of gold.

He turned around, startled, at the sound of the door opening. She looked at him sitting on the porch steps, and then she looked past him to the dark street, a streetlight burning in what seemed to be the center of every tree's leafy crown. She had to leave, she thought. There was no choice.

She saw the boy stand up as she took a step onto the porch.

The next instant, it was as if she had dropped into deep black water. She felt herself pitching forward into nothingness.

Every time she awoke over the next hours or days, the light in the bedroom was different. She lost track of time. Whatever was in the pills Dr. van Dusen gave her made her able to do nothing but sleep. She woke only to creep to the adjoining bathroom and then back to bed. Sometimes when she woke, Dr. van Dusen was sitting on a chair beside the bed, glasses on his nose, reading a book held on his lap.

Once when she woke—she could tell by the light outside the window that it must be early evening—Dr. van Dusen was seated beside the bed, and Mrs. van Dusen was entering the room carrying a tray.

He smiled up at her as she handed him the tray.

I thought she might like chicken, Mrs. van Dusen said quietly, and then left the room.

Ruth struggled to sit up. Dr. van Dusen stood and set the tray on her knees.

On a plate was a scalloped dish of creamed chicken in a pie crust, a spoonful of bright green peas.

Head lolling—it was a struggle to keep her eyes open—she took one bite, and then another. She put down her fork. The food had no taste or smell at all.

Dr. van Dusen glanced up from whatever he was reading.

It's the medicine, he said. Sometimes that happens. The taste of things will come back. It will do you good to eat, if you can.

Ruth ate obediently—fork to mouth, fork to mouth. Flares of panic kept igniting in her belly, and she was afraid she might vomit, but she got to the end of it.

He lifted away the tray when she set down her fork.

A moment later she slipped back again into the flat and dreamless and colorless sleep that felt as if a blindfold had been wrapped over her eyes.

She had fainted on the porch of the van Dusens' house on the morning she had found the boy there, sitting on the steps rolling the newspapers. When she woke in the days ahead, she remembered that, remembered the sensation of her head separating from her body, her body tumbling forward.

Someone—it must have been the boy—had caught her, carried her back upstairs to the bed, but she had no memory of that. She could not make her mind reconcile the fact that the events surrounding what had happened to her father had culminated in this way, with Ruth deposited into the home of the boy on the bicycle. She could not bear to think about her father, but she could not stop thinking about him, either.

She did not know what would happen to her.

She slept. Waking, she would turn her face into the pillow and struggle to fall back down into the blackness. Once, after using the toilet, she dared glance at herself in the mirror. A stranger looked back at her, lips and cheeks drained of color, her hair wild.

One morning—was it the second day? The *third*? How long had she been sleeping?—Ruth woke to the sight of Mrs. van Dusen lowering a tray to the table beside her bed and the unmistakable smell of scrambled eggs and tea. Morning light poured into the room.

She struggled to sit up.

Mrs. van Dusen spooned sugar into a teacup, poured tea from a china pot decorated with pink flowers. She waited while Ruth pulled herself up against the pillows and then handed her the cup. Ruth noticed that her hand trembled slightly, and that there were dark circles below Mrs. van Dusen's eyes, as if the fragile skin above her cheekbones had been bruised.

Dr. van Dusen thought you might feel well enough to eat again, Mrs. van Dusen said.

The eggs smelled wonderful. Ruth ate; the taste of food seemed to have been restored, as well.

When Mrs. van Dusen returned a short time later, she carried a stack of fresh towels.

Maybe you would like to have a bath now, Ruth, she said, though Ruth understood that it wasn't a question.

Ruth watched from the bed, listening to the sound of the water running. She could see Mrs. van Dusen kneeling by the side of the tub, extending her wrist under the tap to check the temperature of the water. Sunlight from the curtained window fell on her head, her hair the same gold color as the boy's.

Finally, Mrs. van Dusen got to her feet and came back into the bedroom. She lifted the tray from Ruth's knees.

Will you be all right? she said. Her eyes sought Ruth's briefly—Ruth nodded—and then moved away again.

When Mrs. van Dusen withdrew, shutting the door behind her, Ruth made an effort to sit up straighter in bed. Her eyelids still felt so heavy. She walked unsteadily into the bathroom, where she closed the door and shed her wrinkled clothes— clothes that seemed to belong to another lifetime—on the floor.

Once she was lying in the bath, she felt better. The water was warm, and when she allowed herself to sink into it, her ears below the surface, the liquid silence was comforting. The water had been scented with something; there were colored rainbows in it, and it smelled sweetly floral. Or perhaps the smell was just from the room's astonishing cleanliness, Ruth thought, lying with her face floating just above the water's surface. Her eyes traveled over the bathroom's shining faucets, the white tiles of the wall, and the gleaming pink-tiled floor. She'd never been anywhere as clean as the van Dusens' house, she thought.

She realized she had no clothes other than those she had been wearing . . . for how many days now?

She had a memory of speaking to Dr. van Dusen at some point, of protesting, of struggling to get out of bed. She had been afraid that he would take her back to the house where she and her father had been living. She did not want ever to see that house again.

What had happened to her father? He must be dead, she thought. Would they tell her?

The memory of him on that day, trying to run, the blood in the air . . . the thought of the blood filled her with pity. Yet she understood that somehow what had happened was not a complete surprise to her. For her whole life her father had been like a man standing alone at night under a lamppost on a street, waiting, and she did not know for what. She thought that what had been between them might have looked like love—they even might have wanted it to *be* love—but it was as if a river had run between them, separating them.

They had been in some way no relation to each other, his blood his own, nothing to do with her,

She began to cry; she had to sink her head under the water to make herself stop.

Out of the bath, she wrapped herself in one of the big white towels, as soft and clean as everything in the van Dusens' house.

In the bedroom, she found that the sheets had been changed, the bed made up again with fresh linens, one corner turned down invitingly. On the chair beside the bed were two new blouses, one with narrow pink stripes, the other pale blue, both still pinned to the shirt paper. Beside the shirts were two

skirts, as well as several pairs of cotton underwear and two brassieres, their cups—excruciating, she thought, that someone had
noticed the size of her breasts, already big—folded neatly inside
one another and slipped discreetly between the blouses. On the
bed lay a pale yellow nightgown and a matching robe. Ruth put
on the nightgown and climbed back into bed. She sensed that
the medicine Dr. van Dusen had been giving her was wearing
off—the taste of the eggs had revived her appetite—but all she
wanted was to be asleep.

When she woke again later that day, the room was filled
with late-afternoon light. She got out of bed and went to use
the bathroom, where she saw that her old clothes had been
removed. She looked out the bathroom window. Mrs. van
Dusen, wearing a wide-brimmed hat, knelt in the garden below
among the flowers.

No sound came from anywhere else in the house.

Where was the boy?

Ruth went to the door of the bedroom and looked out onto
the landing. From the top of the stairs, she could see down into
the front hall. Light came in from the two etched-glass panels beside the front door, and a chandelier distributed colored
chinks around the hall, where they moved lazily across the floor
and walls. Ruth watched the little squares of light travel silently
over the carpet and walls and the slender legs of the hall table.
A clock ticked.

This was somebody's life, she thought. People lived like
this, in a calm and clean quiet. Yet, like a pinch on her arm, she
felt it: was it *too* quiet?

But it didn't matter; such a life would never be her life, anyway.

She fled back to bed. She wanted only to sleep.

Later that evening, when Mrs. van Dusen brought her supper on a tray, the plate held two lamb chops and a baked potato and cooked carrots cut up into tiny cubes.

Ruth's appetite had vanished, replaced by a stomachache, but she ate methodically; she needed to store supplies, she thought. It felt as if a long voyage lay ahead of her.

Dr. van Dusen appeared at the bedroom door, as she finished the last mouthful.

She might like to come downstairs and sit in the living room for a while, he suggested. It's a lovely, cool evening, Ruth, he said. Put on the robe Mrs. van Dusen bought for you.

Downstairs he helped her to a chair, as if she were an invalid.

A polished silver dish shaped like a seashell rested on the table beside her chair. Books with gilt lettering on their spines filled the shelves on either side of a fireplace, which was neatly swept, two polished brass andirons side by side. The upholstered sofa was lined with tasseled pillows. The window by her chair was open, and outside in the garden, the lacy white globes of flowers glowed in the dusk. Ruth felt that she was in a painting of a world, not a real world. She had never been in such a place.

Mrs. van Dusen brought her a mug of Ovaltine on a saucer, a plate with two sugar cookies, an ironed linen napkin with embroidered letters on it.

Then Dr. van Dusen, his shirtsleeves rolled to his elbows, reappeared in the doorway.

Behind him, carrying a folded-up checkerboard, was the boy, the boy on the bicycle.

This is our son, Peter, Dr. van Dusen said. He smiled. But I think you've met.

That night, Peter sat on a footstool across from her, the checkerboard on a folding tray table between them.

Ruth stole glances at him. The part in his shining hair was clean and straight. His eyebrows were straight, too, smooth, delicate lines, his eyelashes dark against his skin as he looked down at the checkerboard.

She could not believe he was sitting across from her.

Every time he took one of her men, he glanced up apologetically.

Sorry, he said, shaking his head

He won three games in a row.

After each one, Ruth was afraid he would pack up the board and leave, but he just set up the pieces again.

Then in the fourth game, as if the arrangement of pieces on the board suddenly leaped into focus for her, she saw a move that would allow her to jump two of his pieces.

She took his men off the board.

Then she looked up.

You *let* me do that, she said.

I didn't see it, he said. That's how it is sometimes. But he was smiling.

She looked down at the checkerboard.

You carried me upstairs after I fainted, she said. I'm sorry.

It's all right, he said. I've carried much heavier things. Then he blushed. It was fine, he said. Don't worry.

She saw in his face that he knew about what had happened to her father and to her, about the perverse and terrible thing from which she would never now be free.

You know why I'm here, she said. In your house, I mean.

He nodded.

I guess you feel sorry for me, she said. But I don't want you to. Pity would follow his understanding, she realized.

I'll try, he said.

Peter had his father's tall gracefulness, the same large blue eyes and high forehead and straight nose. His hair looked so soft that Ruth longed to touch it, to brush it away from his forehead, where it liked to fall. Like everything in the van Dusens' house—Ruth walked through it marveling at the china, the carpets, the furniture she recognized as antiques, every doorknob and mirror and window polished and sparkling—Peter himself was clean and finely made. His hair was full of silver and gold light. His skin glowed.

She found herself looking at the white half-moons on his fingernails, at his wrists, his forearms, the shape of his shoulders under his shirt, the declivity at the base of his throat, his jaw, the curve of his ear.

She was aware for the first time of wanting to touch another person, a boy, of wanting to bring her body close to his.

Sitting at the van Dusens' dining room table across from him in the evenings, which she began to do after the first night of being brought downstairs, was excruciating. She tried not to lift her eyes from her plate, but it was as if her gaze was dragged magnetically toward Peter, and when she looked up he seemed always to be looking back at her. Throughout the meal, while his parents made small talk with each other and with Peter— *How was your day, dear?* Was this really how people spoke to each other?—Ruth felt a racing sensation in her chest. She was aware of her breasts under her shirt, the smell of the perfumed soap with which she'd washed her hair. She felt herself blushing, her cheeks flaming throughout every meal.

She saw, too, that Mrs. van Dusen noticed her feelings, color rising in her own face.

After dinner at night, Dr. van Dusen encouraged Ruth to retreat to the living room, where she was left alone to read. Ruth stood before the shelves choosing books at random, putting her nose to them, and pressing their cool, smooth covers to her cheek.

She could not believe her life with her father was over, gone, that her father himself was gone, probably dead. Because no one spoke to her of what had happened, despite the enormity of the events, it seemed logical to her that people would tell her nothing, that she was owed nothing, neither explanations nor news.

And their life had not been a *real* life, she saw now. It had been a false life, an experiment to which she had been subjected.

Yet she could not let go of its details.

Her father must have carried her when she was a baby. He must have held her, rocked her to sleep sometimes. She remembered holding his hand while crossing streets, remembered the pressure of his hand on her shoulder, briefly, pushing her forward into classrooms, into unfamiliar apartments where a succession of women looked after her when her father was away somewhere. She remembered, oddly, the feel of his hand over her own as she had practiced writing her first letters.

Every night she waited for Peter to appear again in the living room with the checkerboard, but he did not. Sometimes Dr. van Dusen sat with her, reading the newspaper. Mrs. van Dusen brought him a cup of coffee, and he looked up at her then, touched her arm or put his hand on the small of her back as she leaned over to set the cup carefully on the table beside him. Ruth watched these exchanges; this, too, was a revelation to her, how people were with each other. Polite. Intimate.

She sat dutifully with a book, but often she did not really read. She hoped Peter would come join them in the living room, but one evening she watched from the living room window as he headed off on his bicycle after dinner. The next evening he left with a basketball under his arm. Other pursuits had been found for him, she realized.

Sometimes the telephone rang, and Dr. van Dusen rose to answer it, speaking in quiet tones to someone, one of his patients, she assumed. Occasionally he left the house at night with his doctor's bag. One night while he was out, Ruth passed the kitchen on her way upstairs and saw Mrs. van Dusen sitting at the kitchen table, her hands clasped before her. There was no book or magazine or sewing on the table. The kitchen was immaculately tidy, a light on over the stove but the room otherwise in darkness. Mrs. van Dusen did not seem to see her.

In some way, Mrs. van Dusen reminded Ruth of her father. There was something hidden inside her that could not be spoken, she thought.

Every night, Dr. van Dusen left a sleeping pill for Ruth, a tiny tablet in a little dish beside a glass of water on the bedside table. Every night, Ruth took it.

A week went by. Two. Other than the visit from the FBI men one afternoon, the hours passed with excruciating slowness. Mrs. van Dusen continued to bring Ruth breakfast on a tray in bed, as if she were an invalid, and Ruth spent much of the day there, reading or sleeping. Every night she dressed in the clothes that had been purchased for her and went downstairs for dinner. She assumed that Peter did not return to play checkers with her because of her father, because of what had happened to her. His parents—Mrs. van Dusen, in particular— wanted no friendship between their son and Ruth.

She did not know what would happen to her. She assumed that, as the policeman had said, someone would arrive one day to take her away somewhere. A feeling of alert waiting had replaced her impulse to run away, the instinct that had driven her downstairs and outside to the porch on the first night at the van Dusens'. She did not know how to be ready, nor what to be ready for, but her skin prickled frequently with fear. It seemed that no one was to talk to her, to tell her anything. She had the sense that she was on a dangerous kind of probation, that any move was likely to result in catastrophe. She tried to be as quiet as possible, to ask nothing. From the windows she watched Peter coming and going from the house, heard the sounds of passersby or cars on the street, the telephone ringing. But the apparently ordinary life around her seemed both mysterious and out of reach. Such a life would never be her own, she thought. The invisible connections that tied people to places, to each other . . . she did not possess these. Had never possessed them, it seemed.

Then, one evening as she sat in the living room, she looked up to see Peter standing in the hallway. He smiled and lifted his hand.

A moment later, Mrs. van Dusen appeared. Her gaze took in Peter, and then it took in Ruth.

Peter? she said. I need your help with something.

A few minutes later, Ruth heard the sound of the basketball outside, Peter shooting again and again in the twilight at the goal mounted over the door to the small barn behind the house where Dr. van Dusen parked his car at night. The basketball thudded against the backboard, and also, somehow, inside her own body, again and again.

The next evening after dinner, Dr. and Mrs. van Dusen told Ruth that they had found a permanent place for her. She was not to be taken away, after all. A widow who lived in Wells, a patient of Dr. van Dusen's named Mary Healy, was in need of a girl who could help her. She was alone and her health was poor. Ruth understood that the arrangements were being described in particular terms: They were asking her to *help* Mary. They were not saying, *you have nowhere else to go, and we do not want you here.* Yet she understood that the tension in the van Dusens' house had to do with her.

She was not part of their family.

She was not part of any family.

The bad things her father had done, the bad thing that had happened to him . . . people would not want to be reminded of that.

Dr. van Dusen did all the talking during this conversation. Ruth could see that he was concerned that she might cry, though she had not cried once in front of either him or Mrs. van Dusen. She sensed that the decision to find a place for her had come because no authority had yet been found to come get her, and that Mrs. van Dusen—more than her husband—was eager for Ruth to leave. Peter was not present for this discussion, which was not a discussion. Nor had he been there for dinner that night. She would never see him again, she thought, and it was this realization, as Dr. van Dusen explained to her what would happen, that made her eyes fill with tears.

How foolish she was, to want a boy like Peter.

The next day, Dr. van Dusen drove Ruth to Mary Healy's, several blocks away through a complicated tangle of streets. Ruth could see, looking at the houses as they drove past them, that they were moving into a neighborhood of less affluence.

A parcel in her lap held the belongings Mrs. van Dusen had presented to Ruth that morning before she'd left: a handmade sweater—a cardigan in blue wool—as well as an ivory brush and comb set.

It was a complicated fact about Mrs. van Dusen that Ruth

would come to know in the years ahead; she was not unkind, and she was generous—she would give Ruth many gifts—but her generosity was not an easy generosity, nor one borne of joy. It was designed, Ruth came to understand, to protect Mrs. van Dusen from the knowledge of her own loneliness, her estrangement from other people.

Later, after what happened between Ruth and Peter, Ruth threw away all of Mrs. van Dusen's gifts except the books: every item of clothing, including the hand-knit sweaters and scarves and mittens, the embroidered pillowcases, the jewelry box with Ruth's name embossed on it in gold letters, and the gold bangle bracelet, the set of watercolor paints, and the shepherdess figurine.

These were gifts she would have been given if she were actually someone's beloved daughter, she understood. But she was not someone's daughter.

She was not anyone's daughter.

And she was not beloved.

When Mary Healy opened the door of her house to Ruth and Dr. van Dusen, Ruth took in a sitting room crowded with plants on one side of a front hallway, and a dark dining room and kitchen on the other side. Off the back of the kitchen, she discovered, was an annex where Mary, who could no longer walk upstairs, had a daybed and her beloved radio.

Mary, in her early eighties, Ruth assumed when she saw her for the first time, looked as if she had been fattened on something unhealthy. She was missing a foot, the stump of her leg ending in a man's white sock. Her skin shone wetly, faintly green. Sweat stood out around her hairline and on her scalp under her thin white hair.

She was in pain, she told Ruth, but not much, really. She spoke without self-pity, moving through the downstairs of the house on her crutches, showing Ruth where everything was. Plants garlanded the windows, tentacles of greenery running along the ceiling moldings, dead blossoms falling on the carpets.

Mary had written out in a shaky hand a list of Ruth's duties, which she gave to Ruth in the kitchen. The simplicity of the tasks—wash, iron, cook, sweep, garden—reassured Ruth.

But I don't know anything about gardening, she told Mary.

Anyone can put a seed in the ground, Mary said. That'll wait until spring, anyway.

At the bottom of the stairs, Mary stopped.

I can't get up there anymore, she said, holding on to the newel post. But you tell me if there's anything you need. She looked at Dr. van Dusen and then at Ruth. I'm glad to have you here, she said. You've been unfortunate. That's not your fault. I'm unfortunate, too. We'll be a pair, won't we?

The telephone rang, and she went to the kitchen to answer it.

What happened to her leg? Ruth asked Dr. van Dusen when Mary had gone.

She has a disease, Dr. van Dusen said. Diabetes.

Ruth looked away from him, up the stairs toward the dark landing.

It will help her to have you here, Ruth, Dr. van Dusen said. It is not a punishment. Try to see it as an opportunity. Mary is a good person. She has two daughters, but they live in Boston and they can't get here as often as they'd like. She'll treat you well.

Upstairs in Mary's house, Ruth discovered that she could see the ocean from one of the bedrooms, despite that the rooms were crowded with furniture. She left her things there on the bed and came back out to the landing.

Dr. van Dusen was waiting at the bottom of the stairs. He lifted his hand.

Not good-bye, he said. I'll see you soon. I pay house calls to Mary every week.

Ruth raised her hand. I can't pay you anything, she said. For what you did.

Dr. van Dusen closed his eyes and put his hand over his mouth for a moment. Then he took it away.

No, Ruth, he said. No, there would be no need for that, in any case.

After he left, Ruth went back to the bedroom and looked out the window at the tiny piece of the ocean visible between the rooftops. She watched it, as if something might appear there, a ship on which she could sail away.

It was the bedroom she would occupy for the next six years, until she was eighteen years old.

Early on a Saturday evening a few weeks after moving to Mary Healy's, Ruth heard someone knock at the front door downstairs.

Dr. van Dusen stood under the porch light.

Would you like to go for a drive tomorrow, Ruth? he said.

He named a place; she agreed. She did not recognize it as

the place where her father was. She thought Dr. van Dusen was proposing an outing of some kind, that such car trips were what people like the van Dusens did on the weekend.

She hoped she would see Peter.

Peter, however, was not with his father when Dr. van Dusen arrived with the car the next day. Instead, she sat in the front seat as they drove past late-summer marshland from which ibis and herons with their snowy wings and delicate legs lifted off, soaring away as if in accompaniment to the jazz playing on the car radio. Once they stopped for gas, and when Dr. van Dusen returned to the car, he gave her a serious look.

All right, Ruth? he said.

Yes, she said. She was fine.

But she did not understand where they were going until they arrived and she saw the coils of barbed wire, the empty cars in the parking lot. The inconsolable silence of the place was terrifying.

She shook her head, held on to the armrest. She did not want to get out of the car. She did not want to see her father. She felt shocked to learn that he was still alive.

Are you sure? Dr. van Dusen said.

Ruth said nothing. She did not want to think about her father in that place. She did not want to think about him at all.

She looked up at what she recognized was a guard tower, two men with rifles standing in it. She looked down at her hands, turned them over, palms down, in her lap.

It's all right, Ruth, Dr. van Dusen said finally. Never mind. This was a mistake. It's my fault, and I'm sorry. I thought you understood.

He started the car again and turned around. Near dusk, they stopped at a diner and he bought them both hamburgers and Coca-Colas, carrying the food out to the car where Ruth waited.

It's my fault, Ruth, he said again. Forgive me.

He asked about me? Ruth said.

I think he said it was up to you, Dr. van Dusen said after a minute. If you wanted to.

Ruth looked up at the lighted windows of the diner, a man and a woman leaning toward one another across a table, both of them laughing. The woman's hair was red, her lipstick bright.

You don't have to decide now, Dr. van Dusen said. He handed her a napkin.

We can try again one day, he said. If you want to.

One evening just before school began in September, Mary called to Ruth from the bottom of the stairs. From the landing, Ruth looked down and saw Dr. van Dusen. He was dressed in khaki trousers and his shirtsleeves and suspenders, as if he had been taking an evening stroll and had stopped in to say hello, but he did not smile when he greeted her.

In the small front room, the windowsill crowded with plants, Mary's cats prowling a path between the chairs, he asked Ruth to sit down.

Her father was dead, Dr. van Dusen told her. He had taken his own life in prison.

I thought you should know, Ruth, Dr. van Dusen said, though I am sorry to tell it to you. I believe he regretted—here

Dr. van Dusen hesitated, as if searching for the word. I believe he regretted his past, he finished finally.

Mary Healy stood in the doorway. Ruth understood that she'd been warned that Dr. van Dusen would come with this news.

I want you to know, Ruth, Dr. van Dusen said, that there is no need for you to worry about anything. I mean, in terms of money. You will be taken care of.

She's a good girl, Mary said from the door, as if she had been asked to defend Ruth.

Dr. van Dusen glanced at Mary, then back at Ruth.

I know she is, he said.

Ruth looked around the room. Sometimes the act of naming things in her head, crowding her mind full with the words for everything that was in the world, helped her ward off panic, a sensation inside her body that things were speeding up to an unbearable degree.

Leaf, she thought, looking up at the long tendrils of one of Mary's philodendrons. Armchair. Carpet with roses. Moon climbing in the sky. Sound of waves.

Mary came forward on her crutches.

Ruth felt Mary's hand rest lightly on her head.

If she happened to wake near dawn that summer, Ruth always went outside to Mary's front porch. She hoped she might see Peter as he rode his bicycle down the dark streets, delivering the morning papers, but she never did. Perhaps his route did not take him past Mary's house. She thought again and again of her first sight of him, riding toward her with no hands on the bicycle's handlebars, whistling. But most mornings when she woke, the light already streamed into her bedroom, finding a path between the furniture stacked around her. She felt comforted by the barricade of old wicker chairs and tables, the heavy wardrobes and battered desks stored on the second floor of Mary's house.

Mary kept Ruth busy—she was a talkative person, and she seemed to like Ruth's company—and there were always books to read.

Rainy days were most difficult. All her life her moods would be sensitive to the weather.

Gloomy days, Ruth told Dr. Wenning many years later, always made her feel depressed.

Dr. Wenning appeared uninterested in this observation.

Turn on the lights, she said.

Electric light isn't the same, Ruth said. People need real sunlight.

Dr. Wenning was silent.

You're the psychiatrist, Ruth said finally. You should know this.

Bah, Dr. Wenning said. Everyone feels a little blue when it rains except the ducks.

Ruth rolled her eyes. For a psychiatrist, you're awfully unsympathetic sometimes, she said. You know that?

What makes you think psychiatrists are sympathetic? Dr. Wenning said.

She took off her glasses. Fortunately, she said, you and I

cannot do anything about the rain, Ruth. But it is as the poet said: *Be still, sad heart! and cease repining; Behind the clouds is the sun still shining.*

Longfellow, Ruth said. I know that poem.

Is that who it is? Dr. Wenning said. Oh. Well, I cannot remember it all. How does it go? Something, something, something . . . *into every life some rain must fall. Some days must be dark and dreary.*

Ruth remembered the nights over those years with Mary as often dark and dreary.

She was frequently awoken by nightmares. She sat up, heart pounding, her forehead damp. She learned to take a blanket and sit at the top of the stairs where she could hear the sound of Mary's radio. Mary didn't sleep much herself, she had told Ruth, and the radio kept her company through the night. Ruth sat on the landing wrapped in the blanket and leaned her head against the wall, listening to the comforting sound of voices from below. She liked the tones of the sports announcers with their steady patter interrupted by bursts of excitement, the canned laughter from the comedy shows. Occasionally she fell asleep curled up on the floor and woke at dawn to the sound of the surf crashing against the beach a few blocks away.

Of course her nightmares were fueled by the events of her childhood, Dr. Wenning agreed later, by the incident that had taken place before Ruth's young eyes, by an early lifetime of her father's silence and secrets.

One Saturday afternoon near the end of the first winter

that Ruth worked for Dr. Wenning, she looked up from her typing to see Dr. Wenning standing beside her with a cup of tea. Dr. Wenning patted Ruth's shoulder as she set the cup and saucer beside her.

This is chamomile tea, she said. Good for sleeping.

Then she sat down on the chair beside the table where Ruth did her work.

I have been thinking about your dreams, Ruth, Dr. Wenning said. About the problem of your nightmares.

She gestured at the cup.

Go ahead, she said. It tastes a little bit like grass, I think, but it is calming. Try it.

Ruth took a sip. It did taste like grass. She made a face.

Honey might improve it, Dr. Wenning said.

Anyway—she went on as if talking aloud for her own edification—who wants to be frightened to death every night? No one does, of course.

Then she looked at Ruth.

But maybe there is another way for us to look at these dreams, she said.

Ruth's nightmares sometimes were haunted by a firing squad aiming its guns at her and by her own weird, ghoulish rise from the ground again and again. More often, though, the dreams contained the people Ruth imagined her father had wronged. Desperate men in torn shirts, widows dressed in black, and inconsolable children accused her from ruined landscapes, empty barns, and desolate, echoing houses; unplanted fields and streams empty of fish; orchards barren of fruit. In her dreams, Ruth encountered people sitting on porches and staring into space or lying defeated in the furrows of their fields. She ran among them, helpless and guilt-stricken, trying to take them by the arm and rouse them, or to give them money from her pocket.

Dr. Wenning had listened to Ruth's accounts of these miserable scenarios, her face still.

These are no fun, these dreams, she'd agreed.

Ruth did not like to cry, especially not in front of Dr. Wenning. She wanted Dr. Wenning to see her as brave.

I have been thinking, Ruth, Dr. Wenning said that Saturday afternoon. Obviously these nightmares are your imagination hard at work.

There you are, she went on, waving a hand in the air. Your mind rushes in—*gallantly* rushes in, I might say—trying to make reparations, even for crimes of which you are innocent.

These dreams are the dreams of a comforter, Ruth, she said. You want to make *amends* for your father.

She leaned back in her chair and smiled at Ruth, as if she admired this quality in her and wanted to convey her admiration.

Really, your mind is quite *heroic*, Ruth, she said. You want to put it all right, even though of course you cannot. But look how your imagination never rests! Night after night you have these dreams.

She stood up and patted her stomach. I think, Ruth, she said, that you need to be grateful for them.

Ruth gazed up at Dr. Wenning in her drab dress, cinched at her thick waist by a belt.

Two pigs in a gunnysack! Ha ha, Dr. Wenning had said of her own shape. The twin wings of her frizzy white hair bobbed now as she nodded emphatically.

It is a gift you have, Ruth, this ability to see things so vividly, Dr. Wenning said. I think these dreams will end one day, but meanwhile I see them as evidence of your compassion and your imagination. You could not have prevented what happened, of course, but you can convey your sympathy now. Speak to these people when you meet them in your dreams. Let them show you the places where they live, the things they loved and lost. Listen to their stories. Tell them of your own grief. Eventually, I think, you will come to the end of knowing one another, and you will let one another go.

Ruth gazed around at the untidy shelves of Dr. Wenning's office, the books tufted with loose papers, the pewter gray drapes at the tall windows overlooking Center Church on the Green in New Haven, the marble bust of Schiller with his flowing hair and Roman nose.

She tried to imagine speaking to the people she could see so clearly in her dreams in their sad, shabby homes and unkempt farms.

Dr. Wenning had lived during her childhood in the same town in Germany where Schiller had spent part of his own youth, Ruth knew. She liked to tell Ruth about the great beauty of this place: the sloping vineyards alongside the river, the soft shapes of the dark islands in the water, the birches and fir trees, the golden light, the smell of honey in the air, the abbey with its vaulted ceiling and cold air full of ascending currents. Schiller had disliked the classroom, Dr. Wenning told Ruth. He became a poet because of the beauty of the world in which he ran free as a boy.

No one believed in Schiller's idea of the beautiful soul more than Dr. Wenning, Ruth thought.

You have a beautiful soul, Ruth, Dr. Wenning said that afternoon. She patted Ruth firmly on the shoulder again.

Drink your tea, she said. Do not be afraid of these dreams. Imagine that these people are replanting their orchards, rebuilding their barns, fattening their cattle. Try to see everything, remember everything. The sun shining, the rain falling . . .

She looked down at Ruth.

All shall be well, and all shall be well, and all manner of thing shall be well, she said. Do you know these words? No? Julian of Norwich, famous Christian mystic. She had powerful visions, like you, except of course the only person she ever saw was Jesus Christ. Too bad.

After this conversation, Ruth discovered that she seemed at least to be paying closer attention in her dreams. When she recounted them later for Dr. Wenning, she appeared to remember greater numbers of details: the chestnut color of a horse in a field, the steep rise of a dormer and the reflection of clouds in the window glass, the sound of bulrushes moving in the wind at the edge of a pond, the smell in a room of a candle burning.

Did I dream these things, she asked, or am I just making them up right now, telling you about them?

Good question! Dr. Wenning looked pleased. How do they make you feel?

Like . . . well, like the world is full, Ruth said.

Dr. Wenning looked satisfied.

The things of the world will comfort you, Ruth, she said. Love the things of the world.

Ruth spent hours that first summer at Mary Healy's reading.

Mary owned a series of books, *Rivers of America*—bought from a salesman one day when she'd been a young mother, she said—and also a big volume called *Uncle Arthur's Bedtime Storybook*. Ruth read this book over and over again, even though she knew she was too old for it.

When Mary realized that Ruth liked to read, she called around to the neighbors, and soon Ruth had books by Rudyard Kipling and George Bernard Shaw, several volumes of *Reader's Digest* condensed books, Carl Sandburg's *Rootabaga Stories*, a collection of new detective novels—*The Asphalt Jungle* and *Sunset Boulevard*—and also copies of *Lorna Doone* and *Under the Lilacs*. Best was the gift of several novels by Dickens, *Oliver Twist* and *Bleak House* and *David Copperfield*, *Great Expectations* and *Hard Times*.

Sadly, sadly, the sun rose, Ruth read in *A Tale of Two Cities*.

It rose upon no sadder sight than the man of good abilities and good emotions, incapable of their directed exercise, incapable of his own help and his own happiness, sensible of the blight on him, and resigning himself to let it eat him away.

She thought of her father. *Blight.* That was a good word for what had been inside him, she thought, after looking it up in Mary's dictionary. *A ruined state, a destructive force. An affliction.*

Ruth already knew how to cook frankfurters and beans and

scrambled eggs. Mary showed her how to make corned beef and cabbage and vegetable soup, to bake rye bread and a cake made with raisins and brown sugar and Crisco.

The radio was always on in the sunroom annex off the kitchen, and she and Mary listened to baseball games at night.

They played cards.

They never mentioned Ruth's father directly.

Once, apropos of nothing, Mary reached over and squeezed Ruth's arm. You poor kid, she said. You never knew anything, huh?

Ruth shook her head. But she had known *something*, she thought.

Poor kid, Mary repeated.

One evening a few days before the school year began, Ruth and Dr. van Dusen walked to the local school, which was a dozen blocks from Mary's house. Standing outside the fence with Ruth, Dr. van Dusen told her that he had gone to school there himself when he was a boy, and that she would go, too.

Two large oak trees shaded a lawn with bare patches in front of the building. Those trees, he told her, had been much smaller when he'd been a student.

Ruth wanted somehow to make Dr. van Dusen talk about Peter.

Did Peter like the school? she asked.

Peter attended a different school, he told her, a boarding school in Providence, where the boys were taught by Jesuit priests.

Mrs. van Dusen was Catholic, Dr. Van Dusen said.

Ruth felt her stomach drop. This had been her last hope, that she might see Peter at school.

If you would ever like to go to church, Ruth, Dr. Van Dusen said . . . Mrs. van Dusen would be happy to take you.

Ruth looked up at him. You don't go?

Sometimes, he said. But I make house calls on Saturdays and Sundays for people who cannot get out. The priest and I often cross paths, he said, but he is usually the one invited for dinner.

At Dr. van Dusen's tone, Ruth looked up. He was smiling.

Ruth looked away from him at the dark windows of the school. She would not tell Dr. van Dusen that she was afraid of God. Sometimes when she sat on the front steps of Mary's house at night, after the lights in the other houses had been extinguished, she imagined seeing Peter, imagined him appearing suddenly. She did not want to pray for this, though, because she did not think God was reliable; in fact, she thought God, if he existed, was an unpredictable force, as unknowable as her own father had been.

Also, she found it difficult to believe fully in God.

She did not want to say that she did *not* believe in him, though. If God did exist, surely her doubt would bring down his wrath. Better not to direct his attention toward her in any way.

She could wish for things, she thought—wishing was not the same as praying—but she had no faith in either enterprise, anyway.

· · ·

The day before school began, Mrs. van Dusen made a surprise appearance at Mary's house, bringing school supplies and
clothes for Ruth, five cotton dresses and two cardigans, one
white and one dark blue. She also arrived with a lemon pound
cake, paper sacks of peaches and plums, a bouquet of flowers
for Mary, and a vase of tiny flowers fashioned cleverly out of
seashells for Ruth.

Ruth noticed that Mary was a little abashed around her.

It must be tough, being the doctor's wife, Mary said later to
Ruth. You have to be nice to everybody all the time. Still, she's
not an *easy* person, is she? Makes me kind of nervous.

Someone at the police station, Ruth supposed, had spread the
story of what had happened to her father; everyone at school
that fall seemed to know that something bad trailed her. Teachers did not call on her in class, as if forcing her to speak would
be unkind, and for the most part the students ignored her. Her
English teacher was a middle-aged woman named Miss Dougherty. She had a bold manner, and she wore lipstick and blouses
with ruffles. After Ruth turned in her first essay—an account
of the books she had read over the summer—Miss Dougherty
took Ruth to the town library one day after school and got her a
library card. She gave her some clothes, too, a few dresses and
soft sweaters.

I'm too old for them now, she said, looking Ruth up and
down. But they'd be pretty on you.

You watch out for the boys, Ruth, she said. And don't you
bother about those other kids, either, she told her. Just keep

reading. Keep your head down but your chin up. You'll be done with school before you know it, and then you'll go to college.

She looked again at Ruth. Everything will be all right then, Ruth. It'll be better when you're a grown-up. Trust me.

Walking around town one weekend afternoon that first fall, Ruth discovered that Wells had a small art and natural history museum. After that she went often after school, stopping under the portico at the entrance to the building where she turned her back on the front door with its medieval, studded hinges and leaded-glass window and checked her face in the mirror of the compact she had bought at Woolworth's with the allowance Dr. van Dusen gave her. She patted her nose and her cheeks with powder. She wore a dark green beret over her hair and gray wool mittens, items she had unearthed in a dresser and that Mary had told her to keep.

Even though she knew he was away at school, she always imagined that there was a chance she might run across Peter.

A rambling heap of brownstone boulders, the museum had been built originally as a private residence for a cotton baron in the late 1800's. Ruth read this information in a free pamphlet on her first visit, the blurry, mimeographed copies stacked on a spindly three-legged table at the foot of the marble spiral staircase in the front hall. A niche in the curved wall of the stairwell contained a magnificent urn embossed with flowers and Irish harps and trimmed with a design of dogs chasing each other.

From the tower of the museum, Ruth liked to look out over the water, the whitecaps like fins bristling over the surface. The wind came off the ocean and blew a flurry of crimson leaves across the cotton baron's lawns.

In every room of the museum, around every corner, there was something bizarre or horrifying or fascinating or beautiful: a taxidermied monkey's head from Lima, Peru, and a giant clamshell, pearly jaws shining under the lights, fossils of fish and shells and an ostrich complete with an egg. She loved an exquisite, thimble-sized nest woven of down and silver hairs by a ruby-throated hummingbird. The museum's dusty dioramas were mysterious, all inky undergrowth and slanting sideways light in which a mountain lion and a squirrel and a toucanet stared glassily past each other. A bronzed man with a Neanderthal brow and beaded loincloth, spear poised, hung behind a tree so obviously made of paper that the scene seemed both comical and tragic at once.

Paintings hung floor to ceiling in some rooms, many of them so high above Ruth's head that she couldn't see them properly. There were dreamy seascapes, and pictures of flushed maids scattering grain, and glittering still lifes: an ermine hanging upside down, pointed teeth bared, a parallelogram of light captured on a dusky red grape. It amazed her to consider that one man had collected so many things in his lifetime. She hadn't thought before that this is what one might do, if one had money: amass the treasures of the world. She'd only ever thought of her father's dreams: a big house and him all alone in it, room after room, all to himself. She'd never imagined a room for herself in those houses, she realized.

Her solitary afternoons in the museum—its otherworldly isolation, the mute, majestic silence of the extraordinary objects within—offered her a profound comfort during that first year in Wells, filling her eyes and her mind. The rooms were hushed, smelling of the sea and the lemon-scented oil used by a smocked curator's assistant, an old man who nodded at her while polishing the gleaming banister and the glass cases. Wandering through the building, Ruth tried to catalog it all in her head, even the smells: fur and tooth and nail and enamel and crystal and gold, oil paint and silver tarnish, marble and plaster and ancient reeds and papers.

One winter afternoon in the minerals room Ruth came upon an old couple, very well dressed, the man leaning on a silver-topped cane. He and his wife—Ruth assumed they were husband and wife—hung together over the glass-topped cabinet containing the milk-spattered gypsum and the foot-long aquamarine and the bristling geodes. They were whispering happily to one another, the woman's gloved hand nestled in the crook of her husband's arm.

They looked up at her in surprise when she came into the room.

Ruth had begun to feel that the museum belonged to her alone—there were almost never any other visitors—and she backed away, hurrying down the marble staircase. Outside, snow had begun to fall. She walked carefully down the long drive, slipping in her school shoes, listening to the sound of the surf crashing nearby.

The sight of the old couple had made her feel lonely. She wished again that she would see Peter. Occasionally, walking to school or in town to the library or on an errand for Mary, she had the sensation that she had stepped around a corner onto a street where he had stood a moment before, or that she had entered a store he had just left. Once she thought she saw him going into the hardware store on Main Street. She had followed him inside, her heart pounding, but it was not Peter after all.

She did not ever walk past the van Dusens' house, though she thought she knew where it was. And of course she avoided the block on which she and her father had spent their one night.

That winter she made a friend, a girl named Ellie McHenry, whose parents ran a bar and restaurant called the Castle House. Ellie and Ruth had been paired together at school on a history project. In the kitchen of the Castle House, working on Sunday afternoons when the restaurant was closed, they made a model of the Parthenon out of sugar cubes. Sometimes on weeknights Ellie's father paid the girls to wash dishes. Ruth sensed that the Castle House with its sticky tablecloths and noisy bar was not the kind of place where the van Dusens would go.

It was fun to work alongside Ellie. In the kitchen they listened to the radio, tossing soapsuds at one another. At night when they were finished with work and the restaurant was closed, Ellie's mother let them eat lobster rolls or bowls of clam chowder and plates of French fries at the bar.

Dr. van Dusen or his nurse, a brisk woman in a neat uniform, came over regularly to see Mary and give her injections, but those visits usually took place when Ruth was in school.

Sometimes Dr. van Dusen left packages for Ruth, books and clothes from Mrs. van Dusen.

After that?

Years passed, Ruth would tell Dr. Wenning later.

Years passed? Dr. Wenning lifted an eyebrow.

Ruth looked away, out of the tall windows in Dr. Wenning's study in New Haven. She flicked a dustcloth at a windowpane, blinked.

I understand, Dr. Wenning said after a moment.

She got up then and poured two whiskeys, another of her remedies.

Together Ruth and Dr. Wenning sat in silence and watched the sky outside the window. Ruth would never know anyone who could remain silent as long as Dr. Wenning.

It wasn't all bad, Ruth said finally. Then she drank down her whiskey, grimacing.

Of course not, Dr. Wenning said.

Things are never all bad, all good, she said. A lot is gray.

She finished her drink.

I take it back, she said. Most is gray.

Years *did* pass, and then when Ruth was sixteen years old she came out of Mary's house on a Saturday morning near Christmas, tugging her hat down over her ears, a stack of books to be returned to the library in a bag over her shoulder. She hesitated outside the front door, stopping to pull on her gloves.

When she looked up, Peter was standing on the icy sidewalk before her.

He looked older, but there was no question of recognizing him.

His hands were shoved into his coat pockets, his shoulders hunched, his hair wind-whipped. His face had grown fuller and even more handsome, she thought, his head like the glorious beautiful heads on the statues in the museum.

It had been four years since they had seen each other, and Ruth could not believe he was standing there before her now. Yet she had thought of him so often, imagined this encounter so many times, that his presence also seemed inevitable.

Later, he would tell her that usually he went straight from the boarding school in Providence at the end of the school year to a summer camp run by a Jesuit brotherhood in the mountains of North Carolina. These arrangements, Peter explained, were made by his father, so that Peter spent no extended periods of time at home. His mother, Peter explained to Ruth, was increasingly depressed, the treatments she received at a hospital outside Boston briefly transformative but incrementally disabling.

You thought maybe I'd forgotten about you, Peter said that morning.

His eyes never left her face. Do you want to go for a walk? he said.

She came down the steps of Mary's house. You *didn't* forget about me, Ruth said.

I didn't, Peter said. No.

The next summer, the summer between their sophomore and junior years in high school, Peter did not go to North Carolina. He got a job in Wells instead, working at a golf course and life-guarding at the town's swimming pool. On his days off, he and Ruth rode the ferry Ruth had seen from the beach on her first day in Wells. They took it to other towns along the coast, where they sat on the painted horses at a merry-go-round, or went to the movies, or ate lunch at a place that served malted milk shakes and fried clams. Gulls swooped in the ferry's wake, crying and darting down to Ruth and Peter where they stood, holding on to the rusted handrails. In the shade beneath the ferry's narrow metal staircase connecting the upper and lower decks, where no one could see them, they braced themselves against the wall of the cabin and kissed. They had sand in their teeth and in their hair. The ferry's engine throbbed under their feet.

They swam off the beaches in the other towns during these excursions, places where they wouldn't be recognized. They did not talk about it much, but they understood that what they were doing was forbidden, that no matter how irrational or unfair or unkind it was, Peter's mother would be undone by the thought of Peter and Ruth together. They understood that they were governed by a tyranny—Mrs. van Dusen's fragility—about which they could do nothing except what they were doing, which was to disobey an unspoken rule.

Swimming in the ocean, out past the breakers, they felt alone. Under cover of the water, they pressed their bodies together, Ruth's arms around Peter's neck. Ruth had never wanted anything as powerfully as she wanted to touch and to be touched by Peter.

More than a year would go by before they made love for the first time, though, lying hidden in the beach dunes at night.

When Peter returned home during the Christmas break from school during their senior year, he came to Mary Healy's as often as he could, arriving late at night after Mary had retired to bed with her radio. He carried his snow-covered boots in his hand and crept silently up the stairs, leaving the boots to drain in the bathtub.

Mary never came upstairs, and they felt safe up there, lying under the blankets in Ruth's bed and facing each other, the sound of their whispered conversation drowned out by the radio playing downstairs.

Peter was the only person Ruth could talk to about her father, about what had happened.

Ruth was the only person Peter could talk to about his mother.

They'd been so young, Ruth thought later. Oh, the foolish things they'd said to each other. They'd recounted endlessly for each other their first meetings, how much they had thought about each other in the intervening years.

It *was* love at first sight, wasn't it? Ruth said.

Peter agreed that it was.

That spring, Peter was admitted to Harvard, and Dr. van Dusen came to Mary's house to congratulate Ruth for winning a scholarship to Smith. She would need spending money, he said, and he had set up an account for her. There would be money deposited there. She would be taken care of.

You've done a wonderful job, Ruth, he said. We are very proud of you.

But by then Ruth had already guessed that she was pregnant.

Peter came home from school in April for spring break. He appeared at Mary's house very late his first night home, well after midnight. Ruth lay in bed, watching him undress. He tossed his coat on the floor, kicked off his shoes, pulled his sweater over his head. He was elated by the news of his admission to Harvard, hers to Smith. They would be able to see each other often, he said.

He sat down on the bed beside her.

What's the matter? he said.

He fished one of her hands out from under the blankets. Aren't you happy?

I'm pregnant, she said.

He stared at her. Then he closed his eyes.

We were careful, he said.

He let go of her hand and dropped his head into his palms, rubbing furiously at his hair.

Then he reached down, found his sweater and pants, and put them back on. He sat back down on the bed beside her.

What are you doing? she said.

I feel stupid without my clothes on, he said quietly.

She stared at his back. Outside, wind rattled the windowpane, gusts of rain splattering against the glass. The ocean had been stirred up all day. Earlier in the afternoon Ruth had walked alone along the beach.

She had missed two periods by then. She understood what had happened, despite—as Peter said—that they had been careful.

Though she was afraid, she had not imagined that Peter would desert her—she had never imagined that.

You're sure? Peter said.

His hunched shoulders—both boyish and like an old man's—filled her with fear and then with rage.

He *would* leave her, she thought. Of course he would.

No, I'm guessing, she said. Just to terrify you.

She had been warm in bed, waiting for him. Now she felt freezing cold.

Oh, Ruth, he said. He did not turn and face her, did not take her in his arms. He held his head in his hands.

She hadn't actually expected him to be happy. Yet this response, this cold fearfulness in him, took her by surprise. He was being a coward, she thought. She had been braver than he already. She had not cried, not once. They would just make a plan, she had thought.

Oh, *Ruth*, he said again. He clasped his hands around the back of his neck, bowed his head further.

Ruth rolled away from him, pulled the sheet and blankets up over her shoulders.

From downstairs, she heard a sudden burst of hilarity from Mary's radio.

She thought of the nights she had fallen asleep at the top of the stairs, waking cold in the morning, her knees pulled up under her nightgown. She thought of her father mowing the lawn the day he'd been shot, the way she had lifted her legs cooperatively out of his way. She thought about the policeman who had ruffled her hair when he'd dropped her off at the van Dusens' house that night.

Sorry, Doc, the policeman had said, as if she were a stray dog.

Go away, she said to Peter now.

Peter turned on the bed. She knew he was looking at her.

Ruth, he said. I'm sorry. I'll—

Get out, she said. Go away. I *hate* you.

He put a hand on her shoulder, but she flinched away from him. It was easy, at that moment. She actually hated him. How easy it was.

I don't ever want to see you again, she said. If you touch me, I'll scream.

Ruth, he tried again. Don't do this. We—

Get *away* from me, she said.

You don't mean it, he said then.

From downstairs, more laughter, then applause. Dance music drifted up the stairs.

Go away, Peter, she said. I mean it.

There was a long silence, and then the bed beside her rose slightly when he stood.

Please, he said. Ruth?

She said nothing.

Eventually she heard him leave the room. A little later, she thought she heard his footsteps, coming back. She sat up in bed, tears running down her face.

But there was no one there.

She couldn't believe it.

At the doctor's house in Boston where the abortion was performed, Ruth woke from a hazy sleep with fierce pain in her bowels and belly. She lay on a daybed in a room with tall windows and a dark dresser with a bowed front and a mirror in which she could see reflected a framed map—some ancient version of the world—behind glass. How had she gotten to this place? She had no memory of it. Her head felt sore, as if she'd had teeth pulled.

Around her, the house was silent. The door to the room stood ajar. With shaking hands she put on her underwear and her skirt and her stockings, which had been laid neatly on a small table. Her shoes had been placed side by side next to the bed.

Her legs wavered. The floor seemed to pitch. She put her head down between her knees, waited until her vision cleared.

There was no one in the back passage, no one in the large unlit kitchen to which the passage led. She had come to the back of the house, as instructed, earlier that day, and rung the bell just after noon. Now, making her way through a quiet kitchen and parlor, she realized that it was nearly dark outside. She had no idea how to find the back door again. She went through a deserted dining room into what she assumed was the front entrance.

Beside the front door in the shadowy hallway was a coat-rack on which hung a man's black raincoat. The door was flanked by twin panels of stained glass, extraordinarily rich in color, featuring the design of two peacocks, tails spread, flowers climbing up the borders.

Ruth, clutching her purse, her coat over her arm, stared at them, the minute depiction of tiny star-shaped blossoms around the clawed feet of the birds. As she stood there, a set of pocket doors leading to the hall slid open. A woman—middle-aged, her thick brown hair streaked with gray and parted on one side—emerged. Wordlessly, she crossed the hall, never looking once at Ruth; it was as if Ruth were invisible. She opened the front door and stepped aside, holding the door ajar.

If you have any difficulty, she said, you should go to a hospital. But you were never here. Remember that.

Dazed, breathless from the pain in her abdomen, Ruth hesitated. She understood that she was being dismissed, but she did not know how to ask about the pain, whether it was to be expected. As she passed the woman on her way outside, she saw the colors from the stained glass thrown eerily against her neck and face.

Her friend Ellie was waiting in the car on the street outside. It began to rain as Ruth opened the passenger door.

That took *forever*, Ellie said, when Ruth got in the car. Her face was terrified. I've been driving around the block for hours, Ellie said. You look awful. Are you all right?

Twenty-four hours later, Ruth was in bed, teeth chattering, delirious. At first she did not recognize Mary Healy, standing on her one foot in the door of her bedroom.

Mary had never climbed the stairs in all the years Ruth lived with her.

How did you get up here? Ruth said, lifting her head from the pillow.

Mary came in the room and put a hand on Ruth's forehead. When she pulled back the sheets, she gasped.

Ruth gaped down at the blood.

I'm calling Dr. van Dusen, Mary said. What happened, Ruth? What have you done?

After Ruth was released from the hospital, she was brought again to the van Dusens' house. Once again, she understood, there was nowhere else for her to go. Mary, ever more infirm, could not have been expected to cope.

At first, Ruth imagined that some sort of arrangement would be made, that the things she had said to Peter when she had told him she was pregnant would be taken back, that he would be there to care for her. Things would be explained to his parents; Ruth felt as much relief as fear at this idea. She had thought that her solution to the problem of the pregnancy—she did not call it a baby; that would come later, again and again, a grief that would flatten her for days at a time—had been a difficult but responsible one, a kindness to them all. She and Peter weren't ready to have a baby. Ruth wanted to go to college. She was going to make something of herself.

Peter would apologize. She would apologize.

She and Peter would be engaged, she thought, eventually married under the appropriate circumstances.

All would be forgiven and forgotten.

In fact, she learned later, she nearly died of the infection. At the van Dusens', back in the same bed in which she had spent the first days after her father's arrest five summers before, Ruth slept with a similar kind of exhaustion. Mrs. van Dusen brought meals to her, but she did not speak to Ruth. There was no discussion of the happy future that Ruth—foolishly, she finally realized—had imagined. Mrs. van Dusen herself looked terrible, her face puffy and ashen, her hair dull and dry.

Ruth had seen Mrs. van Dusen only a couple of times over the last few years. Peter's descriptions of his mother's illness had made Ruth feel sorry for them all: Mrs. van Dusen's frantic phone calls again and again throughout the day to Peter's father, her hours at church where she held the priests prisoner with her endless talking, the pacing in her bedroom, the hand flapping and the weeping, the raw, chapped skin at the corners of her mouth, the uncontrollable trembling . . . His mother's stays in the hospital seemed to help, Peter had reported, but the effect of the treatments never lasted.

All this, as well as Peter's descriptions of his father's patience, had worked against Ruth's anger at Mrs. van Dusen. Yet one morning when Mrs. van Dusen came in to bring Ruth a tray of tea and toast, Ruth sat up, determined.

Where's Peter? she said.

Mrs. van Dusen's face went rigid.

I didn't know what else to do, Ruth said. I want to know where Peter is.

But Mrs. van Dusen would not look at her.

I can't talk to you, Ruth, she said, her voice shaking. No one here is speaking to you. And then she left the room.

Ruth understood then that she and Peter were being separated. She would not be allowed to speak to him. The van Dusens did not, could not—would not ever—regard her as a daughter-in-law.

Ruth was not a wife for the van Dusens' son, she understood. She was not, as she had known all along, anybody at all.

That night, in her nightgown, gripping the edge of the sink in the upstairs bathroom—Peter already must have been sent away somewhere, she assumed, for the house had been funereally silent—she choked down two handfuls of orange-flavored baby aspirin she found in the medicine cabinet. They felt like dirt in her mouth as she chewed and swallowed them. She managed to get down everything in the bottle and then almost immediately vomited it all up.

Through the sound of her own retching, she heard footsteps hurrying up the stairs.

When she looked up from the sink, eyes streaming, stomach heaving, a mess of orange vomit in the basin and on the floor and running down the front of her nightgown, Dr. and Mrs. van Dusen were standing at the door of the bathroom.

What are we going to do with her? Mrs. van Dusen said. Oh, my god.

Dr. van Dusen stepped into the bathroom. He looked grim, but he rinsed a washcloth and helped Ruth, who was swaying, to sit down on the seat of the toilet.

Put your head between your knees, he said. He put his hand on the back of her head and pushed. For god's sake, Ruth, he said. For *god's* sake.

Years later, recounting the events of that terrible, sad summer for Dr. Wenning, Ruth could still remember the sensation inside her body that night, as if something too large for the space had been wedged into her chest and then ripped out, leaving a gaping hole. The pain of Peter's absence felt insupportable. It no longer mattered to her that he had gone away in cowardice when she had told him to. She missed him so fiercely she thought she could not go on. It was too painful.

Lying in the dark that night after swallowing the aspirin, after a shower and after swallowing the pill Dr. van Dusen held out to her—Take it, Ruth, he said, frowning at her. You need to sleep now—she could still smell traces of the orange-flavored baby aspirin clinging to her breath when she covered her face with her hands. Outside, she heard the rhythmic, sawing songs of tree frogs in the summer night, the percussion of the surf against the shoreline twenty blocks away. From downstairs, she heard the van Dusens' raised voices and then the sound of crying—Mrs. van Dusen, Ruth realized.

A minute later, music reached Ruth, a symphony drowning out the sound of the tree frogs and the beating of the ocean and the grief that Ruth had brought into the house.

She lay in bed in the dark.

She tried to think of what she loved in the world, to name those things.

She loved books.

She loved to eat, crumbling oyster crackers into clam chowder with Ellie.

She loved swimming in the ocean.

She loved her bedroom at Mary Healy's house, the sound of the waves, the strip of sea visible between the rooftops.

She loved Mary Healy, who had been good to her and who had climbed upstairs with only one foot to rescue her.

She had loved, she thought, her father, though he hadn't deserved it, though perhaps he hadn't even been her real father.

She turned her face aside into the pillow.

She loved Peter van Dusen.

As soon as the van Dusens discovered what had happened to Ruth, they confronted Peter, Ruth learned. He had confessed—

yes, he and Ruth had been seeing each other secretly for two years now. They sent him away without delay to relatives in New York City. He was to work for his uncle, who was a lawyer.

Dr. van Dusen arranged for Ruth to spend the remaining weeks of the summer after her recovery working for a friend who ran a camp in Vermont for blind children. For six weeks, Ruth sat in the camp nurse's office, a hot little room whose walls were beaded with amber sap. She read paperback novels and dispensed calamine lotion and applied Band-Aids to the knees and elbows of the poor blind children who came in so frequently with cuts and scrapes. She understood that tending to the children had been someone's idea of penance for her.

At night, left to her own devices, she went down to the lake and swam out far enough that she could not be heard if she cried.

She lay on her back, floating, and looked up at the moon and the clouds, feeling the pull of the water around her.

In a novel, she thought, the protagonist would want to die, would just drown herself. But the reality was actually far worse, she thought; she did not want to die, and yet it was so painful, being alive.

At the end of the summer, Dr. van Dusen returned to pick her up. Getting into the hot car in the pine-needle-filled parking lot, Ruth saw that all her belongings—her clothes and books, her winter coat and boots, everything from her five years at Mary Healy's—had been packed up.

She understood that she would not return to Mary Healy's or to Wells.

What had happened to Mary? she asked Dr. van Dusen. Who was taking care of her?

She's gone to one of her daughters, Dr. van Dusen told her. She had lost her other foot.

I want to write to her, Ruth said.

Dr. van Dusen nodded. I'll give you her address.

For the remainder of the car trip from Putney to Northampton, they exchanged fewer than a dozen words. Ruth did not ask about Peter, and Dr. van Dusen did not offer her any information.

Mostly, she pretended to be asleep.

Ruth's roommate at Smith, a cheerful-seeming blond girl named Louise, had already moved in by the time Ruth and Dr. van Dusen appeared in the door of the room to which Ruth had been assigned in Talbot House. Louise had scattered her belongings everywhere. She talked enough for all three of them, exclaiming with false enthusiasm over Ruth's modest clothes as Ruth opened her suitcases.

Dr. van Dusen stood by silently.

Finally, clearly aware of the tension in the room, Louise left to go see a friend from home who, she said, lived on another floor.

Dr. van Dusen went to the door and looked out into the hall for a minute after Louise left. When he turned back, he pulled the door behind him, but he did not close it all the way.

That opening—as if people would find it odd to discover

them in a room with the door closed, Ruth thought—filled her with anger.

The time had come for them to say good-bye. She understood that she would probably never see him again. She turned away from him, staring blindly into her closet. She would not cry in front of him, she thought.

When he spoke she heard pain in his voice.

Don't worry about your bills, he said. I am not abandoning you, Ruth. I'll see that you have money, whatever you need.

Ruth said nothing.

Everyone makes mistakes, he went on. You and Peter made a mistake, a natural mistake for young people to make. It just . . . it had a sad outcome.

She did not think she could stand to hear any more.

But still he went on. I know you were fond of each other, he said. You and Peter. But you're young. You'll go on.

Yes, she *had* made a mistake, she thought, going to that doctor.

She had made a mistake, taking those baby aspirin.

She had made just about every sort of mistake there was.

That awful night, as she'd sat on the seat of the toilet in the bathroom in her soiled nightgown, Ruth had begged Dr. and Mrs. van Dusen.

Where is Peter? she had said. I want to see *Peter.*

You ended a *life,* Ruth, Mrs. van Dusen had said suddenly, fiercely, from the doorway. She had leaned toward Ruth, her face contorted as if she would spit on Ruth, and Ruth had understood then that no one had forgotten about Ruth's father, either, about the lives he had ended.

You'll see, Ruth, Dr. van Dusen said now from behind her in her dormitory room. But his voice was sad, and she knew he didn't believe it himself.

You'll forget all about this one day, he said.

8

We were introduced in college, Ruth told people later, when they asked how she and Peter met.

Or sometimes she said: Oh, we were set up on a date.

Neither of these statements, she thought, was actually a lie.

In the winter of 1957, by then a senior at Smith, Ruth celebrated her twenty-second birthday. She had a group of friends and plans to go to New York after graduation, where she hoped to find a job in publishing. She'd majored in English. She thought herself a pretty good writer.

One Saturday afternoon that December, someone knocked on Ruth's door in Talbot House. Ruth looked up from her book.

Sally Carlisle, who lived down the hall from Ruth, stuck her head around the doorframe.

Did Ruth want to come along that night on a double date? she asked.

Two Harvard boys, one of them an old chum of Sally's from back home, were on their way, driving over from Cambridge.

Sally had told them she'd find another girl to go along to a party.

Ruth looked out the window. The air was smoky, full of fluffy clumps of snowflakes. She thought about Peter at Harvard, of course. But he would never come over to Northampton on a *blind date*, she thought. Not after what had happened between them.

She hadn't seen him since their last night together, when he'd sat on the side of her bed at Mary Healy's, holding his head in his hands.

It's snowing again, she said to Sally, putting down her pencil and her copy of Horace's *Ars Poetica*. She leaned across the bed and touched her finger to the cold glass of the window. As always when she thought about Peter, there was a war inside her. She missed him. She could not forgive him. She loved him. She hated him.

They won't come in the snow, anyway, she said.

Oh, it's only a *little* snow, Sally protested. And they're already on their way. Come on, Ruth. It'll be fun. Be a sport.

Ruth gazed out the window. In some ways, the years before she had entered Smith seemed far away now, a time from someone else's life. Those years had seen the end of so much, her strange, sad life with her father, her father's fate in prison, her love affair with Peter—its beginning and its end—the terrible abortion . . .

It was possible for Ruth to feel sometimes that those events had nothing at all to do with her. She had made up a story about her past: her parents, Carl and Anita, had been killed in an automobile accident. One tragedy was just like another, she thought. She could tell Carl and Anita's story with some ease now when people asked her about her family. Yet if listeners responded with tears at the news of Carl and Anita's tragic death, the loneliness of the untold story inside Ruth made her stomach hurt.

No one, she believed, wanted to hear the *true* story of her life.

Now she looked back to Sally, waiting impatiently in the doorway of Ruth's room.

Outside, the snow hissed against the window, falling through the bare branches of the trees, over the grass, over the wet, dark line of the street.

Sally clasped her hands, a parody of longing. I *promised* I'd find another girl, she said.

Ruth watched the snowflakes swirling in the milky late-afternoon air. She would need to wash and set her hair. She had studying to do. She didn't want to go on a date.

Who is he, anyway? she said. The other fellow.

Sally hadn't been told his name.

But I'm sure he's nice, she said. He's got to be smart, anyway.

Well, there were men other than Peter van Dusen in the world, Ruth thought. She had gone on very few dates over her years at Smith, but there had to be *someone* to whom she could tell the truth about her past, someone she could know and be known by, someone else she might love one day and who would love her back.

Okay, she said to Sally. But I'll need clothes.

She borrowed a dress of champagne-colored chiffon from Sally's roommate, Barb. She knew it was somehow wrong with her red hair, and she'd need to let out the hem, which would leave a line, but it would have to do, she thought, looking at herself over her shoulder in the mirror in Sally and Barb's room. She had no extra money for clothes. Apart from buying her books for her first semester at Smith, she'd hardly touched the money Dr. van Dusen had written to tell her was in an account for her use. She'd feared she would need it more after she graduated.

Instead she had worked at the library and in the museum. She'd sewn costumes for the theater department, a skill she'd learned from Mary Healy. Other girls, aware that Ruth had no family, gave her clothes from time to time, castoff coats, shoes, or blouses they said were just wrong on them but would look marvelous on Ruth. The gestures embarrassed Ruth, but she accepted the offerings when she'd sensed it would cause offense not to do so. People wanted to be kind.

A few minutes before the boys were due to arrive she bit off the thread between her teeth and shook out the pleats in Barb's dress. She put it on, reaching to zip it up in the back. She brushed her hair lightly, careful not to pull out the wave. She crouched a little to see her reflection better in the mirror. She applied lipstick, patted her nose with powder.

She would not think about Peter van Dusen.

She carried her coat over her arm, as well as a clutch and pair of gloves borrowed from Sally.

Her father had been a murderer and a thief, and her mother was a mystery. But Ruth was . . . well, she thought, she was a young woman at Smith College in the state of Massachusetts.

She would be a famous editor one day . . . or a scholar of

some kind, a professor of art history, maybe, or perhaps a pianist or a painter. She hadn't decided yet which it would be. But first she would go out that evening and have a date, a triumph of will over desire.

You look gorgeous, Sally said, blowing her a kiss from the doorway. See you downstairs. They're waiting.

From the landing halfway down the staircase, one could see through an archway in the hall into the sitting room.

Sally and her date—a hawk-nosed boy wearing a tweed jacket, a ridiculous-looking meerschaum pipe clamped in his mouth—were standing in front of the tiled fireplace.

On the sofa sat a tall young man reading a newspaper, his knees sticking up. One brown sock had slipped down around his ankle.

Ruth stopped. Heat flooded her. In her ears, a clanging sound began.

Peter's hair had been cut short. Gone were the soft, wheat-colored bangs that had fallen over his forehead. Lamplight lay against the exposed back of his neck and across his shoulders. He looked half a foot taller and a decade older than when Ruth had last seen him.

Ruth put out her hand and steadied herself against the banister. The rail felt slick under her palm. Wild joy ran through her.

Peter looked up. He dropped the newspaper. Then he stood up slowly.

Ruth, he said. *Ruth.*

Sally's date gazed back and forth between Ruth and Peter. He took the pipe out of his mouth.

You two know each other or something? he said.

The sitting room at Talbot House was furnished with brown wicker armchairs, standing lamps whose pleated shades were the color of old parchment, rickety gateleg tables where the girls sat to study or to knit and chat or play cards. Heavy plaid curtains hung at the windows. On the mantelpiece stood a stuffed fox, eyes glittering, and a white ermine, perched on its hind legs and lifting a dainty paw, alert in death as in life, both animals a gift from someone, the oddball husband or father or uncle of an alum, someone who had once lived in Talbot. On little pieces of paper tented next to the creatures, a girl had written the names Lucy and Ricky. The ermine sometimes wore a garter around its neck like an Elizabethan ruff, but not tonight, Ruth noticed. With its paw raised, the ermine stared out over Ruth's head.

From the stairwell and the dining room below came the sounds of supper, the rise and fall of girlish chatter. Ruth caught the familiar scent of Saturday night dinner, navy bean soup and gingerbread cookies.

Paradise Pond on campus had been frozen solid for a week. The day before, Ruth had gone with some other girls to push and be pushed unsteadily across the ice in her shoes, laughing hysterically, arms waving. She had no skates and had never learned, anyway, but it hadn't mattered. The snow lay beautifully around them as if painted on the arms of the fir trees.

This was the world to which she had miraculously ascended,

Ruth had thought, she and her fictitious past, her imaginary young parents killed tragically in a car accident: pretty Anita and handsome Carl, both botanists, Ruth had decided. Early on in her days at Smith, Ruth had gone alone to the Botanic Garden to read the plant labels and memorize the names: *Adonis amurensis Fukujukai*, which flowered early, even in the snow. *Abutilon* x *hybridum*, the flowering maple or Chinese lantern. *Aconitum japonicum*, Japanese monkshood.

She'd known nothing about botany, but it was not difficult to imagine a shared history among plants with names derived from Southeast Asia, and it had been easy to invent trips for her specimen-gathering parents to the archipelago of Japanese islands, where they'd wandered the canals lined with willow trees or bathed in the hot springs in the snow-covered mountains, feeding one another sea urchin and black rice from chopsticks. One rainy afternoon, Ruth had sat in the Conservatory for a couple of hours and drawn the orchids with colored pencils, signing the drawings in tiny script—she'd carefully canted the letters backward, unlike her own forward-sloping penmanship—with her fictitious mother's fictitious initials.

It had been work to invent a past, though not much, it had turned out. It had been more difficult to know when to stop, in fact. How tempting it was to imagine what she had never had but had longed for: her mother's famous chicken and rice casserole and Black Forest cake, her father's skill on the dance floor.

In the sitting room of Talbot House now, Peter—Peter who *knew* her, who knew everything about her—looked up at her.

She had forgotten what it was, to be known.

Peter did not move. She knew he awaited her judgment,

THE LAST FIRST DAY

and that a judgment was forming inside her, though she did not yet see its sentence. She wondered what would happen if she just turned around and went back up the stairs. Would he follow her?

She could see, at least, that he was as shocked as she was.

Well, it was a *blind* date. She supposed he hadn't been told *her* name, either.

She thought about Carl and Anita, the depth of love she'd imagined between them. Browsing one day in an antiques shop in Northampton, she had found an album of old photographs, its heavy leather cover embossed with a fleur-de-lis, and she had slipped from its pages two pictures: Carl and Anita leaving the church, both smiling happily, one of Anita's tiny gloved hands on Carl's arm, one raised against a shower of confetti. The other was a picture of Carl and Anita and infant Ruth, the baby's bonneted face invisible, her christening gown in a drape over Anita's lap, Carl's hand on Anita's shoulder.

A Christmas tree had been behind them in that photograph, the electric lights little blurs.

Ruth had known it wasn't real, of course—wasn't *her*—but sometimes she took out that photograph and stared at the baby.

She'd had to produce the pictures only a few times over the last several years, carefully rewrapping them in tissue paper afterward and tucking them away again in her drawer. She had been moved, doing this, had found herself near tears.

She had depended on Carl and Anita, she knew, the mute testimony of the anonymous photographs. She had come in some way to love their story, these two young people who had adored and admired each other, and who had loved her, too,

243

who had loved a world of curling vine and tendril, of blossom and leaf, of greenhouses filled with scented flowers and cool dirt, warm air from the heaters high overhead stirring the fern-like leaves of the towering cycad.

On the stairs now, her feet seemed to have disappeared beneath her. Yet somehow she descended the final steps.

She came into the room.

Peter held out his hand and she came forward and took it.

When they touched, Peter held tight to her fingers, and for one more moment she thought of Carl and Anita, whoever they really were, as they'd left the church that day after their wedding, heading into the future together.

Then she let them go. She wanted to let them go. She had never really known them, never really loved them, she knew.

How are you, Ruth? Peter said.

Fine, she said. Her face felt strange, rigidly grinning. How are you?

Then she took her hand away and fished frantically in the little clutch Sally had loaned her for her handkerchief, because she had begun to cry. She pressed the handkerchief to her eyes.

Excuse me, she said from behind it, but it was the joy she knew was on her face that she was trying to hide.

From his position at the fireplace, Sally's date put his arm around Sally and pointed at Peter and Ruth with his pipe.

Well! he said. That's what I call a reunion.

They went to the party with Sally and Ed, as it turned out the pipe-smoking date was named. A crowd of people milled in someone's apartment—Ruth didn't even know where they were; the snow-filled night had gone past the car windows in a blur—with everyone smoking and drinking and laughing. Ruth heard nothing of the conversations going on around her. People kept shaking her arm and shouting things.

What? she would say, turning to them, feeling dazed. *What?*

Finally, after a few minutes of Ruth and Peter staring at each other across the room, Peter made a gesture; he would go find their coats.

Ruth ducked into a bathroom. A narrow shelf above the sink was crowded with bottles of perfume and lotion, talcum powder spilled messily over a woman's kimono draped over a radiator. The room smelled girlishly sweet.

She stared at herself in the mirror.

Was this really happening? she thought.

Outside, she and Peter stopped on the sidewalk under the cone of light from a streetlamp and turned to face each other, snow falling fast around them. They were almost the same height, Ruth only a few inches shorter than Peter. Snow settled on his shoulders, his collar, his hair.

Tonight, she said. Did you know it would be me?

He shook his head. It's not the first time I've tried to find you, he said, but I was just as surprised as you were.

Ruth blinked against the snow falling onto her eyelashes. *What?* she said.

A bunch of times this fall, Peter was saying. Last year, too, and the year before.

She felt the air around them, colder than it had been earlier. He reached out and took her hand, laced her fingers between his own.

She had not been wrong, she thought. All those times she had somehow *felt* him near her . . . she had imagined that it was just a kind of wishing on her part.

He was still talking.

I came as often as I could get here, he said. I don't have a car, so it was whenever someone was coming from Boston, and I could get a ride.

Wait, she thought.

I saw you four times this year, he was saying. Once going into the library, once on the sidewalk in Northampton outside the post office—you were eating an ice cream cone—once on the steps of the Hillyer, once in the Botanic Garden. You were with another girl in the garden, a blonde, much shorter than you. You had on a blue dress that time.

He gestured to her neck, indicating a shape.

Her blue dress with the sailor collar, she thought.

The suffering of the last three years, the loneliness of it, came up inside her. She took her hand away.

He had been here, he had seen her. He had not spoken to her.

Her ears started to ring. She put her hands up to her head and closed her eyes.

I thought you hated me, Ruth, he said, and she heard the pleading in his voice.

I didn't know if you would ever speak to me again, he said. Ruth, take your hands away from your ears. Look at me. I didn't know what to do. I know I made a terrible mistake. All this time, I've hated myself.

He took her hands away from her head and held them in his own.

Please, he said. Please don't tell me to go away, Ruth.

She allowed herself to fall against him—she had felt it happening inside her, like sliding down a mountain—her head resting against his chest.

He put his arms tightly around her. Oh, my god, he said.

Don't cry, she said warningly.

I won't, he said, but she knew he was.

And she was, too.

At the familiar feel of his body against hers, in the smell of his skin, in his presence again, she could not bear the remembered loss of him. His long wool overcoat against her cheek was silky.

What if it *hadn't* been me? she said. Tonight?

I didn't think it *would* be you, he said. Ed just said he was coming—he had a date with this girl he knew from home—and he asked me to come along. I'd taken every chance I could get. I always thought I would see you again, and that one day I'd have the nerve to talk to you.

When you came down the stairs? he said. I couldn't believe it. I just couldn't believe it.

Ed had given Peter the keys to the car. Apparently delighted to play witness to Peter and Ruth's meeting again, he said he'd take care of getting Sally back to Talbot House and hitch a ride with someone back to Boston. Peter drove out of town in the snow until they found a motel outside of Northampton, a place with a sad yellow light over the office door and a frozen pond next door. Ruth had to hunch down in the front seat of the car, watching Peter through the motel's picture window, while he paid the owner inside and was given a key. In those days, at certain places, they wouldn't let a couple stay if they weren't married. People had to produce rings for that sort of thing.

She'd be in trouble for failing to turn up for curfew at Talbot House, she thought, but the snow was a good excuse. She would just say she'd been stranded somewhere, that the phone had been out of order.

It wasn't as if there was anyone to whom the house matron could call and report Ruth's misbehavior, anyway.

In the motel room, a painting of a stormy sea, the frame visibly sticky with dust, hung over the bed.

Peter closed the door behind them.

There was a prickly green bedspread on the bed.

It's a cliché, Ruth said. It's horrible.

She put her hands over her face.

Peter took off his coat and wrapped her in it, then in his arms.

It was freezing in the room. They got under the blankets, but they didn't take off their clothes. Everything that had happened between them was in the room with them, everything they had lost.

They kissed, holding on to each other.

I'm sorry, Ruth, Peter kept saying to her. I'm sorry.

He held her face, stroked her hair. When she began to cry

again, he extricated an arm from their embrace to retrieve a handkerchief from his back pocket.

It's all right now, he said. Don't cry.

Later, she woke. She'd been asleep, she realized, but something had woken her. A sound outside? Then she realized what it was. Not a sound, but quiet. The snow must still be falling.

Beside her, Peter spoke. Are you awake?

She turned to face him. She couldn't believe it. There he was.

He rolled toward her and brought his forehead down to touch hers. Ruth. Will you marry me? he said.

Okay, Ruth said. Yes.

Then she started to cry again.

I'm not ever going to be able to remember anything about our life without feeling sad, she said.

He found his handkerchief, handed it to her.

We're going to be happy, Peter said. I love you, Ruth. I've always loved you, and I always will love you.

I can't stand it, he said after a minute, watching her cry. What I did to you.

Stop, Ruth said. She rolled over and blew a breath toward the ceiling, patting her cheeks. She made herself stop crying.

It's enough, she said. We did it to each other.

Later, when she woke again. Peter lay next to her on his side. His arms were around her.

I thought I'd dreamed this, she said.

He kissed her. No dream, he said. Promise.

• • •

At some point over the long night, he told her that he'd been at Yale the day before, where he was applying to the doctoral program in American history. After the interviews, walking back to the university's guesthouse in the bitter cold, he'd stepped into one of the chapels on campus to get out of the wind.

I just sat there, Peter said. I thought about all the letters I'd written to you and never mailed. I thought about all the times I'd seen you but been too afraid to speak to you. But I knew I had to try again. Even if you still hated me, I had to know that.

The next morning, he said, he had taken the train back to Boston, and the friend who had picked him up at South Station—that had been Ed—had said to him, Hold on to your hat, Pete old pal. We're going to Northampton.

It just felt like a sign, Peter said. Like I was being given another chance.

He pulled Ruth against him.

And there you were, on the stairs, he said. More beautiful than ever.

What will happen, Ruth said. What will happen when we tell your mother?

Peter rolled onto his back, pulling her with him.

Well, she's not—, he started. She watched him look up at the ceiling.

She's not exactly . . . anyone we know anymore, he said.

Ruth rested her head against his chest. She thought about Mrs. van Dusen, about how clean she had kept the house and garden, about her chapped lips and trembling mouth, about how she had dressed up on Sunday mornings to go to church. She'd worn a little hat with a veil, and white gloves.

Does she still go to church? she asked. She remembered Peter's accounts of his mother's increasingly bizarre behavior, her daily visits to the Catholic church and the hours spent on her knees, her distress.

Someone usually takes her to Mass when she's home, Peter said. Or my father will do it, if she says she wants to go. They have friends—really, my father's friends—who come by and pick her up. But it's just . . . she's just going through the motions. Or else it upsets her.

They lay in silence for a while.

Then Peter said, She's mostly at the place now, where she gets the treatments. When she comes home, she's . . .

He stopped again, and then he drummed lightly on Ruth's shoulder with his fingertips. He didn't finish the sentence.

Ruth thought about the night in the bathroom at the van Dusens', the terrible taste of the aspirin in her mouth, the look on Mrs. van Dusen's face.

I'm sorry, Peter said. She wasn't—she isn't—a bad person.

She hated me, Ruth said.

She didn't hate you, Peter said. But I know it looked like that. She was just—I don't know. Afraid of everything.

I know, Ruth said. I know that. I could tell, even from the beginning, I think. Only I didn't know what it was, that she was sick.

Someday we'll forgive her, Peter said.

Ruth turned her head to look at him.

I'll try, she said. To forgive her.

Me, too, Peter said.

Later, though, Ruth thought it was a blessing that they

decided to wait until the end of the academic year before telling his parents, that in fact Peter's mother died before hearing
the news that Peter and Ruth had found each other again and
intended to marry. An autopsy showed that her death was the
result of a ventricular dysfunction, Dr. van Dusen told Peter, the
defect present but undiagnosed all along. A seizure induced by
the electroconvulsive therapy triggered an episode of arrhyth-
mia from which Mrs. van Dusen's heart failed to recover.

When Peter finally brought Ruth home with the news that
they would marry, Dr. van Dusen—who looked to Ruth sad
and terribly thin—embraced her.

I'm glad, Ruth, he said. I'm so glad.

Peter was admitted to Yale's graduate program, and Ruth and
Peter moved to New Haven immediately after their commence-
ments. Peter gave Ruth an engagement ring; they would marry,
they decided, the next spring, in 1958.

Don't you just want to get married now? Peter had
asked her.

I want to do things the way *normal* people get to do them,
Ruth had said. I want to be an engaged person for a while, with
people congratulating me.

On a windy, rainy Saturday afternoon a few weeks before
the wedding, Ruth arrived at Dr. Wenning's office for work,
as usual. By then, she had been working for Dr. Wenning for
several months. She had already told her the story of her life.
Something about Dr. Wenning—her own tragedy, probably,
Ruth thought—had made it impossible to tell her the fib about

the young, beautiful, fake botanist parents killed in an automobile accident.

Ruth hadn't even hesitated before telling her the truth.

That Saturday, Ruth came in to Dr. Wenning's outer office, taking off her raincoat and stepping out of her shoes, which were soaked. She hung her raincoat on the coatrack and went to the door of Dr. Wenning's study.

Dr. Wenning was seated at her desk. She looked up.

Nice weather for the ducks, she said. I thought you might not come.

An enormous, expensive-looking box tied with a wide green silk ribbon was propped on the extra armchair chair across from the desk.

Ruth looked at it.

Yes, yes. It's for you, Dr. Wenning said, following Ruth's gaze. She took off her glasses. Who else?

She put her glasses back on and pantomimed peering around comically, as if she might have overlooked someone standing in the shadows.

Open it! she said.

Ruth had wanted a wedding dress, but she had confessed that, under the circumstances, the usual sort of wedding gown—seed pearls and Alençon lace and cascades of white chiffon—seemed foolish. She would feel ridiculous in such a costume, she'd said.

I'm not exactly . . . you know, she had said, a virgin in white.

Dr. Wenning had waved a hand.

Virgin, *schmirgin*, she said. Who cares? You think all those girls in white are virgins?

The box on the chair was full of pale blue tissue paper. Ruth peeled back the layers. Inside was folded a dove gray suit and a matching pillbox hat with a dotted veil. The material was full of watery light.

Ruth lifted out the jacket and held it against her. It was beautiful.

Across the desk, Dr. Wenning took off her glasses again.

Good color for a redhead, she said.

She replaced her glasses and folded her hands over her belly.

Who wants to be a virgin, anyway? she said. They have a terrible life, those virgins, someone always trying to sacrifice them.

Ruth could not speak.

Never mind, never mind . . . Dr. Wenning waved her away. I have no daughter, as you know, she said. So . . . it is my pleasure.

They were words Dr. Wenning said a lot.

It was always her pleasure to listen to Ruth, or to give her a book, or a record album, or to pick up the check at dinner.

Let us go have some refreshment, she would say, hooking her arm in Ruth's as they were leaving her office on Saturday afternoons, and she would buy them pie and coffee at the deli across the street, or a draft ale at a bar.

After a while, Ruth realized she had begun saying it, too.

My pleasure, she said to Peter, when he thanked her for bringing him a sandwich at the library, or ironing his shirt, or typing a paper for him.

When he leaned his head against her shoulder in gratitude,

or hugged her, or held her face and kissed her, she thought: My pleasure. My pleasure.

Ruth and Peter were married on a Sunday morning in early May under the Apse Memorial Windows in the Battell Chapel at Yale. Ruth carried a bouquet of yellow daffodils. The party was small.

Dr. Wenning was in attendance, along with Dr. van Dusen and Peter's thesis advisor from Yale, an elderly, stooped scholar from England with whom Peter had a formal but affectionate relationship. Two of Peter's friends from Yale stood with him, and Ruth's friend Marnie Lawrence drove down to New Haven from Northampton, where she had stayed after college to work in the Neilson Library.

The day was misty and cool, the scent of lilacs in the air.

The group lunched afterward at Mory's Temple Bar, where they had the Cream of Baker Soup and lamb chops.

Ruth drank too much champagne, for which she had a weakness.

That afternoon, she and Peter drove in Dr. Wenning's car, loaned to them for the occasion, to Cape Cod, where they had rented a cottage for the weekend.

Ruth fell asleep in the car and woke only when they left the paved road to rumble along the bumpy track to the beach.

Opening the car door when they stopped before the cottage, Ruth took in the familiar smell of the ocean. It was dark, the night sky star-strewn. She sat for a moment, breathing deeply.

They carried their bags inside. The cottage smelled of mildew, and Ruth opened the windows and pulled back the bedspreads to air the sheets.

Then they put on sweaters and took a blanket from one of the narrow little twin beds and went out to the beach. The wind was very strong. Ruth shivered under the blanket, and Peter shifted to sit behind her, wrapping his arms around her and resting his chin on her head.

The sound of the surf was too loud for conversation. Ruth watched the whitecaps on the water in the moonlight. She felt as she usually did at the edge of the ocean, both thrilled and a little frightened. She also felt very young and very old at the same time. It had been a long road, getting to this point, she thought.

She tilted back her head to look at Peter.

He leaned down, as if she'd said something.

What? he said.

She shook her head.

She thought, but did not say: I am afraid of loving you this much.

He kissed her. She could still taste the curry on his breath, from the Cream of Baker Soup at lunch.

There had been no one to give Ruth away at the chapel that morning, but she had told Peter that she didn't mind.

She didn't want to be *given* away, anyway.

I'm not an object, she said. I give *myself* to you, she told him.

In fact, she said, I fling myself at you.

That sounds good, he said. Please do.

Later, in one of the little twin beds, which they had pushed together, he said, You won't ever leave me, will you?

No, Ruth said. I won't.

9

When Peter was offered a job teaching at the Derry School, he and Ruth bought their first car for the trip, a used Ford station wagon with wood-paneled sides. Peter drove and Ruth held the map on her lap, following their route up the coast through Connecticut and Massachusetts and Rhode Island and into Maine. Wyeth, a decrepit mill settlement of gray-shingled houses and a brick factory, was one of the last towns on the map, nearly at the Canadian border. The buildings, close by the road's shoulder, had a despairing look.

Despite her high spirits when they'd set off before dawn from New Haven that morning, Ruth felt another of the waves of trepidation that had been assailing her ever since Peter had accepted the job.

Who knew whether they would be happy in this place?

Peter had been elated by the offer, which had come to him through a friend at the Divinity School in New Haven.

Though he could have taught at the college level—he'd had

two offers, in fact—Derry's mission of educating impoverished boys in the wilderness appealed to him.

Ruth had been less certain.

It's in the middle of nowhere, she'd said at one point. And what do you know about tree chopping or woodworking, anyway?

I'll learn, Peter said.

And they'll all be desperately needy, Ruth said.

They'll be orphans and hoodlums. Peter seemed cheerful about this fact.

Ruth had felt stung by his reference to orphans. It wasn't like him, to make light of the circumstances of her life. Finally she'd said, Well, just don't come near me with any buzz saw.

In bed that night, she had lain next to him, pretending sleep.

I know you're not asleep, Ruth, Peter had said finally into the darkness.

He'd rolled over to face her. I was teasing, he said. About the orphans. I'm sorry.

I know, she said, but she wouldn't turn toward him.

After a minute, Peter reached over and rested his hand on her rib cage, gave her a little squeeze.

She was afraid, she knew, of what lay ahead. Peter would be brilliant; of that, she was sure. But she had so little confidence in herself. What would *she* do? Would she make any friends? It was always so complicated, carrying around this story about her past.

Peter nuzzled close to her, pulling her hips into him.

Don't worry, he said, and she had to close her eyes shut against the tears suddenly there.

They'll love you, he said.

I'm not worried, she said.

But when they made love that night, she wept, as she sometimes did.

It was true, she knew, that being abandoned—not once, but twice, if you counted both the mother who had given her up and the father who had gone to jail—was an indisputable tragedy in her life. Sometimes she thought about the woman who had given birth to her, imagined that she, like Ruth, longed to be reunited, mother and daughter. But mostly she didn't like thinking about it, about whatever had made the woman who was her mother give away her baby. The idea of it was too close to the abortion Ruth had needed to choose for herself.

At least I'm lucky about Peter, she'd said to Dr. Wenning.

Dr. Wenning had agreed.

Ruth knew that Dr. Wenning thought Peter was the universe's way of providing compensation for Ruth's earlier suffering. She thought Dr. Wenning had a little crush on Peter, and she accused Peter of encouraging this. He brought Dr. Wenning flowers, offered his arm in a gentlemanly fashion when the three of them went out to a concert or to dinner, as they occasionally did.

You don't *always* have to be so chivalrous, Peter, Ruth said to him once. It gets on a person's nerves, you know.

Fine, he said. I'll do my best to be hateful.

But he would never be hateful, Ruth knew. He was the most well-intentioned person she had ever met.

From Wyeth, the road to the Derry School passed through a forest of white pine and hemlock and yellow birch, the sunlight filtering daintily through the leaves. A few miles to the east, too far away to be visible through the trees, lay the plain of the Atlantic Ocean.

She had been glad they would be near the ocean again.

Reading about that part of the country before they'd arrived, Ruth had discovered that the twigs of the birches along the roadside could be broken off and chewed for their distinct wintergreen flavor. That day, the windows of their car rolled down, Ruth detected the scent, so bracing she could almost taste it.

As they approached the campus through the forest, the atmosphere around them gradually brightened. Then the peaceful, sun-struck lawns of the school appeared around a bend in the road: a jumble of roofs, the sweep of the old oaks' branches, the diamond patterns of paths faceting the lawns.

It had been a sight so surprising, so magical, that both she and Peter gasped.

Peter whistled. Not so shabby, he said. Pretty nice for those orphans.

Ruth shot him a look, but she, too, was enchanted.

If she couldn't be happy here, she thought, she couldn't be happy anywhere.

Their first apartment was above one of the stone garages, a big room with a kitchen counter and appliances along one wall under a series of transom windows, and a tiny bathroom with an old claw-footed tub. The room was furnished with a double bed and an uncomfortable mattress, too short for both of them, and two windows with a view of the small lake. They arranged their table, a maple drop-leaf that seated the two of them, beneath one of the windows. Ruth loved looking out at the water when they ate their meals.

In a dormered attic above the big room, Peter set up his desk and typewriter, an Underwood Noiseless.

Ruth fell asleep many nights that first year to the dampened sound of its keys being struck as Peter worked on his lesson plans over her head.

Their housing at Derry was provided as part of Peter's salary. For the first time in her life, Ruth didn't need to work. In New Haven, she'd held three jobs, one as a part-time secretary in the biology department at Yale, and another on two evenings a week at Filene's, where she'd sat behind the perfume counter on a stool—her supervisor didn't like her towering over the customers—garbed in a white clinician's coat that had made her feel absurdly important. And once a week on Saturdays she had ridden her bicycle across the Green to work for Dr. Wenning, though often all they did after a while was talk.

That first fall at Derry, while Peter taught his classes and went to meetings and ran around coaching the boys on the basketball court, Ruth began work on a novel. She sat at their little table and wrote by hand, eating toast and drinking tea, looking up between sentences and watching the reflection of the trees in the surface of the lake as the leaves changed color. She had studied American literature at Smith, had loved it all indiscriminately—Willa Cather and Whitman, Emerson and Thoreau.

But it was difficult, she discovered. The struggle of it wore her out. Still, she tried to feel hopeful. She swept and polished their rooms, she washed and ironed Peter's shirts and undershorts and khaki pants and handkerchiefs, she sewed skirts and dresses for herself, and she cooked dinner every night—dishes overly ambitious and too expensive for just the two of them, duck à l'orange and lasagna with a béchamel sauce and standing rib roasts. She wrote detailed letters about her life to Dr. Wenning and to the few friends from Smith with whom she had kept in touch.

They were all married, these friends, like Ruth.

Two had had a baby already, and another was pregnant. Ruth tried not to mind about that.

So far she had not been able to get pregnant.

Pregnant *again*, she sometimes reminded herself, and then sat alone in the bathroom, the water running, so Peter would not hear her cry.

A novel! her friends said by reply. How exciting.

Yes, and I'm trying a play, too! Ruth said in her letters back. And I'm also painting! And I have time to play the piano! I'm definitely improving.

But she could not avoid the worrying sense that she was casting about wildly for something to do that felt meaningful, that her protestations to her friends and to Dr. Wenning were an unconvincing disguise for the loneliness she felt.

• • •

A few weeks after classes began at Derry that first fall, Ruth and Peter were invited to a cocktail party at the headmaster's house. Ruth agonized over what to wear. Finally she chose a long, gold-colored quilted skirt she'd found at the Junior League Thrift Shop in New Haven and had thought very grand. That evening, glancing into the headmaster's living room from the front hall—the house that would become her own ten years later, when Peter himself was offered and accepted the position—she saw instantly that the skirt was wrong.

The other women in the room, though there were only a handful of them, wives of teachers, were dressed for the party in trim, short dresses and pantsuits.

A smile plastered to her face, her long red hair pinned up fussily, Ruth shivered as Peter lifted her coat from her shoulders and made introductions. Her bibbed white blouse, too, was wrong, wrong, wrong, she thought. She looked like Miles Standish.

Ruth's working on a novel, Peter announced proudly as they all stood around with their drinks in hand. It's going to be terrific.

She wanted to die.

By the first Christmas at Derry she had begun to dread the parties.

The handful of wives who lived on campus often left these affairs early, if they came at all, to go home and fix dinner for their children. There weren't many women at the school who were her age to begin with, and the few who were seemed to

Ruth bewilderingly angry, full of complaints—when Ruth ran into them at the post office or the grocery store in Wyeth—about the school or their children or their husbands or the boys.

It was true that many of the boys *were* trouble. It was part of the school's mission, after all, to educate those who'd had no opportunity to prepare for it. Ruth understood from Peter that there were teachers who felt the place was beneath them. She knew, too, that Peter's enthusiasm for the challenge—his credentials were strong enough to have won him a job almost anywhere—was a mystery to some.

For Peter, she understood, teaching was a source of happiness. He was energized by the boys and by their rough ways. He tended to see the best in people, and he came home full of stories about their triumphs in the classroom, delighted by the ways in which he saw their lives being shaped for good. He rarely doubted that a boy would succeed, and somehow, Ruth thought, his certainty communicated itself to them. At dinner he regaled her with stories about them, their misdeeds and their achievements.

Don't you ever *dislike* any of them? Ruth asked once, feeling peevish.

I don't like what they *do*, sometimes, Peter said. But I try not to dislike *them*.

Well, Ruth said, *I* dislike some of them.

I know you do, he said. But they think *you're* fetching.

Try harder to make friends, Dr. Wenning told her, when she went back to New Haven to visit and confessed that she was lonely.

Why don't you have a tea party or something?

I can't have a tea party, Ruth said. There's no one to invite. For a *party* you need more than one guest.

Okay. Have someone for dinner, Dr. Wenning said. Just one person. Make one of those fancy dinners you've been working so hard on.

Ruth went back to Derry and tried to strike up a friendship with an English teacher at the school, a spinster named Ann Kressman with a gentle voice and a sweet face, whom Ruth imagined was in her early forties. Ruth approached her in the library one day and began a conversation about Edith Wharton, and eventually Miss Kressman herself invited Ruth for tea at her house on campus. Ruth tried to tell herself that she'd enjoyed the occasion—though in truth it had all seemed stiff and formal to her; she'd felt silly sipping from her teacup like an old lady—but she issued a reciprocal invitation, which Miss Kressman accepted.

Ruth went to great lengths for the occasion. She made a chiffon pineapple daisy cake ringed with a fussy barricade of sponge ladyfingers that kept falling over.

On the agreed-upon Saturday afternoon, Miss Kressman failed to appear.

When Ruth finally reached her on the telephone on Monday, Miss Kressman behaved oddly. She apologized. Oh, dear, she'd had the date wrong, she said. Yet her tone—injured, faintly hostile—somehow implied that it was Ruth herself who had made the error, then compounded the mistake by forcing Miss Kressman into politely accepting blame.

Eventually Ruth came to understand that Miss Kressman

wanted to be kind—she was capable of entertaining Ruth at her own home, a beautifully decorated little cottage, where they could peruse her admirable library and talk about books—but somehow she just couldn't bring herself to visit Ruth.

The evening of the failed tea party, Ruth, depressed, served Peter cake for dinner. He ate three pieces of it. Ruth pushed a ladyfinger around on her plate. The cake had been a visual failure—one side had toppled over completely—but it tasted all right.

Is it me? Ruth said. Is it something I do?

Of course it's not you, Peter said.

Ruth toyed with her fork. Well, obviously I did *something* wrong, she said. Why don't I have any friends here?

There aren't a lot of options, I know, Peter said. Don't worry. Keep trying.

That night, they went to bed early. They left the dishes and the cake on the table. In the morning, Ruth threw the rest of it in the garbage can.

Determined to be supportive of Peter, to be a credit to him, Ruth continued to make an effort at Derry that first fall and winter. She retired the quilted skirt she had once thought so handsome. On another trip to New Haven to see Dr. Wenning, she went shopping at Filene's and bought a black pantsuit with a tunic top and bell sleeves; she tried it on for Dr. Wenning, who assured her that it was elegant. But each time Ruth faced one of the social events at Derry, her heart pounded with anxiety as she dressed. She grew light-headed. It felt as if mice scurried over the skin of her belly.

One night shortly before the first Christmas at Derry, Peter received an invitation to a formal dinner at the headmaster's house.

Am I supposed to come, too? Ruth asked.

I'm sure you are, Peter said. I think it's sort of a holiday party.

In attendance would be a bishop from Maine's Episcopal diocese, Peter had been told, and the executive committee of the school's trustees, three who were also ministers. Peter's energy and charisma, the success that first semester of the boys he taught, had attracted notice, and Ruth understood that the invitation to join the older men that evening was an important occasion for him.

A half hour before they were due to arrive, Ruth lay down on the bed in her slip. After a minute, she got under the covers.

I'm sick, she called to Peter, who was shaving in their tiny bathroom.

Peter came into the room and sat down on the bed beside her, toweling dry his hair.

No one talks to me at these things, anyway, Ruth said. That one man who teaches Latin, the one who wears that furry vest? What's it made of, anyway? A cowhide? He spoke Italian to me all night last time, even though I told him I didn't *know* any Italian. And he has dandruff in his eyelashes.

Peter rubbed his head with the towel.

I'm too shy a person for these things, she said. She closed her eyes.

Just leave me here, she said. Really, I'll be fine.

On the bed beside her, she watched surreptitiously as Peter

draped the towel around his neck and tugged on either end, like a boxer. He gazed at the floor, frowning.

She felt a flare of resentment. He didn't understand. He had a *job* here. He was an important part of things. She was nobody.

Ask them questions about their lives, Peter said. People like to talk about themselves.

She knew he was tired. He'd been working hard, staying up late at night, preparing for classes, and there was an endless procession of extracurricular obligations: meetings for the school's newspaper staff, or the student government association, or sports council hearings, duties for which Peter always seemed to have been volunteered by his older colleagues. But she felt rebuked, misunderstood, as if he'd said her shyness was only a veneer—a lion pretending not to be hungry around a gazelle—like it was something she could put on and take off at will.

She turned on her side away from him.

Don't condescend to me, Peter van Dusen, she said. I know how to talk to people, if I have to.

The room was cold. Despite herself, she began to shiver. This always happened when she was upset. She turned her face into the pillow.

Peter put his hand on her back.

Why was there no one to whom she could turn? she thought. Dr. Wenning was hours away. Ruth had no friends nearby, and no parents, no *mother*, as Peter well knew. Peter's father was the closest thing she had to a parent, but she couldn't talk with him about any of this, about how useless she felt sometimes. All kinds of things were happening out there in the world—President Eisenhower had signed the Civil Rights Act a couple of years before, and there were sit-ins all over the South, the wonderful young John Kennedy had won the Democratic nomination, and Ruth and Peter hoped he would become President—but meanwhile she felt as if she had been banished to a desert island. Many of the women she knew from Smith were married, or trying to be, but she knew others who were writing for magazines, who were lobbying for women's rights, including better pay and birth control. Gloria Steinem, who had been a couple years ahead of Ruth, had already published her extraordinary account of working as a Playboy bunny with its famous last line, the sad girl who waved good-bye to Gloria as she gathered her clothes for the last time. *See you in the funnies.*

What was Ruth doing? Nothing.

She stared at the face of the clock beside their bed.

It's not a cowhide. It's actually a deer hide, Peter said after a minute. The vest that that guy always wears.

His hand was warm against her skin.

Ruth rolled back over to look up at him.

And he shot the deer himself. Peter made a face. Don't ask him for the story, he said. You'll regret it.

She put her hands over her mouth.

Then she reached up and put her arms around him. I wouldn't think of it, she said. But I still don't want to go.

Peter let the towel around his waist fall away and joined her between the sheets.

I'm sorry, he said into her neck. I know it's lonely here for you, Ruth. I appreciate everything you're doing to help me. I wish you had a friend here. You will. I know you will.

You'll find your place.

They were late to the party that evening, holding hands and running across the silent campus. Many boys had already left for the holidays; in another day or so, they would all be gone, those with no families to the homes of parishioners for Christmas.

They arrived at the headmaster's house red-cheeked and breathless. Ruth saw instantly that she was the only woman present. The headmaster, whose wife had passed away some years before Peter and Ruth moved to Derry, seemed surprised to see her, which made her think that maybe he had intended for Peter to come alone, after all.

She felt mortified. When the headmaster took their coats, she shot Peter a furious glance.

He looked back with a helpless expression. Sorry, he mouthed.

When they were seated at dinner, the bishop, a lean man with extraordinarily tufted eyebrows, offered a prayer.

Thank you, God, he said, for the state of Maine. Thank you for the care of these boys into whose lives we have been privileged to extend the powerful rays of your generosity.

Ruth felt her stomach rumble loudly with hunger.

The bishop's eyes were closed, his fingers laced beneath his chin.

Down the table, all heads were bowed. The bishop opened

his eyes, gazing down the table as if he might have heard Ruth's stomach, and then closed them again.

In the name of Jesus Christ our lord, amen, he said.

During the meal, Ruth could see Peter trying to catch her eye across the table, but she wouldn't look at him. Neither man seated beside her spoke to her beyond extending the usual sorts of politeness.

And how old are *you*? the man to her left asked, as he sawed away at his beef.

Ruth repressed the urge to ask him the same question. What kind of question was that, anyway? she thought.

To her right, a bald gentleman with veins in his nose inclined his head when she told him her name, and then called her Beth and later Bess and finally—clearly with no idea of her name but apparently unconcerned about this—Susan.

Ruth did not bother to correct him.

She said hardly anything during the meal. She felt beaten down by the occasion, by the fact that the headmaster had not expected her, though he had greeted her kindly, calling her my dear and steering her toward the fireplace, putting a glass of sherry—which she drank down almost immediately—in her hands.

All the joyfulness of her earlier lovemaking with Peter, the comfort of his love for her and hers for him, their happy race across the snow-covered campus, felt extinguished.

She gazed across the dinner table at the waving lights of the candles. An image of her father in his suit pants and white shirt stepped before her, as it sometimes did when she felt most low.

She put down her fork. She put butter on a roll and stuffed it into her mouth so she wouldn't cry.

After dinner Ruth smiled and shook hands dutifully around the room.

We're glad you're here, my dear, the headmaster said. Your Peter is doing a super job. Derry's lucky to have him.

Someone helped her into her coat, and then the headmaster opened the front door. She and Peter stepped into the darkness, calling good night.

The headmaster closed the door behind them.

Ruth registered the silence around them, the night sky bristling coldly with stars. The temperature had been below freezing for several days, but Ruth felt feverish. She unbuttoned her coat as they left the driveway and turned down the lane back toward the center of campus. The loose tops of her galoshes—Peter's galoshes, actually—flapped around her calves. She'd been in too much of a hurry to leave to buckle them properly.

Peter walked in silence beside her.

I wasn't supposed to be there, she said.

I guess not, Peter said, but there wasn't any harm in it. They were glad you were there. Anyway, I'm sorry.

Do you want to know what people asked me tonight? she said finally.

Peter said nothing.

Someone asked me my name, she said. Someone else asked me how *old* I was. She puffed out a breath. And, before dinner, three people asked how we'd met.

Peter hunched down inside his collar. She could tell he felt wearied by her.

Well, it *is* a story, he said.

Ruth shot him a look of anger. It's not the kind of story you *tell* people, she said, and you know it.

She slipped on the path in her open galoshes, felt cold snow against her ankle.

They want a *love* story, Peter, she said. Hearts and flowers and doves.

We have love, he said. He tried to catch her hand.

We have terrible things in our past, Peter, she said. My father is not dinner table conversation. Nor is an abortion, for god's sake.

They almost never talked about that time. She'd said that last part because she felt mean.

Peter, striding along beside her, said nothing.

It was always like this between them, she thought help-lessly. She said too much; Peter said nothing at all.

It was not that they ever disputed Ruth's past, the tragic business of Ruth's father and the way in which Ruth and Peter had been delivered to each other. There was no disput-ing those facts, of course, or any part of their shared history, the time before their marriage, the doctor who had ended the pregnancy, nearly ending Ruth's own life as well. But what was she to *do* with her past, she thought? What was she to do with the loneliness and sadness that came up inside her sometimes, the way those feelings transformed so quickly into anger?

Ah, Ruth. Do not *punish* yourself so, Dr. Wenning had said to her once. Your childhood would explain a lifetime of bad behavior in very many people. You are not a bad person because you feel sad sometimes. And that boy Peter loves you. You know he does.

Still, Ruth knew that it was difficult to live with someone who struggled as much as she did sometimes. She wished she could believe in God. What a relief it would be. But she just couldn't manage it. In truth she sometimes felt repulsed by the idea of a God who seemed to preside over so much suffering in the world. And she was equally repulsed, though she knew it was uncharitable of her, by what she saw as the credulousness of those who *claimed* to believe—or perhaps, like Peter, really *did* believe—by the kneeling and rising and murmuring of prayers and singing.

Something about it, about even Peter's faith, struck her as smug and horrible.

How are you so *sure*? she asked Peter once.

I just am, he said. I don't know why or how.

Simple as that? Ruth said.

Well, not simple, he said.

No, she cried. It's *not* simple!

You're right, he said. You're right.

She put her head in her hands. I can't fight with you, she said.

I'm trying, he said. Give me credit here.

Oh, for heaven's sake, she said.

In general that first year at Derry, Ruth tried just to follow Dr. Wenning's advice.

Once every few weeks, she packed a sandwich and a thermos of tea and drove from Derry to New Haven, where she sat in Dr. Wenning's office and tried to help her with her increasingly disorganized papers, meanwhile listening to Dr. Wenning opine about the mental habits of the optimist, exercises of positive thinking designed to help Ruth defeat the voices of despair inside her.

You must alter the schema, Ruth, Dr. Wenning advised. Reject the sad ending. Concentrate on what is *now*, on the extra-*or*-dinary present!

Afterward, they would go out for dinner at the Italian restaurant Dr. Wenning liked, where the owner kissed Dr. Wenning's hand as if she were royalty and took her shabby old coat from her shoulders as if it were a full-length mink.

Dr. Wenning spoke to him in rapid Italian; some of his relatives, too, had died in the war, she told Ruth.

We have that in common, she said. Also the experience of national shame.

Ruth and Dr. Wenning always ate the same thing on these occasions—eggplant Parmesan or spaghetti with vodka sauce—and shared a bottle of wine, and then Ruth would spend the night on the itchy little sofa in Dr. Wenning's study at her house, driving back to Derry the next day feeling restored and more hopeful.

I'm sorry, Ruth apologized to Dr. Wenning on one of these visits, after a long afternoon of complaining. All I do when I see you is woe-is-me. You just bring it out in me.

You are not my patient, Ruth, Dr. Wenning said kindly. You are my *friend*. I want to listen to you. You listen to me as well, you know.

Dr. Wenning was fond of quoting Whitman and Rilke,

especially, and she gave Ruth many books over the years, mostly novels and poetry. Ruth also read lots of popular psychology books, though Dr. Wenning tried to discourage her from this.

Enough Freud, Ruth! she would cry, springing up in frustration from behind her desk. What you need is novels. You need music, sex, food, dancing, wine, jokes . . .

What do you call a cow, lying down? she said. *Grrrrround* beef!

On Dr. Wenning's advice, Ruth played tennis with Peter as often as he could find time for it, and she walked three miles every day, learning the country roads and the paths around Derry. In her correspondence with friends, she tried to be entertaining, telling little stories about happenings at the school and describing the boys and the flora and the fauna. She looked up the names of the birds and the wild-flowers.

She was a regular visitor at the school's library, where she wandered self-consciously through the stacks. There were few women at Derry, and Ruth, with her red hair and height, felt herself especially noticeable. But she made her way through one or two novels a week, Dostoevsky and Flaubert, Tolstoy and Hardy. She toiled away at her novel and at her play, trying to have faith in herself and in the process, faith that all the creeping forward and crossing out and gusts of excitement and bleak periods of nothingness, when she couldn't seem to imagine what came next, would end up finally in a complete story.

On the night of that first horrible Christmas dinner with the bishop and the board of trustees, however, Ruth felt that all her weeks of determined effort—of self-improvement and patience, of taking care of Peter—had been a waste.

She had made no progress in acquiring serenity or contentment. She was as full of wanting things—things she couldn't exactly name—as ever. She was tired of housekeeping. She was tired of being just a wife. She was lonely.

Beside her on the path, Peter took off his gloves and stuffed them in his coat pocket. He unbuttoned the top button of his overcoat and blew out a tired breath.

Ruth watched these movements through narrowed eyes.

As usual, she thought, Peter would not fight with her. He *never* fought with her.

She was sorry that she'd spoken. It wasn't Peter's fault that those old men were rude. Why hadn't she just tried harder to be nice to them that night? Why hadn't she wanted to charm them? What was wrong with a little charm, anyway?

At last Peter said, Well, you don't have to mention those, um, darker aspects. He tried to take her arm.

For gosh sake, Ruth, he said. Slow *down*.

She thought but didn't say: But if I don't mention those darker aspects, then there's no *story*.

Instead, she said, No one ever asks what I'm interested in or what I studied or what I hope to do with my life. It's as if they think that meeting you is the only thing of consequence ever to have happened to me.

Peter didn't say anything.

She'd hurt his feelings, she knew, but despite her effort to be rational, she felt too wild to care.

She wrenched her scarf from around her neck, where it

felt like it was strangling her. Her stride could be longer than Peter's, if she wanted, and all she wanted at that moment was to stalk away from him, to run through the snow.

If I can't ever tell anyone the true story, she burst out finally, then no one will ever *know* me.

It had begun to rain, a fine icy sleet almost invisible except in the halos of light around the lampposts along the path.

You *can* tell them, Peter said, trying again for her hand. You *can.*

She snatched her hand away.

She knew better than that, she thought. Some stories you simply could not let out into the open.

That night when they got home, Peter hung up his coat and began to gather his books from the table.

Ruth, still in her coat, watched him balance his grade book on top of the stack and tuck it under his arm. Where are you going? she said.

I'm going upstairs, he said. I need to do a little work.

Ruth said, The semester's over, Peter.

He didn't look at her. I know, he said.

Fine, Ruth said. Go ahead. Go do your important work.

He didn't say anything. She watched him leave the room, closing the door quietly behind him. She threw her gloves at it.

She stood in the center of their room, listening, expecting to hear soon the sound of Peter's old typewriter, but there was only silence from overhead.

10

The woods into which Ruth wanders early one lambent June morning nearly sixty year later, when she is eighty-five years old, are filled with ghost ferns and lady ferns and wild columbine and wild ginger, species of plants common to the part of the Adirondacks in which she and Peter made their home following Peter's retirement from Derry. Ruth, always the student, always in search of knowledge, purchased dog-eared field guides to the area at the local library's annual sale when they first arrived. She has struggled over the years to discern one fern from another.

The Robust Male fern, she has fretted to Peter, looks inconveniently a *lot* like the Lady in Red fern.

That's us, Peter said. The Robust Male and the Lady in Red.

Ruth rolls her eyes at him, but she laughs. He is so corny, she thinks.

She sets off just after seven thirty, in the morning's delicate light, along the fire road that runs past their house. It is a familiar path, a mowed blaze perhaps twenty feet wide, thick in midsummer with goldenrod and purple ironweed but now shorn low and easily traveled. The dog—an old, fat, sheepdog-beagle mix named Nanny, whom they'd agreed to adopt from a neighbor after his wife's death and his subsequent move to an assisted-living facility near his son in Florida—comes with her.

The dog worships Ruth and Peter equally and hates to have

either of them out of her sight. She has powerful herder genes in her, as Peter has observed. She is tormented by Ruth's habit of solitary walks, wanting equally to be with Ruth and to be with Peter, who more and more often stays behind these days, content to sit on the deck and read—or just *look*, Ruth thinks—while Ruth takes what Peter calls her constitutional.

Ruth has done a lot of coaxing and cajoling, a lot of handing over of dog biscuits, to get Nanny to come with her this morning. For several hundred yards, for as long as the house remains within sight, the dog runs back and forth between Ruth, making her way slowly up the clearing, and Peter, sitting on the deck, leaning forward in his chair to shoo Nanny away when she returns to him, assuring her that she will be happier on a walk with Ruth.

Ruth turns at one point to call Nanny again. From the deck, she sees Peter stand up to lift his hand to wave good-bye to her.

She waves back.

Finally, the fire road drops over the rise, and the house is out of sight at last, as is Peter with his ravaged face, a consequence of the disease that has failed yet to kill him, though it has transformed his once handsome, gentle features into a rough wooden carving of a face, a face on a totem pole, Ruth thinks. She can still see in her husband the man he once was—she will always think him beautiful—but strangers often stop at the sight of him, nearly seven feet tall, hands like big spiders flapping at the ends of his frail wrists, heavy head balanced on his warped, elongated spine. His eyes are hooded and sleepy-looking. When he smiles, his jaw unhinges.

Come on, Nanny, Ruth calls. Come with me.

The woods on either side of the fire road are crossed with sunny ridges and deep, velvet glades, pierced by long columns of filtered sunlight and filled with the trickling sounds of water, where springs bubble forth here and there among the tumbled rocks, their arrangement the silent, motionless aftermath of once massive glacial upheaval. Ruth has read about the geologic history of the area, about plate tectonics and sedimentary structure. She knows that this place where she stands once rippled with the fluvial processes of the Susquehanna River. It feels so solid underfoot, she thinks; it is difficult to imagine these hills in motion. She feels small as she walks, aware of her footprints, the tiny, receding figure she must have seemed to Peter, standing on the deck and waving.

The day is already warm, and Ruth moves out of the bright sunlight and into the dappled shade at the edge of the fire road. It will be hot by the time she returns, she knows. She has brought water, carried in a special flask with a comfortable padded shoulder strap, which Peter gave her last Christmas.

The dog following closely at Ruth's heels is panting, her barrel chest heaving. In the end, it is more troubling for Nanny to have Ruth straying far from home than it is to leave Peter behind safely at the house, and she has elected to follow Ruth, but Ruth knows that it was a painful choice.

Poor old Nanny, Ruth says to the dog.

She slows, to allow Nanny time to recover.

You're doing a fine job, she says, stopping finally to pat the dog and stroke her back.

The dog, never good at making eye contact, averts her gaze but moves closer to Ruth's leg as if to protect her from threat.

I promise we won't go far, Ruth says. Poor old Nanny, she says again. You're such an old worrier.

Sometimes Ruth is gone on one of her walks for a whole morning—she gets a second wind some days, and she feels as if she could walk forever—but it makes Peter worry if she is gone too long. She will not go far today, she thinks. She is tired.

But how easy it is to be led deeper into the woods, which this morning, Ruth begins to notice, are filled with the strange spiral webs of orb weavers. Some of them are a foot or more in diameter, utterly fantastical things, and they hover in the woods as far as she can see in every direction. The finely spun rings of the webs are backlit by the rising sun, the empty bull's-eyes of their centers surrounded by halos of filament suspended among the branches of the wild hydrangea and the elderberry.

She marvels at the gleaming architecture strung all around her. She can see as many as a hundred of them—no, two hundred, she thinks, or three—gazing in astonishment.

Look, Nanny, she says.

She wants, for a moment, to return to the house and get Peter, to bring him here to see this extraordinary sight, but she knows, even as she thinks of it, that by the time she can return and rouse him, the light will have changed and the webs will have vanished. Or, not so much vanished but become invisible. It is only an accident of the light that she has happened upon this strange phenomenon, this wonderland.

He can't really make such a journey with her anymore, in any case.

She bends to inspect a web nearby, sees a single fly netted in its center, wrapped in a sarcophagus of silk thread.

Behind her, when she glances back, Ruth can still see the brighter light of the clearing on the fire road, but the ferns grow so thickly here that it is not difficult to drift into the woods and to move among the big old trees. Nanny comes behind her, trampling a heedless path.

After a while, Ruth is thirsty. She unscrews the cap from her water bottle, drinks deeply. She looks down at Nanny, her mottled tongue hanging, and she pours some water into her cupped palm for the dog to drink.

Nanny laps at Ruth's palm, her tongue thick and surprisingly strong.

As Ruth bends over, she feels her legs waver beneath her.

Let's sit, Ruth thinks. What's the hurry?

Come, Nanny. She puts her arm around the dog's soft, heaving flank.

Hours and hours of light, she thinks, lying back among the ferns and staring up into the cathedral space. Green days. Mineral nights, full of sparks.

What could be more nicer than this? she says to Nanny.

Silence.

She opens her eyes. She wants to sit up.

What could be *nicer*, she corrects herself, surprised. She knows better than *that*.

High above her, the trees are rocking. Ruth feels, for an instant, a giant genuflection of the earth under her back, as if the mountains are boiling, swelling beneath the surface. Then all is still again. But she realizes that she cannot move her hands or her legs.

Her eyes traverse the green swaying overhead.

The dog's breath on her face is, briefly, hot and foul. She turns aside to avert her mouth; she wants first to vomit and then to laugh. Nanny is gone.

Come back, she thinks.

A moment later she feels Nanny's worried tongue on her neck, along her hairline, against her closed eyes, then a flickering of something—fingertips—against her cheekbones and across her chest and arms. A tickle. A plummeting descent— she feels her feet skitter against shale—toward sleep. She fights it, knowing.

She does not want to leave Peter.

Then she is awake. Once more she opens her eyes—it is so bright, though, she cannot open them for more than a moment—and it is Peter, looking down into her face.

She smiles at him—beloved Peter—and at the green, glowing world beyond him.

Shining day, she thinks. Perfect light. What a spectacle it all is. How happy she has been, after all.

It is past noon by the time the dog finally abandons her position at Ruth's side, having sat there through the morning, snapping at flies as they approached Ruth's nose and open eyes and mouth. She hurries home, following her trail.

In the flat light of midday, the host of spiral orbs, as Ruth predicted, is no longer visible in the woods.

When the dog appears, weaving rapidly down the fire road toward the house, nose to the ground as if tracking prey, Peter is standing on the deck under the hot sun, both hands gripping the railing.

Ruth? he calls when he sees Nanny. *Ruth!*

But the dog, he sees finally, is alone. No one follows her down the clearing.

11

The night after that awful dinner at the headmaster's house, Peter having retreated upstairs to the attic with his grade book and his papers under his arm, Ruth stared at the door through which he had disappeared.

She wanted to throw something.

She kicked the table leg, hard, hurting her foot, and then she looked around, her chest heaving. There were plates on the shelf, two glasses upturned in the dish drainer . . . but no, nothing breakable. She couldn't bring herself to throw anything breakable.

She went over to the dresser beside their bed, wrenched open the drawers and began emptying them, tumbling blouses and brassieres and socks and Peter's sweaters to the floor. From the closet she snatched shirts from their hangers, hurling them behind her. She picked up a book and threw it as hard as she could onto the bed. Then she threw another, and another.

She got down on her knees and heaved Peter's shoes out of the closet into the room behind her.

She paused. She felt sick, sweat on her forehead. What else? What *else* could she do?

She tugged the bedclothes with their cargo of books to the floor. She beat a pillow savagely against the table, the sofa, the armchair she had laboriously recovered in pretty orange fabric, hurting her fingers for days with the awful upholstery tacks.

The pillow exploded. Feathers filled the air.

She went to the bookshelf and grabbed the stack of pages that was the play she'd been writing, having long since given up on the novel. She paused for a minute; she would never be able to put it all back together . . . but, oh, what a pathetic thing it was anyway, her *stupid* play—and then she flung the pages onto the floor.

They fanned out, sliding across the floorboards.

Standing in the middle of the room, she looked around.

There was nothing else she could touch without doing real damage, she realized. She had to get out of there.

She listened. Upstairs there was silence, though Peter must have heard her, she thought.

Had heard her and didn't care.

She ran, stumbling, down the steep staircase. At the bottom, she opened the door and then slammed it so hard behind her that it bounced back open and struck the wall, where it stood open. She heard the report of it hitting the wall behind her, but she was already running.

* * *

Later, when she got back home, she found Peter sitting on the floor.

Clothes and feathers and shoes were everywhere around him, the contents of the bookcases in a heap.

A bottle of Scotch stood on the table.

He looked up when she came in the room.

In his lap, he held a stack of papers, the pages of her play. He'd begun sorting the pages into little piles, she saw, trying to put them in order.

There were feathers stuck to the back of his sweater and one in his hair.

He looked away from her. You scared me, he said.

I know, she said. I scared myself. I'm sorry.

Peter took a drink from the glass on the floor beside him, and then he got to his feet. He walked over to the bed and heaped the covers back onto the mattress. Then he crossed the room and pulled Ruth roughly against him.

Don't ever do that again, he said. You promised, Ruth. You promised you wouldn't leave me.

I won't, she said.

That wasn't leaving, anyway, she said. That was . . . steam.

They were wild with each other that night, a mixture of pain and anger and desire and love.

In bed, in the darkness, the weight of Peter against her felt like the deepest kind of consolation and forgiveness.

She had walked that evening across the mostly deserted campus, her head down against the wind. The icy rain had turned to snow again, but at first she hadn't felt cold; she'd been giving off heat like a furnace, making a penumbra of warmth around her, her breath a cloud.

Her hair, though, was quickly covered with snow. She'd shaken her head, lifting her face to the sky, blinking against the numberless, endless, falling snowflakes, the darkness lit from within as if an enormous lamp burned somewhere high above her. She took deep breaths, trying to calm herself.

The snow fell so thickly that soon the paths were covered.

When she felt slippery grass underfoot, she could tell she'd veered off the path and lost her way. She fell down but scrambled immediately to her feet, an explosive energy inside her. She could walk all night, she thought. She could walk forever. She'd just keep going.

Soon, though, she felt the land beneath her feet shifting down the grade. Was she near the entrance gate? Were those massive dark shapes ahead the old oaks?

She fell again, sliding downhill for several feet. The cold of the snow on the back of her neck and down her collar was shocking.

She lay on her back, watching the air above her swarm with snowflakes.

She was a bad person to have hurt Peter in that way. She was a bad person to have made such an awful mess of their lovely apartment.

She felt cold and wet and very tired. How could she have behaved so badly?

She sat up in the snow, brushed her hands against her coat and got to her feet. Where was she?

She turned around. In the distance, through the falling snow, she could see that a few lights were on here and there in the school's buildings, high up in the darkness above her. She knew there was still a handful of boys left on campus, those who would be picked up in the next day or so by families taking them in for the holiday.

They must be reading now late at night, she thought, those left-behind boys, or asleep, their cheeks resting on the open page.

How lonely the lights looked, the solitary lights of orphan boys.

Over the years she had accompanied Peter from time to time when he had night duty, a responsibility he maintained through the years, even when he was headmaster. They had climbed the dormitories' creaking stairs and walked the halls together, Ruth reading the names of the boys printed on the cards taped to their doors, looking at the notices on the bulletin boards for club meetings or study halls or upcoming football or basketball games, the times of church services, the routines for fire drills. Sometimes Ruth brought oatmeal cookies and thermoses of hot cider with them, a late-night surprise for the boys. Sometimes Peter had to stop to quiet a rowdy group swinging from their bunk beds, or to tell a boy to turn out the lights, putting his head around a doorframe to say sternly, settle down now, lights-out, time for shut-eye.

She wished she were there now, opening her coat and unwinding her scarf, smelling the heat of the radiators, walking the halls that smelled like boy.

When she had been a child, she remembered, on Sundays she had laid out her clothes for the school week ahead, deciding what she would wear each day. She had lined up her skirts and blouses in her closet so as to have them in order. Mary had taught her how to sew a blouse, how to make darts.

She had a sudden memory of the kerchiefs she had sewn from scraps, of her first clumsy attempts at knitting. What a sorrowful thing she had been.

But now, here she was.

It had ended after all, that sad childhood.

She looked up at the hill, the solitary lights floating here and there in the darkness.

Those hoodlums and orphans, she thought.

Surely there was something she could do for them.

That night, she had started to pick up the clothes strewn over the floor.

Just leave it, Ruth, Peter had said of the disarray. It's okay. Come to bed.

He fell asleep almost instantly after they'd made love, a combination of whiskey and relief, she thought, his arm draped over her, part embrace and part restraint.

Ruth lay awake. She would have to confront the chaos she'd created, everything helter-skelter in their apartment, in the morning, she knew.

She thought about Mrs. van Dusen and her troubled mind, her shining floors and windows, the glacial beauty of the surfaces in her house, the sad years during which Peter had watched his mother disappear. She thought about what it must have been like for Mrs. van Dusen to lose so much, herself, her husband and her son.

She thought about her father, the tongue twisters he'd practiced in the mirror during her childhood, watching himself in the mirror.

Daddy draws doors. Daddy draws doors. Daddy draws doors. Tommy Attatimus took two T's, tied them to the top of two tall trees.

Then, in her mind, as she had so often over the years, she made her apologies on her father's behalf to the men who were said to have died at his hand. She would never understand what her father had wanted, what he had feared, what he had hated.

There was his voice, a whisper in the darkness. Going, going, gone.

Forgive him, she thought.

Beside her Peter sighed. His breath smelled like Scotch.

She thought about her mother, whoever she had been. She must have had her reasons.

She thought about Dr. Wenning, the men and women who came to her with their burdens and their grief. My friends, Dr. Wenning called them.

Ruth had not understood that, at first.

Under the weight of Peter's arm, Ruth settled herself more deeply into the mattress. She closed her eyes and remembered the scattered lights on campus she'd seen this evening, imagined every one of them going out, one by one, every orphan boy laying down his head on his orphan's pillow in the breathing silence of the dormitory.

She was not alone here.

There was a place for her beside Peter, with these children.

Go to sleep, boys, she thought. Good night and sleep tight. And she sent her love toward them across the campus, through the cold and the night and the bright snow falling, a light in the material world.

ABOUT THE AUTHOR

Carrie Brown is the author of six novels and a collection of short stories. She has won many awards for her work, including a National Endowment for the Arts fellowship, the Barnes and Noble Discover Award, the Janet Heidinger Kafka Prize, and, twice, the Library of Virginia Award. Her short fiction has appeared in journals including *One Story*, *Glimmer Train*, the *Georgia Review*, and the *Oxford American*. She taught for many years at Sweet Briar College in Virginia, where she lives with her husband, the writer John Gregory Brown. She is now distinguished visiting professor of creative writing at Hollins University.

A NOTE ON THE TYPE

This book was set in Caledonia, a typeface designed by W. A.
Dwiggins (1880–1956). It belongs to the family of printing
types called "modern face" by printers—a term used to mark
the change in style of the type letters that occurred around
1800. Caledonia borders on the general design of Scotch
Roman, but it is more freely drawn than that letter. This version of Caledonia was adapted by David Berlow in 1979.

Typeset by Scribe, Philadelphia, Pennsylvania

Printed and bound by Berryville Graphics,
Berryville, Virginia

Designed by Iris Weinstein